Praise for *Guardian*

"Part mystery and part paranormal fiction, the story is ripe both with anticipation and emotion, and the satisfying ending with a cliffhanger successfully sets the stage for the series finale. Dark and moody, the novel makes for a thoroughly engrossing read. Lovers of supernatural mysteries will want to take a look."

Prairie Books Review

Guardian

Book Two in the Legacy Trilogy

MARK J. CANNON

IGUANA

Publisher: Meghan Behse
Editor: Owen McEwen and Heather Bury
Front cover design: Ruth Dwight (designplayground.ca)
Cover photograph: Andrey Svistunov, Unsplash.com

ISBN 978-1-77180-520-9 (paperback)
ISBN 978-1-77180-521-6 (epub)

This is an original print edition of *Guardian*.

To Phil,
Having someone believe in you is incomparable!

Prologue

Two Alone

2005

The appearance of the O'Connell's two-storey, reddish-orange brick farmhouse opposite the traditional red barn, seemed warm and inviting. Its long gravel laneway, leading up to the elevated property over a hundred feet from the main road, was picturesque. To the right, a healthy, dark green cornfield was separated from the property by several tall walnut trees. The front left leading up to the house had a spattering of dogwood and maple trees in full bloom. The house, with its wrap-around porch, white-trimmed windows, and fascia boards, was emphasized in contrast to the well-maintained lawn and landscaping surrounding it. Completing the look of a family home, a rope swing for the kids to enjoy hung from the branch of an old elm tree not far from the front of the house. It was a portrait of a warm and joyful existence of country living. This was where Jacob and Sara O'Connell chose to build their family.

Before a crisis occurred in the summer of 2005, Sara looked at her life with confidence and clarity. Everything she attempted to bring to the surface of her thoughts beyond that damaging moment was opaque from a deep and unforgiving grief. Collapsed on the kitchen floor of the farmhouse with her feet tucked under her thighs and her shaking frame slumped over, Sara was despondent. Yet the infirmity of her muscles from shock and exhaustion would not stop her from grasping her dead husband, Jacob, and sliding his limp body along the hardwood floor, resting his head in her lap. Her immutable wailing at the injustice of the guardian's rule — the only rule that mattered in this consequence — silenced all else in their immediate range.

Her pleas with this secretive and mysterious world of guardians to return her husband proved futile. Life could not re-enter Jacob's body. Even after incorporating her life to support one of their own, the guardian rule stood firm and final — taking a life forfeits your own. Her emotions leapt beyond anger, quickly building to an internal rage at this deplorable and implacable source that took her love. Attempting to close off to it all, she gently caressed Jacob's serene face, repeatedly and softly sliding her thumbs over his eyelids, as if to say goodbye. She murmured, "It's going to be okay, honey." This was a phrase Jacob often used, spoken when calming and comforting her or uttered in dire moments of need.

Jacob's death revealed a level of darkness that forcefully injected itself into the O'Connell's lives, resulting in this calamity. With such awareness, all Sara could muster was to curl herself into the fetal position on the floor. She wrapped Jacob's lifeless arm around her shoulder, mooning countless intimate moments. She was falling into a rapidly expanding abysm, seeking comfort in memories of happier times. Somehow, with this new reality facing her, an awareness arose telling her she needed to consciously repel what would be an easy slide into a chasm eternal. Sara's fear and pain were consuming her, forcing her to shut down for survival's sake.

§

When Sergeant Paul Kelley entered the O'Connell's residence through an open front door, he was met with a gentle breeze that carried a light scent of lavender. He recognized this smell from a single meeting with Sara. She left an impression. Paul's partner, Officer Sean Murphy, rushed directly to Sara and Jacob on the floor and quickly dropped to one knee to assess what lay before him. After a few seconds, Murphy looked back to Paul with a limited shake of his head, sadly making sense of the depth of Sara's inconsolable cries. With a rattled, choking breath to clear his throat, Paul moved swiftly to clear the rest of the house of potential danger. With the O'Connell's best friend, Pat Keegan, found dead early this morning followed now by Jacob, Paul didn't expect to find anyone upstairs, at least not alive. The search ended at the master bedroom.

The scent of lavender was invaded and spoiled by Jonathon Vargas's overpowering cologne. It almost disguised the horrible odour of feces and urine that emanated from his evil corpse. "Son of a bitch!" Paul grunted out, knowing Vargas killed Pat Keegan earlier that day. *Serves you right, you fucking piece of shit!* Paul thought, wanting to spit on the man. He also wanted to pull his gun out and shoot him a few more times. Paul stood motionless in the hallway fighting to maintain his composure. Two men he had known and admired were dead on the same day.

Paul was an ominous figure in his black uniform and camouflage bulletproof vest. He was undoubtedly strong, but what happened on this day was difficult for him. After several moments, he reached over to his left shoulder and squeezed the button on his mic. "All clear." *(static)* His voice was weak, barely audible. "Dead body on second floor." *(static)* "Rear, right bedroom." *(static)* He turned the mic off and took a deep and shaky breath. Lowering his head, he released a suppressed sigh of failure.

He reluctantly turned his attention in the direction of the kitchen downstairs. He made slow pronounced steps in his black heavy-duty boots, moving down the hall toward a scene below he simply didn't want to acknowledge. An entirely devastated Sara O'Connell, lying on the floor with Jacob's arm wrapped around her, was almost more than Paul could take, professionally and personally.

1

The Longest Day

2005

PART 1

A small celebration of life for Jacob O'Connell, forty-three years old, had come to a tearful end. An emotionally exhausted Sara O'Connell brought her two children home. Mary, six, and Ben, four, were both well fed and very tired as Sara put them to bed. After that task was completed, a large glass of chardonnay invited Sara to come and curl up on the sofa. There she would watch the sun fall over the horizon to signify the end of this heartbreaking day.

As stoic as Sara remained throughout this ordeal, it was this day with her children that proved her biggest test. Muscles and bones saluted her collapse, and her body gave in to its own weight, reluctant to move. She was finally weakened enough to allow herself to be awash in sorrow. She muffled her cries into one of the sofa's cushions. Her fatigue gave her permission to drift off. The last thing she saw as her eyes blinked, barely fighting the coming slumber, was the light over the barn door. The light's sensor, automatically reading the dusk, set the illumination into motion and glowed a yellow orange before slowly reaching its full capacity. The amber colour emanating from that bulb was familiar to Sara. It was the same colour that she witnessed coming from Jacob's hands when he saved her life in the past. A smile appeared on her face as her eyelids fell for the last time. She was left feeling a familiar warmth flow throughout her body as she recalled the times her lover had wrapped his strong arms around her in a gentle embrace.

PART 2

After such a time filled with grief, Sara was experiencing a moment of comfort, curled up on the sofa. Without notice, she quickly slid into a dreamscape that she wanted no part of. This particular dream had occurred for the first time when she was pregnant with Mary. To her relief, over the last year it had vacated her nights. The familiar and chilling atmosphere shifted. Now she was being warned that this was more than an incubus, that this darkness was real and had eyes upon her yet again.

The view out the farmhouse's living room window slowly narrowed, morphing into a long, dark, and unrecognizable corridor. She sensed cold hands hovering just above the back of her neck. Her body tensed with such severity that her shoulders pushed up into the base of her skull, building pressure. Sara began a distorted and slow-moving walk down a seemingly endless hallway. The walls were a foggy perimeter blended with moving light and dark shades of amaranthine. She suddenly found herself in the Clarington apartment she and Jacob once rented above their shop. She made a slow shuffle to the living room window, arriving to see a forceful and voluminous rain. Sara could barely make out the outline of a man no more than thirty feet kitty-corner across the street.

Strong gusts of wind pushed the rain across the road in sheets, blurring any detail of this mysterious individual. She replayed this dream many times before, but this time a far more intense fear came with it that grew like ice flowing up the length of her spine. In front of her eyes, she was forced to watch as the telephone pole shrank to the size of a fence post. The rain had kept its force but changed direction, falling straight down. Abruptly, the intense flow surrounding the man stopped. It was as though someone reached in with both hands and pulled the rain apart in opposite directions like vertical blinds being opened. And there stood a relatively young man, unknown to her, in his early thirties by her guess. He stood with an unnaturally straight back, seemingly stilted, and his shoulders stooped over with his arms slung at the sides, motionless. He wore an open, black blazer with a dark grey collar-neck sweater and matching black pants and shoes.

Initially, his head pointed downward with his shoulder-length, thin, black hair parted to one side. Unexpectedly, his head raised, exposing pale white, almost translucent, skin. He had fiery brown eyes, pronounced with slices of dark green and ochre throughout the iris. Looking up at Sara, his form was a frightening figure. However, there was a fluidity to his face, constantly shifting in appearance, akin to a reflection in a rippling pond. And it was so much so that when the dream concluded, she could never form a proper picture of who she was looking at. This created a violent shake in her, with intense rising and falling waves of warm and cold tingling skin. Instinct took over and she grabbed both sides of the window frame to steady herself for what may come. Within seconds, she was being pulled away from the window by her lower abdomen back toward the corridor. She hung on so fiercely, her back arched to the point she felt it would snap in half.

Before being pulled away, she felt compelled to look down at the man outside one last time. But just then his head snapped perversely and tilted sideways as he looked up into her eyes. He forced her to watch as his eyes rolled vertically in his head before turning solid black. When she thought it done, the wavy slices of green and ochre rolled across his eyes horizontally. It terrified and repulsed her so that she instantly became nauseous, her stomach rolling. She knew he was the controlling force pulling her toward the increasingly dark hall behind her. And what waited there was death. His face developed a sickly sinister smile, sickening her more. She squeezed her eyes shut and screamed, "NO!" long and loud, finally waking herself from the hellish spectre.

Sara sprung straight up on the sofa and wiped away a layer of perspiration from her cold, clammy forehead. She was breathing deeply in between sobs. "What in God's name was that?" That wasn't Vargas this time. "What was ... who was that sick thing?" After those words spilled out of her, she reached behind and grasped her Granny Millen's handcrafted afghan to wrap around her shoulders. If nothing else, the thought of family would warm her.

2

Malignant Growth

2005

PART 1

A miserably cold and damp October rain fell the day Dylan Matthews showed up in Clarington. He arrived a few short months after Jacob O'Connell and Pat Keegan died along with Dylan's biological father, Jonathon Allan Vargas. The stamp on the letter Dylan was carrying was from the law office of Brimmage & Tyrell, located near the town core. Their law office was in a converted dark-orange-brick, three-storey century home. The area had been revitalized with wider streets, sidewalks, and landscaped boulevards accented with black cast-iron light posts and frosted-white globes. Dylan stood still, staring at the front entrance of the office, looking unsure of what to do next. He dropped his worn and filthy backpack to the ground and secured it between his feet. He ran his tongue around the inside of his mouth, tasting his bad breath as he felt the rough surfaces of his unbrushed teeth.

Dylan's mother hadn't told him much about who his father really was. She refused. This created a level of animosity between mother and son. The story she told him was of a brief relationship. His father was an abusive drunk and left when she became pregnant — never to be seen again. The end! The last thing Michelle Matthews expected of the man who raped her was that he would keep track of his illicit child.

It was a most disturbing thought to discover that her rapist had stalked and studied her from the shadows. After being raped by Vargas while working in a restaurant in B.C., she always feared he was capable of returning to kill her.

Dylan walked up the cobblestone path toward the entrance, his pack slung over one shoulder, as he continued to survey the area with a scowl of contempt.

§

Not a full hour later, Dylan stood inside Clarington's recently restored town hall. His face remained stained with misery and antipathy. *If I see any more of this fucking swank, I'm gonna puke!* Dylan thought to himself, seeing a continuation of renewal. The faux-granite countertops, with clear maple borders, covered a large area approximately twelve feet long on all four sides in the centre of the large atrium-style reception. Inside, a few desks, a copier, and several plants brightened the encampment of bureaucracy. Currently, there was one employee on duty. Around the perimeter of the bright, orange-painted walls, doors led to various offices. And beyond reception, a very wide and open set of stairs went up and down two levels. Signs indicating the direction of services were small and easy to miss when walking in as a first-time visitor.

Dylan stood at the counter where an information sign hung above his unnoticeable stature. There was a low cut-out in the counter at desk height where Shelley Randall was furiously typing away with her earphones stuck in.

"Um … my name is Dylan Matthews, and my father worked in the Building Department and—"

"It's downstairs. Can't you see the signs?" Shelley blurted out, rudely interrupting Dylan, while pointing to the sign but not looking up at him.

He slammed his hand on the countertop, a sound that echoed throughout the large space.

"If you could get your head out of your ass for two seconds and shut the fuck up, I'll tell you what I want. Now, if you interrupt me, I'm gonna come inside your little fucking kingdom there…" Dylan said, pointing to her workspace.

He leaned over the counter with a piercing glare when he spoke to Shelley. She froze momentarily, shocked by his demeanour. She reached for the phone to have someone remove him. Dylan didn't hesitate to put his hand on top of hers before a call could be made.

"Don't do that," Dylan said, with a low-toned growl.

"What do you think you're doing? Who do you think you are to grab my hand like that?" Shelley said quickly, feeling her authority and yanking her hand away, repulsed by his touch. When she turned to call out for help, a man from the Town Planning Office happened to come out and was quick to come to Shelley's aid.

Barely audible, Dylan whispered to Shelley, "You'll pay for that."

The police were called as a result of Dylan's defiant and forceful behaviour. The precinct was less than five minutes away, and he was quickly removed from the building despite stating his purpose for being there. Shelley was somewhat shaken over the incident, but she felt relieved when her favourite police officer, Sean Murphy, arrived to ask who Dylan was and what he wanted.

"Something about his father worked here in the building. But I know everyone here and no one has a son named Dylan Matthews, I'm sure. Then he said he was Jonathon Vargas's son. Like, come on. Which is it already, ya know?" Shelley said through smacking gum, holding her hand to her chest and appearing frazzled. Shelley was the type to be oblivious to the smaller details. It turned out to be a shock to the system for Shelley and Sean Murphy when they learned Dylan was telling the truth.

PART 2

"I just found out a little while ago who my father is … was!" Dylan said, holding the large tan envelope from the lawyer's office, a business card attached with a paperclip. "I got a call from my mom that a lawyer here was trying to contact me for an inheritance. So, I came here to get his stuff he left in his office, but that bit—" Dylan stopped himself before the derogatory remarks about Shelley came out and got him into further trouble.

"So your dad's Jonathon Vargas, eh?" Murphy's query came dripping with a sense of disgust. Dylan couldn't help but pick up on it. Dylan just stared at Murphy. "I guess Vargas didn't care too much about what he left behind the day he decided to kill Pat Keegan and abduct Sara O'Connell."

"I guess. Can I get his stuff and get out of here? Please?" Dylan asked, clearly offended and agitated. He had obviously been told by the lawyers what his father had done. Officer Murphy walked to the storage area inside the building with Shelley and Dylan so he could retrieve the items his father had left behind and leave. Murphy made sure to walk him out of the building.

Shelley looked to Murphy. "When he said his father worked here, I had no idea he was Vargas's son. That scares me, I have to say."

"If he comes around here or bothers you, don't hesitate to call. Okay then." Officer Murphy was eager to return to the precinct and tell his boss who he had just met.

"I appreciate that. Thank you."

Shelley's usual flirting with Murphy, although toned down, couldn't have been more obvious or unwanted. Watching Murphy get into his cruiser from the steps, Shelley looked up to the sky and made the sign of the cross and kissed the crucifix hanging around her neck before she went back inside. She was a few steps toward the building when a cold wind picked up, lifting her skirt along with the hairs on her body. It spooked the superstitious lady. She turned around and saw the sky shifting from grey to black over the lake in the distance. She took it as a warning for her to beware of the man she just encountered. She wasn't a seer by any means, but she believed in signs, and that was one to her.

Murphy reported back to the precinct and without delay went straight into his boss's office.

"You're serious, Vargas has a son? That's hard to believe. And not exactly what I needed to hear. God damn it!" Sergeant Paul Kelley said as he slumped back in his seat, chewing on his pen.

"Yes, sir. Seen the paperwork from the lawyer myself," Murphy was quick to respond.

"So, what did he raise a stink at the town hall about?"

"He was there to pick up personal crap from Vargas's office, but I guess Miss Randall was rude to him. I could've charged him with mischief, but I thought it best he just took care of business and got the hell out of there. And hopefully, here altogether," Murphy said, with a raised brow.

"Sit down, Murph. Shut the door first," Paul said, sitting straight up in his chair. Paul spoke to Sean in a near whisper. "Well, him leaving is a nice thought, but you said he's inherited Vargas's house, right?" Paul asked the question and waited for confirmation.

"Sadly, yeah. According to the lawyer's letter."

"Then he might just be here for a while, and if he's anything like his old man—"

"No, he's selling it. Well, that's what he said to me," Murphy interrupted.

"Well good then." Paul took a relaxed position in his chair. His body language looked more positive and calm. He let out a short exhale of relief.

"Yes, sir. It is good."

"Record?" Paul queried.

"Oh yeah. Assault mostly, but he had a good lawyer. Here's the scary one." Murphy leaned forward in his chair. "Attempted sexual assault but knocked down to simple assault because of some idiot judge. It's just as well he gets the hell out of here. But he's just going to end up being a problem for someone else, I'm sure of it. He'll probably cash out and party his face off and end up back in the system. These guys are all the same. A revolving door. But he won't be our problem. I hope," Murphy said, unsure of his words.

"Just make sure that he doesn't go near the O'Connells or the Keegans while he's here. If he does that then he gets the treatment and a ticket out of town," Paul said, standing up from his chair.

"Without a doubt. Yes, sir!" said Murphy, shaking his boss's hand before exiting the office.

PART 3

Dylan sifted through his father's house like he was robbing the place, caring only about objects of value. His last stop was in the basement. Seeing a few tables with toy soldiers and battle scenes, Dylan held out little hope for anything of value but was surprised.

"Uh ha!" he grunted as he peeled away a piece of scotch tape at the back of the desk's main drawer. The tape had been holding a key for a safety deposit box. From experience, Dylan knew where to look. He didn't expect much of anything else after scanning the different paints and brushes on the desk with a giant illuminated magnifying glass attached to a long adjustable folding arm.

To his surprise, he found a large binder under a supply of toys inside a box. He pulled out what he guessed would be magazines or photos of model toys, but they were something beyond anything he had seen before. These weren't magazines that were sold in any kind of retail store — for shockingly understandable reasons.

"What the fuck? Wow, you were one sick…" Dylan's orations stopped, and his opinion of the father he never knew was suddenly one of a fellow compatriot in depravity. The more he looked through the images of detailed rape and murder scenes, the more excited and aroused he became. His admiration for his father rose to a level similar to that of a devoted follower of a cult leader. Learning that his father had been as enraged and psychotic as he was finally explained and justified his own desires, urges, and overall behaviour.

Continuing to look around, all he could see were white walls and a concrete floor painted light grey. Even the floor joists and floorboards above were painted white and mostly cleaned of cobwebs. Dylan shook his head at the detail, neatness, and cleanliness.

He turned his attention back to this large binder of magazines but discovered there was more than just perverted periodicals. Deeper inside there was a scrapbook with pictures, articles, and wisps of different-coloured hair glued to some of the pages. It would have been a prize piece of evidence for any detective pursuing a serial killer or rapist. The articles, cut out of newspapers, were about his victims. A sickening volume of victims. It turned out that many of the failed interactions Vargas had with Sara correlated with another person being viciously raped or murdered. In Vargas's mind, Sara was his prized possession to be cared for until it was time for something else.

Dylan was amazed the police missed this on their way through the house after his father's death, not looking past the top boxes of toys and supplies. But outside of trophies memorializing his accomplishments, his father's obsession with Jacob and Sara O'Connell was clear. The file Dylan was carrying held the autopsy report, along with his father's savings and returns on investments, which were substantial. All of this would be a lot for any normal individual to take in. For Dylan, the day's lottery was the treasure trove that showed the different victims. It wouldn't take him much of the day to put together a plan to carry on where his father left off; however, it took him only seconds to commit to the decision to begin.

Something else caught Dylan's attention in the basement. It would be his greatest discovery and the greatest gift he would receive from his father. It never dawned on the police why an adjustable heat grill would be on a cold air return duct. Its location was entirely misplaced. One of the many jobs Dylan had and lost over time was work as an HVAC labourer. Removing the grill and reaching deep inside, he discovered Vargas's journals inside a leather pouch. He found several five-subject notebooks that contained his personal documentation of stalking, rape, and murder, and, of course, evasion. Eventually, Dylan would simply refer to these notebooks as his "murder books," including the devil's bible.

Expeditiously, the house went on the market and sold within two months. It would later be razed to the ground by the new owners. Dylan loaded up what he wanted of his father's possessions into Vargas's mint-condition blue Cherokee. With that completed, he headed out of town. It was the apocalypse of his old life and the rebirth of a new one as Jonathon Vargas's son.

3

Demented

2006

On a cold February night, approximately two months after Dylan Matthews left town, Shelley Randall was settling into her recliner to watch her favourite show, *The Sopranos*. Five minutes had passed when she realized her dog, Joey, wasn't barking at the back patio door to be let back in as usual. She knew that in this cold he wouldn't last too long outside before he started complaining. She grabbed her winter coat, slipped her bare feet into her winter boots, and stepped out onto the rear deck and began calling. She could feel the cold dry air burning the insides of her nostrils. She closed the gap in her unzipped parka and continued to look about the yard, calling out for Joey. Concerned the dog hadn't answered yet, she gingerly stepped down the snow-covered wooden steps from the deck and ventured deeper into the backyard.

Shelley was a friendly and outgoing woman in her mid-forties who always dressed to make a statement. Although she exuded a strong exterior, inside Shelley could be reserved and demure, and at home it was sweats and t-shirts. Her life was work at the building department, volunteering in the community, and the balance being a homebody with her dog.

Still unable to find her furry companion, her concern quickly turned into fear. Rows of walnut trees and bushes on either side of the long and narrow backyard made it that much harder to make anything out. On the overcast winter night, the darkness seemed to envelop the yard in shadows.

Unable to find Joey, her fear increased to panic as she continued to yell out for her beloved pet. Suddenly hearing him barking, she turned back toward the house. His barks sounded muffled. Seeing Joey barking at her from behind the glass of the patio door gave her an instant fright. Shelley felt her stomach muscles firm up, yet she felt empty inside. Her brief happiness in locating Joey turned into an intensely cold chill that deeply penetrated her — but not from the weather.

That's impossible. He couldn't get back inside. I didn't leave the door open. Oh my God! Who's in there? The thoughts bounced around in her mind.

Just then, her overly friendly dog turned toward the dining room, wagging its tail. Shelley was shaking now, knowing someone was in her house. She tried to lick her lips, but her mouth turned dry. She felt her knees become weak. Nonetheless, she apprehensively walked toward the back deck. Joey disappeared out of sight, and the barking stopped. Now she was truly terrified. She wondered if he was hurt or if the intruder had left.

"Joey!" she screamed out.

Running as fast as possible in her unstrapped boots, she cleared the few steps onto the deck with such speed she almost slid into the patio door. To her relief, Joey had returned to the door, tail wagging at high speed. When she opened the door, Joey jumped straight up onto her thighs. She picked him up, hugging him with her body twisting back and forth. Reality was quick to return, reminding her that someone had to have come into the house to let Joey in. She slipped her boots off and tender-footed herself toward the front of the house to find the entrance door ajar with no one in sight.

§

Shelley's next-door neighbour, Gabor Barany, hung his head down. "Ah! I should have realized. I should have known something was wrong with all the lights going out at once. What's the matter with me?" Gabor asked. His Hungarian accent became thicker the more emotional he became.

"You can't blame yourself, Mr. Barany. It's not natural to pay that much attention to your neighbours. Unless, of course, you're the snoopy type. Which clearly, you're not. So, to double-check, you're sure you didn't see anyone hanging around? Any people you haven't seen before in the neighbourhood lately? Did she have any guests yesterday, or recently?"

Mr. Barany was becoming frustrated with the series of questions coming at him when the answer to all of them was "no." "I'm sorry, officer. Nothing comes to mind. I haven't seen anyone new around here that I can recall. I'm sorry. I wish I could be of some help to you. Shelley is such a sweet girl." He put his head down again, shaking it in disbelief. "I guess I have to say *was* now."

While the questioning of Shelley's neighbour was happening next door, Paul Kelley was in the house dealing with the aftermath of her demise. "Why in God's name would anyone want to hurt Shelley like this? Jesus Christ! What kind of sick son of a bitch. I can't believe this is happening here." Sergeant Kelley said, slowly standing up and briefly examining Shelley's body that was spread out on her blood-soaked bed. He repeatedly looked at the blood spatter on the ceiling and wall, then back to Shelley. The cuts on her body were savage and numerous, indicating a psychotic rage and possibly a personal connection. But the crime scene investigator was quick to note she was attacked standing up and in her robe. She had also received multiple contusions to her face, indicating she might have been incapacitated briefly before or during the attack, possibly having something to do with the sexual assault that occurred. The investigator held up Shelley's robe and showed Paul the holes in the front of it. She saw her attacker up close before she died.

It was after she was placed on the bed and stripped of her robe and pyjamas that the other stab wounds came. The blood cast off from the knife meant that she had still been alive when she was stripped, viciously attacked, and repeatedly stabbed.

What happened to Shelley occurred a little over seven months after Pat Keegan was murdered. Paul couldn't remember there ever being a homicide in Clarington before Pat's murder, so this was disturbing and frightening. Knowing Shelley was Sara's good friend, Paul felt obligated to inform her before the day was out.

4

With Conviction

2006

PART 1

Any light or noise pollution that penetrated the solace around the O'Connells' home was easily noticed. Snow clouds had blanketed the sky over the last few days. On this cold and blustery night, the howling winds were picking up speed as they swirled around the house and barn. With one light over the barn's old hayloft, and the others mounted on either side of the entrance door, it was total darkness around the property. Just after eight p.m., Sara finished tucking her children into their beds for the night. She thought of having a relaxing cup of tea to ease her own approaching slumber.

After the goodnight hugs and kisses concluded, Sara closed her daughter's bedroom door. Suddenly she caught some movement to her right at the end of the hall. A familiar feeling overcame her — one where time stood still. She felt the air coast around her, cooling and falling into suspension. Her focus sharpened, and she experienced time in slow motion. She felt a gentle coolness puff at her eyes, forcing them to blink and open wide. Her pupils expanded, as black as the sky, taking in everything. Her smile evaporated, replaced with a chilling look of dread. With limited movement she began scanning the hallway.

A black wave darker than night with no particular form had entered the window at the end of the hall. It slithered in from the left and slowly crossed the glass. Visually illuding, it appeared to flow from inside the hall to the outside. It cut back and forth through the windowpane then disappeared out the other side of the frame, causing the wallpaper to swell for a moment before dissipating. Sara's knuckles turned white as she gripped the knob of Mary's bedroom door. As fast as she could move her free hand, she flipped the hall light on, but it didn't reveal anything.

It had been a long day of travel and meetings with a new client and suppliers, so Sara wondered if she was seeing things. In the time it took to shut the light back off, she floated between fear and confusion, and anger and sadness. Even though logic prevailed, her heart felt crushed from such a fright. She held her hand to her chest and allowed herself to exhale, then drew a deep breath.

"God, help me," she whispered.

Staring out the window at the end of the hall for what might further develop, Sara saw a set of headlights in the distance. To ease her mind, she blamed it on a shadow created from the reflection of a passing car.

"Come on, Sara! Shake it off. You're seeing things." Her quiet words came out as she rapidly rubbed the outsides of her arms to take the chill away. She continued down the stairs and into the kitchen to put the kettle on when she saw another set of headlights. Carrying on with her simple routine, she tried to put normality in front as a challenge to any manifested darkness to try and confront her. She was grateful the shadows being created now were from lights coming up the long gravel lane toward the house.

That's odd. Who would be coming here this time of night? Sara wondered, slowly tiptoeing across the hardwood floor. Arriving at the front door, she peeked through the flower-patterned sheers to see a police cruiser come to a stop. It surprised her to see Paul Kelley get out of his cruiser and not his personal vehicle as usual. Six months on since Jacob's death, Paul, his wife, and their kids had all become friends with Sara and her children. "What's he doing here?" She wondered aloud but then thought, *I hope it's nothing serious. Oh, maybe he's just stopping by to ask about another play date for the kids. I hope it's nothing serious.*

She quickly rolled those thoughts around in her mind as Paul neared the steps of the porch. Before he reached the door, Sara was quick to swing it open with a greeting. "Hi, Paul. What's got you out here on such a miserable night?"

Paul took his hat off and held it to his side.

"May I come in, Sara?"

PART 2

Sara could see fine snow blowing around like a small cyclone under the outdoor light of the barn. Holding the entrance door open for Paul, he walked through, unable to hide his nervousness. Sara invited him over to the kitchen table and began making tea for both of them. Tending to the kettle, Sara was slow to turn from the cupboard to look Paul in the eye. For a moment, there was an uncomfortable silence until Paul forced out an awkward smile then went back to looking around at random items in the kitchen, softly tapping his fingers on the table. Paul perceived the silence as an agreement not to discuss anything until the tea was served, but Sara couldn't wait that long.

"So, you didn't answer me. What's going on, Paul, to have you out on a night like tonight?" Sara spoke with her back pushed against the cabinets, her hands firmly gripping both sides of the black granite countertop. Paul looked down briefly and wiped his hand back and forth across the kitchen table as if wiping away crumbs.

"Ah, I'm sorry, Sara, but I've got some bad news." Sara's knees began to bend slightly. "I'm sorry. There's no easy way to tell you this. I just came from Shelley Randall's place. She was murdered sometime last night." Paul thought it best to get it out directly, no sugar coating it. "I'm sorry, Sara. I know how close you two were."

Sara stood still, staring straight across the room over Paul's head. She was wearing a sweatshirt and a pair of grey track pants with her high school logo on them. To Paul, she appeared warm and cozy until she folded her arms, and a slight tremble became noticeable. She looked as though a sudden chill had come upon her, but Paul knew better.

"Best we can figure right now is it happened late last night between ten and two," he said, lowering his head again. Still uncomfortable, he began shifting in his chair and became fidgety. He looked back at Sara. She continued to stare without a word.

"Are you going to be okay, Sara? Do you need me to call someone for you? Heather, maybe?" Paul wasn't quite sure what to say next. He felt a nervous heat rising and a tingling through his chest and neck. In the struggle to think of something else to say, he could tell he was about to start perspiring, feeling his face heating up and moisture in the nape of his neck. Just as he was going to suggest something else, Sara finally spoke.

"What's going on around here, Paul?"

Her question sounded more like an accusation, and he was about to reply when some tears rolled down her cheeks without a sob.

"This kind of stuff doesn't happen around here," she continued, holding her arms out. Sara usually spoke expressively, often descriptively using her hands, but this was more than usual. There was no denying just how upset she was becoming. "You know what I mean? This is a small town!" she said forcefully, pointing in the direction of Clarington.

She stopped briefly and looked up, worried she had raised her voice too high and had woken up the kids. Her voice resumed at a normal level. "Other than Pat, how many murders have happened in this town in all your time here, Paul?" Sara inquired, her eyes widening and becoming dark again.

"None that I can recall," he said in a sombre tone.

Sara finally managed to make it to the kitchen table with two cups of tea, and they sat and discussed what happened to Pat and Shelley, and the evil behind Jonathon Vargas.

"No matter who you find who did this to Shelley, there's something else at work here. There's something else responsible for all of this happening," Sara said, looking Paul in the eye.

Paul looked confused. Just when he thought Sara was done speaking, taking a sip of her tea, she quickly set it down and firmly gripped his forearm on the table, squeezing it hard.

"I don't know if it's from here originally, or if it has just come here recently," she said, sitting back and continuing with small sips of her tea. She had an odd expression as she looked at Paul over the rim of her cup without following up on her statement.

In the preceding months, Paul had gotten to know Sara. He believed this wasn't normal behaviour for her. He continued watching her expressions while she spoke of things he had never considered in the everyday world that he lived and operated in. Then Sara reminded him of what was in that report on Vargas, which Jacob obtained only a few short weeks before he and Pat died.

"Think about it, Paul! What possesses a man to travel three thousand miles to kill the child of his stepfather? Because the stepfather disciplined him, and the daughter got on his nerves when he was a ten-year-old kid? I mean, come on!"

At that point Sara was leaning over her cup of tea with both forearms on the table, talking to Paul as if she were sharing trade secrets. Paul sat back. He looked tired as he considered what she was saying. His expression became one of a man trying to solve a riddle that had just been proposed to him.

"I don't know, Sara. But yeah, it's extreme for sure."

"I know you don't want to hear this, but I think the operative word here is *possesses*."

Sara nodded her head and resumed drinking her tea.

5

Awareness

2011

PART 1

Sara knew that Mary's abilities as a seer were increasing. Sara never applied a label to herself and her own abilities nor to what her daughter was becoming. Mary's dreams of Vargas being mean to her father when she was only three years old suggested to Sara that her daughter was seeing things as they were really happening. This didn't develop for Sara until she was pregnant with Mary. Mary's dreams, with a child's view of a potential danger to her father, were just as much a mystery to Sara as her own dreams and visions of Jacob were. Sara didn't want to discuss the issue with Mary. Even when Mary would foresee some of the smaller inconsequential things in life, Sara felt it best that it was left to develop on its own. Mary would ask Sara about her dreams from time to time, but her abilities didn't become a focal point as she was growing up. Sara made sure of that.

Ben's glowing hands at his father's gravesite suggested to Sara that her son had the same abilities his father had. She briefly wondered if he had tried to heal his father and bring him back to life on the day Jacob was buried. Considering the reality of what Jacob was, Sara thought it absurd that a child would reach that far.

She concluded it had to be an unsuspecting instinctive reaction. And for several years that followed, Ben never exhibited any further signs of his ability that Sara saw. As with Mary's talents, Sara decided not to raise the issue with Ben for fear of how he would react and what he might say to others. In the time since Jacob's death, the subject of what his father had been, and what abilities that provided him, was never a topic for discussion. And for good reason.

As with Jacob's parents, Sara's priority was to protect her children from exposure, especially Ben. Any of this coming into the public's eye was a fear never far from Sara's thoughts. Until anything more became necessary, she quietly observed. Even when Jacob brought a bird back to life at four years old, he wasn't aware of what he had done. That in itself was a blessing for Irene and Thomas. As a grown man, Jacob would eventually go to his mother for help while trying to understand what was happening to him during his awakening as a guardian. Sara wouldn't have that luxury. As time passed, Sara would come to learn just how different one guardian is from the next.

It was the last week of June and the beginning of summer. A light breeze came in from the southwest off the lake that felt like a soft and warm silk sheet gently caressing the skin. It was seven-thirty p.m., and there was plenty of daylight left for "The Soldiers Three" to press on with their outdoor adventures.

Sara was at the kitchen sink preparing snacks for the kids and keeping an eye and ear out for the infantry men weary of battle. Blake McFarland, eleven years old, was an introverted, sullen child. He was skinny with straight dirty-blonde hair and blue-grey eyes. He was significantly smaller than the other boys. Shane Lindsay was a wild red-headed kid who lived on a farm just under a mile north of the O'Connells. He was always on the go and was often found working by his father's side. And Ben, with his scruffy, dirty-blonde hair that hadn't turned completely brown yet to match his eyes, was thrilled to have his friends over. He was an inch or so shorter than Shane, and for the most part a quiet kid, but today's excitement created a boisterous commanding leader on the battlefield.

Sara always had a shaky stomach when Ben had friends over and tonight it was in full flop mode. Zoom! One went by. Zoom! Another dashed in the opposite direction. And occasionally all three boys would be in full flight together, running from or toward the enemy's army of invisible combatants. The yelling about whatever imaginary adventures they were having kept Sara smiling. Nervous, but smiling knowing they were safe and having fun.

Feeling confident the boys were fine, Sara joined Mary in the living room. She was watching the latest episode of her favourite show, *Degrassi*, on the wide screen. Being such a devoted fan, twelve-year-old Mary remained quiet as a mouse. Wearing her denim red-and-white-striped overall shorts, she lay on her belly with her elbows down and her chin propped up in the palms of her hands. She was locked in on the screen. Her knees were bent, and her socked heels banged against each other as she buzzed with anticipation for what would come next. After ten minutes of mostly silent mother–daughter time, Sara was shocked to hear Mary pipe up in the middle of a scene.

"You need to check on the boys, Mom. Something's going to happen," she said, in a monotone voice without moving an inch, staring at the television screen.

What Mary said, and the way she said it, gave Sara an awful chill. She jumped up from the arm of the sofa and ran outside calling Ben's name. She made a quick prayer that her appearance would stop something bad from happening. She didn't make it to the corner of the porch before she ran into Ben and Shane. Their faces were frozen in fear, and they were both out of breath. They frantically tried to get their words to the surface.

"Mom, you gotta come. Quick, Blake fell for real. He fell out of the swing tree, and he's not moving. Quick, Mom. Come on!" Ben said, grabbing Sara's hand. All three ran to the old elm tree in the side yard. Sara's stomach was in knots as she held her breath.

PART 2

Only steps behind Ben and Shane, Sara arrived to find Blake lying motionless at the base of the elm tree. The fall had left him with a serious head injury and a huge welt under a severe gash on the side of his forehead.

"Oh my God!" Sara whispered to herself, shocked by what she saw. She was trying not to scare the boys any more than they already were. Bending down, she started calling Blake's name while she checked his neck for a pulse. Afraid to pick Blake up, Sara turned to Ben with a serious look.

"Ben, honey. Go tell Mary to call 911. Tell her what happened."

Ben stood motionless, seemingly entranced, staring out to the tree line that separated the yard's grass from this year's wheat crop. Ben was locked in on the last big walnut tree closest to the house. Sara looked up again.

"Ben!" she yelled.

Shane could see what was happening, and he pulled on Ben's arm. "Come on, Ben. Let's go!" he squawked, trying to urge him into action.

Sara felt a faint pulse on Blake's neck but worried it was diminishing. She looked back at Ben, wanting to shake him into action. She saw a look on his face that she hadn't seen since he ran back to his father's casket on the day of the funeral. Holding Blake's head, Sara strained her neck to turn and look out to the walnut tree to see what Ben was staring at, but she couldn't see anything with the setting sun in her eyes. Shane's voice and constant tugging at Ben were beginning to grate on her. When she turned her attention back to the boys, Ben's gaze was eerily locked in on Blake.

"Mom, you should take Shane into the house now. Go on now. Go in the house," Ben said with a vacancy in his voice. As strange as the sensation was, Sara felt she had no choice but to listen to her son. Without wasting another second, she rose to her feet and reached out for Shane's hand. The slack-jawed look on Shane's face was one Sara knew would come with many questions. But better the questions than for him to witness what she knew was about to happen.

When Sara reached the house, she stopped for a moment to glance back at Ben. She saw a familiar glow around his hands that was already dissipating. She was amazed and terrified at the same time. She went into the house with Shane but stopped halfway to the kitchen where the phone was located.

"Maybe you should go back and stay with the boys, Shane. That might be better," Sara said, turning to look him in the eye and nodding in the direction of the yard.

Without hesitation, Shane bolted through the door, stomped across the wooden deck and made a dramatic leap onto the grass before continuing the race back to his friends. When he arrived at the tree, he saw Blake sitting up against its base. He looked as though he had just woken up from a nap, squinting his eyes at the brightness of the sun. Ben had taken a rag that the boys used as their imaginary company's infantry flag and placed it against the cut on Blake's head. Blake held the field dressing in place and kept pressure on it until Sara could tend to it.

For the rest of the night, the boys stayed in and played in Ben's room. Shane seemed to forget all about the call for an ambulance. Blake's gash was a scratch by morning with help from the anti-bacterial ointment and bandage Sara had applied the night before. And because of Ben's helpful hands, Blake's cut and bump were barely noticeable. No frantic ambulance trip to the hospital or call to concerned parents required. But the boys had a story to carry with them for as long as they could remember it.

Sara's relief that Ben hadn't been exposed as being the same as his father couldn't be measured. When she looked back on this day, Sara could see the white aura of a figure next to that walnut tree. But the day it happened with the boys there, she brushed the image off as the falling sun playing tricks on her eyes. Every time Sara drove in and out of the property after that day, she always looked to that tree. Although she felt mixed emotions, it always brought a smile to her face.

6

Virulent

2016

PART 1

With small runs of time in and out of jail throughout his life, Dylan Matthews eventually met the kind of people he wanted to benefit from knowing. Dylan's last assault charge landed him twenty-six months in jail, which meant federal time.

This is where he met one of his future partners, Joe Miller. They were released within a couple weeks of each other and ended up at the same halfway house. Dylan was small potatoes compared to Joe, who served a long stretch for armed robbery, attempted murder, and conspiracy to commit murder. Joe became an underling to a white supremacist gang in the penitentiary in order to get protection. He wasn't trying to stay clear of any particular group of people. Joe generally pissed off everybody he came into contact with at one time or another.

Joe had a grating personality with a horribly negative attitude, an unparalleled sense of entitlement, and a know-it-all mouth to top it off. It was a constant barrage of "fuckin'" as an adjective, or "fuckin' eh, fuck me, for fuck's sake" and on and on. Protection came at a cost, however. A cost that he was under constant pressure to pay off now that he was on the outside.

In their first three months at the halfway house, the only free time the men were allowed was to look for work or for legal and medical appointments. Joe was being pressured to walk away from parole and deal drugs full time. He was smart enough to know that if he walked away, he would end up back in prison to finish the seven years left of his sentence, plus another year for running. For now, he made trips only for job interviews or for grocery store or pharmacy runs with strict time limits. It wore on him, but it wasn't prison.

Dylan took the initiative and delivered some staples to Joe, unsolicited. Everything Joe experienced in prison taught him that nothing was free. Initially Joe accused Dylan of trying to buy favours. Joe had the muscle, experience, and temperament to seriously hurt Dylan. He was taken aback when Dylan rose from where he sat on the edge of his bed and walked toward him.

"I couldn't help hearing you telling the house dick you didn't get your cheque yet. So, I got mine plus I had a little saved up. There ya go! What goes around—"

Joe cut Dylan off but brought his aggressive tone down. "Okay. Got ya. Hey, thanks, man." He peeked inside the bag and discovered a porn rag wrapped in a newspaper. "I'll get you back as soon as I get my cheque." Joe's words came quick with the experience of dealing in favours.

Dylan knew better than to waive off the offer to let Joe pay him back. After all, he had graduated from the teachings of master manipulation from what he read in his father's murder books, building on his own natural abilities. Those books had become so important to him that he put them in a safety deposit box after using them, every time. Then he started creating his own.

Dylan knew what he wanted from Joe, and he had the financial means, and then some, to get him away from the local chapter of the Heritage Men. As time went on, the pair got along famously.

And when the time was right, Dylan put his real skills on display for Joe.

Dylan followed Joe down to Mechanic Street where Joe was meeting up with his meth supplier as pre-arranged by the higher-ups. Dealing meth for the gang was the main way Joe could pay back the protection he received in prison. However, Joe argued with the supplier about his cut. This presented the perfect opportunity for Dylan to perform.

PART 2

Barry Kitchen supplied crack and crystal meth, among several other drugs, with a good cut going to the Heritage Men. The house Barry used for transactions was a long-abandoned, post-war, one-storey brick bungalow. Two blocks north of a defunct railway line, three other condemned homes sat across from an old machine shop factory. The street was an image of abandonment with its concrete sidewalks and curbs broken and cracked with knee-high grass and weeds growing out of them. Before completing their transaction, Barry and Joe walked up and down those beaten-up sidewalks discussing potential pricing for grams, eight-balls, and quarter ounces. They finally made it back to the house, which was trashed with holes punched and kicked into the walls and doors. Everything was covered in graffiti. The floors were equally disgusting.

As they were getting ready to wrap up their transaction, they saw one of Barry's foot soldiers just inside the door. He looked like he was lounging, laying back on a once yellow velour chair. His throat had been slit from ear to ear, and he was completely soaked in blood.

Barry was through the door first. He was in pure shock and was slow getting his guard up as he took a double take.

"What the—" These were the last words ever spoken by Barry Kitchen.

Dylan quickly turned the corner and, ever so calmly and smoothly, buried a large butcher knife in Barry's throat and pushed it out through the other side of his neck, along his spine. Joe was frozen and all that could be heard was the gurgling sound of Barry trying to draw a breath while holding his lacerated windpipe.

Dylan pulled out the knife and was instantly hit with a high-velocity stream of blood that sprayed straight out, all over his face and chest. His reaction was eerily calm as he rapidly stuck the knife into Barry's heart as many times as he could before Barry crumpled to the floor.

Next time it's the heart first, then the throat. Less spray, Dylan thought.

There was still no movement from Joe who stood with his mouth agape. His eyes bounced around the room from Dylan to the two dead bodies. When the gravity of the double homicide finally registered, he stammered his words.

"Wha … fuck, Dylan! What fuckin'. What the … what the fuck is wrong with you, man? For fuck's sake! This is serious jail time, you fucking idiot!" Joe forced the words out, restraining himself. His paranoia kicking in, Joe hoped no one could hear him, wanting desperately to yell at Dylan. Joe's new psychopathic friend looked down at Barry, then back to him, as he wiped the blood from his face.

"Come with me. And don't worry about the noise. No one can hear us," Dylan said, deadpan as could be.

Seemingly unconcerned, he walked to the rear of the house where the kitchen was located. He wiped his hands with his shirt then grabbed a kilo of crystal meth from inside one of the cabinets and tossed it to Joe.

"Here, this is yours. Where did they expect you to hide that, up your ass?" Dylan giggled as he started washing the blood off with water from a large plastic bottle.

"Kidding, buddy." Joe could see Dylan was a well-prepared and experienced killer. Despite Joe's time in jail, that still disturbed him. After he finished cleaning the blood off, Dylan took a big swig out of his water bottle and offered some to Joe, who declined.

Dylan dried off and put a fresh shirt on. Joe was still stunned and unsure of what to think, say, or do. He started to pace back and forth from the entrance where Barry's body lay and back to Dylan in the kitchen.

Dylan turned to Joe. "We should probably go," he said calmly and walked out the side door and down the steps.

PART 3

Joe was blown away and at a loss for what direction to take.

"Are you coming?" Dylan asked, carrying the bloody t-shirt in one hand and a small bottle of lighter fluid in the other.

Dylan tossed the shirt in an old burned out, rusted metal drum outside. He soaked it in lighter fluid, threw the empty bottle in, and lit a match. The pair stepped over the broken wire mesh fence in the backyard and into a weed and rubbish-filled alley. When they were a few steps down the lane, a small explosion from inside the metal drum unceremoniously announced their exit. Joe would never look at Dylan the same way after that day. Dylan was already aware how much his attack on Barry would change the dynamic of their relationship. He was counting on it.

Before things went any further between Joe and Dylan at the drug house, Dylan informed Joe what he wanted from him for the kilo of meth, and that was a new I.D. All Joe had to do was contact one of the higher-ups in the gang and ask why Barry hadn't contacted him to tell him where to meet yet. His alibi was easy. He was always being monitored at the halfway house, so what little time he had was wasted because Barry was a no-show. Once he had calmed down, Joe realized that Dylan had given him a leg up. Dylan had taken his time to find the right person in prison who he could manipulate for his needs on the outside. Play the long game, as his father often wrote in his journals. This was his reward.

Joe's personality type was reactionary. His temper was what would lead him to actually kill someone. He normally didn't have the same desire or joy of the hunt the way Dylan did. After being betrayed, Joe was driven by the baser instinct of revenge. He was on the hunt for someone specific. He had thoughts of little else since going to prison, but revenge was out of reach for him. As the light came on for Joe, he realized Dylan was a means to an end for him. But Joe didn't realize just how well Dylan knew him.

Before purposefully going in different directions, Dylan used Joe for his connections and paid for his new identity. He changed his name from Dylan Matthews to Nathan Jona Gravallos. Joe was still on parole, which meant every move he made had to be approved. Unless he became exhausted by it and ran. Dylan convinced him to stay put and lay low for a while longer. Joe found work at the wholesale fruit and vegetable market in the south end of the city, and "Nathan" headed back to Clarington for what he thought of as surveillance.

In Clarington, Dylan planned to take over his father's watch of the O'Connells and began building his own plan for the long game. As he learned from Vargas's journals, the pleasure in stalking someone came from the preparations and the long haul, which made the final scenes all the sweeter. If he needed to release pent-up anger in the interim, he could go back to the city for that. Dylan took a job with a landscaping company that had a contract for the municipality. This worked out perfectly because the company's clients included the Clarington Collegiate Institute, where Mary and Ben attended school. Dylan also revelled in being so close to Shelley Randall's house.

With a new name and look, he could now hide in plain sight.

7

Vulnerabilities

2017

Ben went through puberty just as awkwardly as any other boy. Growing quickly, he appeared to be advancing to the size and look of his father. He excelled at most sports and at the age he was now, his biology was becoming competitive, but sports still ruled over girls.

It was early morning just before school started. Ben and his teammate, Daryl Boudreau, were practicing in preparation for the upcoming basketball championship. Daryl, six-foot-two, and Ben, five-foot-ten, made a great duo. Daryl had the look of a sports star. He was overly handsome with soft brown eyes and long lashes that drove the girls crazy.

After a quick breather, Ben had possession of the ball, and Daryl was on defence. Ben started dribbling in from the outside, forcing Daryl to come out and challenge him. It could have been some water he spilled on his sneakers during their break or drips of sweat on the floor, either way it caused Daryl to slip. Daryl couldn't get his arms out behind himself fast enough to stop his momentum, and he awkwardly fell to the floor. He cracked the back of his skull so hard it echoed throughout the otherwise empty gym. His head bounced off the floor twice before his body went limp, his eyes briefly rolling back in his head before they closed.

Ben's movement was so quick his sneakers squeaked on the hardcourt as he came to a stop. In a flash, he was at Daryl's side calling out his name. "Hey! Daryl! Dude? Daryl, you okay?"

When Ben began to shake Daryl, he saw a significant pool of blood forming on the court beneath his head.

"For real, bro, come on. I don't need this shit right now. You don't need this shit either. Jesus, Daryl. Wake up!" Ben's words were pushed out. He didn't want to be overheard by anyone. It wouldn't be long before classes started, and students started filling the halls.

Ben flashed back to when he was ten years old. This time he was wiser and composed enough to take a few seconds to check Daryl's pulse before attempting a rescue. Daryl's pulse was indeed becoming faint and fading. Holding his ear to Daryl's mouth, Ben could barely feel a breath. His friend was losing his life. He was slipping away.

Ben cautiously looked around. He bolted over to the bench and came back with a towel in hand. He instinctively looked to the bleachers and exits to make sure no one was around. His attention swiftly returned to Daryl. Squatting next to his chest, Ben put the towel under his head to stop the bleeding. With one last look around, he placed his hands on Daryl and covered each side of his cheeks, temples, and head. This was the part that would elude his memory, but his natural abilities drove him. He kept his head down and his eyes closed until he felt Daryl move. Ben felt the most bizarre sensation of his brain shutting off like a light switch, no awareness for the short time it takes to do what he needs to. It would remain a puzzle to him.

Just as Ben was finishing and Daryl started to stir, someone walked into the gym. "Hey, guys. Is everything all right? What happened?" asked a soft female voice.

Ben was becoming aware far sooner than he had experienced before. He could hear footsteps getting closer and he began shaking like a leaf, concluding he was caught.

"Shit! Well, I suppose I can't hide it now. Come on, Daryl. Time to wake up." Ben said to himself, hearing whoever it was nearly upon him now and the voice piped up again.

"Hey. Oh my God, Ben."

Ben was still shaking, feeling like he had a fever bringing perspiration to his forehead, building up and dripping down his nose. He was between panic and anger of potentially being exposed. He realized the voice he was hearing belonged to his sister, Mary, standing right behind him. This instantly provided him with a sense of comfort and protection.

Ben could hear the door to the gymnasium opening again. "Ben. Hurry! Someone's coming," Mary urged in a raspy whisper. With her fear building by the second, Mary heard a mumble come from Daryl.

Thank God, she said to herself, spinning back around to see how Ben and Daryl were doing. Mary assumed it was a student who opened the door and let go for some reason, much to her relief. *Maybe it was just somebody fooling around. God, I hope nobody saw anything.*

On bended knee, Ben looked down on Daryl with a smile. "You gonna be okay, bro? You took an extra cringey splash there."

Daryl looked at Ben with a bit of a simper and without a word extended his arm. Ben locked their forearms together and pulled Daryl and himself up off the floor.

"Wow! Look at all that blood. Is that all mine?" Daryl asked while feeling the back of his head, sounding punch drunk as expected.

"Yeah. You took a good whack, dude. Might want to see the nurse. She might send you to the hospital to get a few stitches," Ben said nervously, motioning to Mary to grab the other towel off the bench. She came over and took it upon herself to start wiping the blood up off the floor.

"We should grab a shower," Ben said, gently leading Daryl with his hand behind his back.

"Yeah. Sure, Ben," Daryl willingly followed.

Leaving the gym, he stepped like he was crossing a pond on rocks that weren't in a straight line. This was quite concerning to Ben and

Mary, and they raised their eyebrows to each other. Walking toward the exit of the gym, Ben stopped for a moment and vomited into the large garbage can next to the double doors. He stood back up and wiped his mouth like he was simply spitting. Normally it would be expected that Daryl would ask Ben if he was all right, but the thought, along with many others, didn't register.

8

Prescience

2017

PART 1

Mary's hair was a darker auburn in the winter months. In the summer, the sun brings out highlights similar to her mother's bright red hair. Ben recognized the colour and style from the far end of the hall just as he was catching up with his friends.

With the basketball championships behind him, Ben had just come out of the showers after several vigorous matches of volleyball. Ben wore his father's old, beat up, dark brown suede coat with a pair of faded and ripped blue jeans. He completed the look with black Dayton's, also his father's. Ben kept his hair buzzed on the sides with dyed-blonde streaks through the rest of his thick, dark brown crop. Lately when Sara would see Ben coming or going, she would think, *I know, I know. There's nothing I can do about it. It's the style now. Just let it go.* She imagined herself having to say this to Jacob over his disdain for Ben's style.

Tonight was date night with his girlfriend, Diane Westbrook. But his plans had changed, and he would be staying in town overnight. Ben wanted to tell Mary he wouldn't be home on this Friday night so she could pass it on to their mother as opposed to the usual interrogation that would ensue if he had asked her himself. It was the plans he had with Diane for the next day that were important to Ben, several rare hours of privacy while Diane's parents were away. It was too cold for the beach, but that wouldn't stop Ben and his friends from having a bonfire on the Friday night. Ben and Diane were as close as teens can be, but there seemed to be an adult manner to their relationship. Neither became overly excited at the prospect of being with the other, or so it appeared. How they felt for each other was as close to teenage love as could be, yet they displayed a mature attitude about it. But for now, Ben's mission was to pass off the information to Mary, so he could take off with his friends.

Standing in the middle of the hall lined with beige metal lockers and a terrazzo floor of various shades of white, black, and brown, Ben suddenly turned to his friends. "Guys, hang on a sec."

Leaving his compatriots momentarily, he ran up behind his sister and tapped the back of her right shoulder as he snuck around to her left.

"Oh. Real funny, pinhead," Mary snapped at her brother for acting juvenile.

Moving around to stand in front of her, Ben grabbed her shoulder to bring her to a stop so he could speak with her. They both stopped cold, frozen in the middle of the school's corridor. They both saw the same thing at the same moment. Seemingly locked in, it took a few seconds before Ben could let go of his sister's shoulder. It took a few more before either one of them acknowledged what just happened.

Finally, Mary reacted. "Please tell me you saw that. I don't know how, but you did see that, right?" Mary's voice sounded somewhat desperate. Ben started backing away from his sister into the crowded hall, people side-stepping him, some bumping into him.

"Ben!" Mary's tone evidently demanding and frightful.

"Yeah … I did. I'll talk to you later … at home, tomorrow."

He was attempting to be dismissive, but his face had a lost, bewildered expression and he struggled to find the words, unsure which way to turn. His face clearly indicated to Mary just how much that vision spooked him, having never experienced such a thing.

What Ben said was to placate Mary in the moment, but he had no intention of revisiting this vision. He wanted no part of it. Although the vision wasn't new to Mary, its content spooked her too, and for the second time in the same week. The first time was directly following Ben saving Daryl's life. It wasn't exactly a reward for helping her brother. Now that Ben had seen what Mary had, it allowed him to find some empathy, realizing just how disturbing her dreams and visions could be.

Ben wasn't with his friends too long before his phone buzzed in his back pocket. It was a text message from his sister.

{*Text me b4 it gets 2 late 2nite, k?*}

She received a {*K*} in response from Ben.

Ben and Mary shared a slightly blurred vision of looking into a mirror and seeing a bloody Shelley Randall in her bed. They also saw somebody's arm holding an equally bloody, large butcher knife.

Mary eventually learned the truth about Shelley Randall from her mother. Although, it was a quick, varnished version of how she was murdered. Sara waited until the rumours drove Mary crazy with questions before she would discuss what happened to her friend.

Mary would not learn of the rape or the gory crime scene details from her mother. Most of those details came from her dreams and visions that matched up with what gossip she heard locally. None of her dreams or visions revealed the attacker's face and that would drive her crazy at times. She did know, by pure instinct, that whoever it was, she and Ben would be running into him at some point in time. Mary hadn't shared this with her mother as for now the content was too sensitive for her. However, not too long into the future, she would feel the need to share everything from her dreams and visions with Ben. After today's vision, she wondered if her dreams were getting closer to revealing Shelley's killer.

PART 2

During high school, Mary never had a full-time boyfriend for more than a few months. Mostly she dated, and not much of that. She was quite shy with boys, and most of them had difficulty approaching her because she was a naturally beautiful girl like her mother. Most boys were intimidated by that and the ones with the nerve to ask her out were jocks, and they weren't Mary's type. And she would never ask a boy out. She wasn't a prude. It was something her Grandmother O'Connell told her when she was young, and it stuck. Even in her last year of high school, she rarely dated, putting all her efforts into getting good grades in preparation for university in Vancouver for a degree in journalism. Mary's tendencies toward journalism began shortly after her father died. Between her family and Uncle Pat's family there was a lot of speculation around the deaths, and it started Mary asking questions. Even though she wouldn't push her mother any more about Jacob's passing, her inquisitiveness only grew.

After today's vision, the bus ride home would be a quiet one now that Ben was gone with his friends for the weekend. The last leg of the drive was the longest with Mary being the last student to be dropped off. Heading home, Mary could see the random oblong patches of snow still clinging to the edges of the farmer's fields. With only pines and cedars providing colour along the way, Mary felt like she would never escape winter's grasp, despite April's arrival.

In this moment, she wished only to rid herself of thoughts about the vision she and Ben had just shared. Popping her ear buds in so she could drown out her thoughts and their effects, she cranked her favourite tunes and opened one of her books. She also ran pictures of the University of British Columbia campus in Vancouver through her head. The buildings and grounds were beautiful enough to distract her for a little while. It was still early in the year, but she was thrilled and scared at the same time about her thoughts of living in another province.

Before long, she drifted off to sleep. Occasionally jostled with the odd bump, she slept most of the way home. The ten minutes to the farmhouse from the second-last stop were long enough to fall back into a familiar and unwanted dream. Once the bus hit a certain speed, the tires produced a sound, a hum that worked like a pacifier for

Mary. Without any conversation to stimulate her, she would occasionally drift off with her head against the window. Mary had never set eyes on Dylan Matthews before, that she was aware of, but she dreamt of him not long after she turned seven years old. The first dream was in the beginning of February 2006, just before Shelley Randall was murdered. The dream may have been an omen, but she was only seven then, incapable of interpreting any part of the dream let alone understand what was happening. As time went on, the same dream would visit her once in a while.

Sara was pulling Mary on an orange, hard-cast plastic sleigh along the snow-covered road past Shelley Randall's house. It was so quiet and peaceful, she heard only the crunching of snow under her mother's feet, and nothing else. It was a beautiful evening with the fresh, powdered snow highlighting some of the trees in suburbia. Not long after New Year's, many of the homes' exteriors were still alit with glowing multicoloured bulbs from Christmas and that included Shelley Randall's. The picture on the moment was completed with a clear, bright sky thanks to a full moon. With a blanket of stars, it looked like the cover of a Christmas card. The lights inside Shelley's house were on as well, and she stood in front of the living room window, her eyes black with fright, but Mary did not realize what was happening.

"Mommy, Mommy, look it's Shelley," an excited Mary shouted out, rapidly waving her bright red mitten to the house. This time Mary raised her voice thinking her mother couldn't hear her. "Mommy … Mom! Look it's Shelley. Aren't you going to wave to her?" Mary asked, curiously disappointed. She looked to her mother only to see her continue to look straight ahead.

"We won't be seeing Shelley anymore," Sara said, her voice bereft of emotion. When Mary turned back to Shelley with a pouty lip, she was startled to see a man wearing all black come into view at the side of her house from the rear. When all this was happening, it seemed to Mary that while the sleigh was moving forward, they were still in front of Shelley's house, not gaining any ground in this bizarre dreamscape.

"*Mom, who's that?*" *No reply came, so Mary asked with urgency as the man slowly approached the side door of the house.* "*MOMMY!*" *she yelled out. Just then this man came into view standing at the door, clearly lit by the overhead light. Mary froze as this stranger locked eyes with her, and it was only his eyes she could see clearly, his face was a moving fog. Terrified now, Mary couldn't squeak out another sound, but she was trying to. An unknown force in the dream kept her voice silent, no matter how hard she tried to scream to get her mother's attention. That's when the man held his forefinger to his mouth to shush her as he slowly slunk down and in rubbery form slipped under the door and into the house.*

Mary was horrified, frantically thinking this strange man with alien-like flexibility was going to hurt Shelley. All of her screaming to her mother, and then to Shelley, went out of her mouth as a near-silent whisper. The last thing she saw before waking up each time was this mysterious prowler standing inside the house several feet behind Shelley, slowly approaching her from behind and about to pounce. And all Mary could do was watch on in horror. Shelley may have been waving back to her, but she was otherwise lifeless and oblivious to the danger coming up behind her.

Mary would often wake up from this nightmare yelling out for her mother.

9

Forward

2017

PART 1

Sara's mood received a boost of optimism with the fresh smell of spring brought from deciduous trees shedding their protective shells and sprouting their baby leaves. For Sara, life in Clarington had constant reminders of Jacob. Those memories were everywhere she turned and had become too much. The cumulative effect of relentless sorrow ultimately led to her decision to make the move to British Columbia. For more than one purpose, she decided to give up her share in Able Hands and move across the country.

Sara had learned to stand her ground against evil, but she became more cognizant, nervous, and fearful for her children as they became older. This was the biggest motivator along with the fact that Mary was going to be in university in Vancouver for at least four years. Sara had never forgotten what happened to her good friend Shelley, and time didn't soften that pain. She was convinced that Shelley's death wouldn't be the last in this area, and she wasn't going to risk her children to the dark force she sensed nearby.

She wanted a completely different environment and lifestyle when her kids made the turn into adulthood. Of course, she would have to deal with the blowback from them upon sharing the news. She expected a certain degree of rebellion typical of most teenagers, but she knew it would mostly come from Ben. She didn't need to be a seer to know that.

Ben and Mary were developing more diversely compared to their parents. Sara started becoming sensitively intuitive to what Jacob was experiencing after she become pregnant with Mary. Sara could sense when Jacob was in the proximity of anything dangerous. That was something that scared her, which in turn could wear on Jacob's nerves. Her dreams at night came with one view of looking at Jacob, and a daydream provided something completely different — the perception from his eyes.

Not long ago. Mary had approached her mother to ask more about her father's death, but Sara remained apprehensive. Knowing the gifts Jacob was born with, all Sara knew of a guardian was the apparent punishment for killing someone, whether they were good or bad. Even with Ben having his father's abilities, Sara chose not to dig deeper into what Jacob had been. After all this time, it was still too painful to pull back that bandage, but she instinctively knew that was about to change.

Sara watched her children closely for any developments that could be a danger to them. She knew her daughter was acutely perceptive and was never satisfied with the circumstances that surrounded her father's death. Sara did her best to get through telling Mary about that awful day, but she stopped short of telling her about her father's abilities and the actual cause of his death. For the moment, all Sara would offer up was that an unknown issue with his heart caused it to fail from the extreme stress of that day. She still felt the need to keep her kids away from the whole story to protect them until they were older, but that time was here. Like it or not, Sara would end up having this conversation with Mary just before the move west. She chose to wait to tell Ben, knowing her intentions to move would be enough for him to handle for now.

Sara tried to talk to Ben after he saved Blake, but he was uninterested in what he could do and wanted no part of talking about it. It was embarrassing to him, like an affliction. As a mother, Sara had most of the common worries any mother would, but what the kids inherited from their father increased her stress exponentially. There was no denying that Ben was Jacob's son. He was a handsome kid with the best of his parent's good features. He was getting taller by the day and had a muscular body. Even though his dark brown hair had blonde highlights, the way it was cropped at the sides gave him a tough look similar to his father's. Normally, Ben was a warm-hearted kid with a rare patience about most things. However, when it came to matters of the heart, or his convictions about his life being interfered with, his patience flew south. And this is exactly how he would perceive Sara's announcement to move.

PART 2

With a ninety-six percent grade average, Mary chose the Simon Fraser University halfway through her final year in high school. After her graduation, the move on to university was imminent. In Ben's case, leaving the only home he has ever known would be much harder to do. With several friends and his girlfriend from Clarington, these emotional bonds would cause a difficult separation. Sara expected a large degree of grief from him and was prepared to deal with it. She sat on the swing sofa on the porch next to the front door, appearing approachable as always. The rattle from the bus's engine as it dropped the kids off was distinct to Sara's ears. Unlike the rattle in her stomach. Nervously rubbing her hands together, she anxiously waited for Ben and Mary to come walking over the hill of the long gravel laneway.

"Hi, guys. How was your day? School will be coming to a close before you know it. You must be excited about that, right?" Sara asked, unable hide her apprehension.

"What's the matter, Mom?" Mary was quick to ask. Ben stood still, holding his backpack strap while it rested on the ground.

"Listen, you two. I need to talk to you about something. This is important, and I need both of you to listen and understand, okay?"

"Sure, Mom," was the unanimous response.

They sat down on the sofa, one on each side of their mother. It was obvious that Sara was having difficulty getting this conversation started. She wasn't one to be apprehensive nor unsure of herself, so she simply blurted it out. "We're going to move to B.C. so we can be closer to Mary while she's in university. And after four years, I'm assuming we will stay there. What do you two think of that?" Sara asked, followed by a deeply nervous and pronounced swallow.

"Well, Mom—" Mary started to respond when Ben stood up without a word and stomped his way inside the house, slamming the door shut.

"Okay. Now we know how Ben feels about this. I expected that. What about you, sweetie? Are you okay with this idea?" Sara asked, wanting Mary's blessing.

"What is it, Mom, that makes you want to leave here? This is the home you and Dad worked so hard to have. I thought you wanted to stay here forever. I mean, all of his things are still here and ... well, I don't know. It's definitely weird, but if this is what you really want to do, then I'm all right with it. I'll support you." Mary's words came calmly and sincerely.

In his room, Ben waited with his outrage brewing inside him. He perceived it as the "fix was in." The decision was already made without his input. Which, technically, it was. Not too long after, Sara came up to talk with him. Before she could complete a sentence, his response to the idea came out.

"No way! You've got to be freakin' kidding me! This is extra B.S.! I'm not going! No way, no how! I have friends here. Diane is here. I have a life here. I don't want a life in the mountains somewhere with a bunch of hillbillies and goats. Forget it ... not gonna happen. For real, this is total crap! No way! Is this what putting Dad's pictures away was all about? What's your plan? To move away and forget about him?"

Sara didn't say another word in response to Ben's diatribe. She looked at him in a way that told him he had pushed the envelope too far. She turned around and walked out slowly, gently closing the door behind her before proceeding down the hall and back downstairs. Ben may be young, but like his father, his expressions and words could cut like a knife.

§

An unexpected but welcomed warm breeze blew in through Sara's bedroom window in late spring, waking her up feeling refreshed. A number of weeks had gone by since she broke the news to the kids that they would be moving to the Okanagan Valley in British Columbia. As much as she could explain, the kids would never grasp the depth of her feelings behind her decision. She knew it was going to continue to be difficult to deal with Ben. It would have to be done carefully, and with a great deal of love and patience, for him to accept what was going to happen. However, at some point Sara would have to put her foot down about that fact, no matter the difficulty. She would also need an ongoing salary with two growing adolescents to care for and one of them going to university.

Sara became a member of an architects' association in Canada shortly after graduating university. She had designed a beach house for a client when she and Jacob were just starting out in the old, converted garage in Clarington. It won her an award for the best original residential design that year. She received a monthly newsletter since, and this is where she started researching architectural firms in B.C. It was from the association's directory that she learned of Cailey & Higgins Design in the Okanogan Valley. They were a rather large firm with their head office in Vancouver. Most of the work they did was commercial, and their biggest client built medium to large resorts and ski lodges. It would be a new and exciting challenge for Sara.

It was heart breaking for her to sell her share of the company she loved building and being a part of. The other partner in the company, Heather Keegan, had remarried J.C. Cameron, the company's foreman. They would keep the business well in hand. Heather's daughter, Melissa, returned home to take over the company's bookkeeping from her mother. And a new junior architect was hired on at Sara's recommendation. In a way, the business was staying family oriented for the most part.

Sara compromised by keeping the farmhouse in the family. If Ben or Mary so chose, the house would be there for them later in life. Sara decided on a young couple in Clarington to take over the place on a five-year lease.

There were several heated discussions in the weeks prior to the move. To ease Ben's aching heart, Sara assured the kids that she could afford to send them back for holidays and special occasions. She hoped that would help soften the blow and make Ben more pliable in the inevitable move that lay ahead. Even though Ben was handy with tools and occasionally fixed things around the house for his mother, he didn't have the desire for construction his father did. Maybe it was his way of standing out as his own man and not be seen as a follower or cashing in on his father's money. Either way, despite the many traits and characteristics that he shared with his father, he wasn't following in his footsteps, except being a guardian. Although he had little memory of his father, Ben felt a connection to him living in the farmhouse. He would ultimately learn that connection wasn't bound by location.

10

Gloss

1990

In the mid-eighties, Jacob O'Connell was an assistant site supervisor for Henderson Construction & Design Ltd. He had worked on a commercial project in Toronto that was a renovation and addition, expanding a café and adding a bakery to the rear. Years after the successful completion of Sam's Café, Jacob and Sam built a friendship that started with their shared interest in fine carpentry. Time passed and Jacob received a promotion at work for his performance on jobs such as Sam's. A celebration of dinner and drinks for his achievement was held by his bosses. The drink portion of the evening was held at a dance club. That is where Jacob met a dancer who periodically looked at him like she was scared of something or someone. Not too late into the evening, on his way to the men's room, Jacob had spotted her apparent boyfriend or client slamming her around in one of the V.I.P. rooms, so he intervened. After Jacob threw the man to the ground, the bouncers quickly broke up the fight and that was that. Jacob didn't give the incident another thought. He did, however, take notice of the dancer's green eyes, similar to Sara's, striking in contrast to her blonde hair.

Wanting to get home to Sara, Jacob was quick to call it a night and left to hail a cab. Strip bars weren't the kind of places Jacob frequented. He preferred to play pool or darts at pubs similar to the one Sara worked at when Jacob met her for the first time as adults.

While standing outside waiting for the taxi, Jacob saw one of his bosses, Blair Dickson, arguing with the very same man he had pulled off the dancer earlier. It didn't appear to be anything more than a heated argument, so Jacob turned away from it. He did find it a curiosity that Blair would be talking to that kind of man to begin with. He raised his eyebrows and shook his head briefly and let the thought slide from his mind. The cab came and Jacob settled into the back seat for the near thirty-minute ride ahead of him. The beers and shots of Jameson, on top of a hard day's work, had caught up with Jacob, and he quickly nodded off. His dreams were strange and unfamiliar, commencing under the current circumstances and ending in him yelling out the name Carol upon waking.

He rubbed his bloodshot eyes and tried to clear his pasty mouth while he exchanged looks with the cabbie.

"Sorry about that. Bad dream, I guess. Huh, the funny thing is I don't even know a woman named Carol." Jacob's words were sluffed off by the uninterested driver, and just as well Jacob thought. Within a minute of arriving home, Jacob paid the cabbie with a ten dollar tip and steadied himself on the asphalt driveway once he was out of the cab. He rubbed the side of his head and tried to rid himself of the smell inside the cab.

Jesus! Nothing about that dream made any sense. And who the hell is Carol? The girl looked like the dancer, except for the business suit. Jacob's thoughts were summed up with a giggle.

The name of the dancer from the strip bar was Misty Lane and the man in the V.I.P. room was her agent, Joe Miller. If Jacob had learned their names, he might have heard a story from Sam of how he gave her a job when she arrived in town. And not long after, the agent, who was never a regular or seen in the café at all, suddenly became a steady customer and was quick to put his moves on Misty for his own needs. An undesirable man by Sam's standards, and Jacob would, without a doubt, agree wholeheartedly.

Misty was young, just turning eighteen, but she was becoming educated in the seedier side of life thanks to the likes of Joe. He had a business with an apartment above it. It was in a small strip mall next to a coffee shop among an urban sprawl. From there he ran Crystal Management Services, a booking agency for dancers, but he had few clients. He used the business as a cover for his many illegal activities, such as, but not limited to, selling drugs and fencing stolen goods.

Misty was pregnant at fifteen but lost the baby from a fall. The gossip in her small town was too much to bear. When her father made it clear he was ashamed of her, Misty ran away from her home in Nova Scotia when she was sixteen years old. She survived by dancing in some of the dirtiest establishments along her slow trek to Toronto.

Sam was quick to notice Misty the day she arrived in his café, cold and hungry, with one of those faces that could look sixteen or twenty-six. Sam was a good man, and as much as he had come to care for Misty, he couldn't pay her enough to survive in the city on her own. As a result, Misty was eventually enticed to let Joe represent her, and she was lured by the significant income that dancing provided. Sadly, she left Sam's employ and ended up moving in with Joe as his girlfriend and him as her agent. The night in the strip club had no direct impact on Jacob, but there ended up being some indirect actions that had an impact on his place of work due to Blair Dickson's association with Joe Miller. Lives would be changed irrevocably from their interaction.

11

Repurpose

1990

Before heading to the police academy in the fall of 1990, a clean-cut Evan Quinn earned his way by waitering in a popular bar and restaurant. He made fairly decent tips that would help with the upcoming weekend with his new girlfriend, Linda Bradshaw. This weekend was supposed to be special, just for them alone, a first.

A good-looking, six-foot-tall, muscular man, Evan walked beside the train, trying to match its crawl to the right location on the platform. Linda saw him from her window seat, and she gave him a shy, honest smile that put Evan in a twist.

Wow, she's beautiful! he thought. *Her ... just everything.*

Images of different scenarios kept running through his testosterone-fuelled head. He wanted to sigh, but his taut stomach muscles wouldn't allow it. So far, he was moving with relative grace while watching her train come in. Not paying attention to his steps, he tripped over a crack in the platform. After three or four truly ugly flopping steps, like a newborn calf on ice, his attempt to correct his trajectory failed spectacularly.

At the moment of impact with the train station platform, Evan could see the face of a woman he didn't know. A mysteriously beautiful woman appeared like she was floating through the ripples in the taupe-coloured coffee that spilled into a puddle on the platform in front of him. Linda's image injecting itself into his peripheral vision quickly brought him back to reality. His purpose for the day had been temporarily reimagined, but he would need to stand and confront what was waiting for him. Evan was there to meet Linda, but she paled in comparison to the woman he had just seen. He was amazed at what he saw after he picked himself up from the platform and got a proper look. He was stunned by her overall look. She had dark black hair and lily-white skin and wore dark red lipstick. She looked back at him with her emerald-green eyes. Evan felt trapped, smiling at the beauty in front of him while trying to make his way to the train. For one magical moment in time, Evan was frozen still and all else that surrounded him turned to fog. Luckily, Evan's trance lasted only the few seconds it took for her to walk away.

Evan still managed a pleasant day with Linda, spooning on the grass down by the beach in the tourist town of Port Credit. There was far too much talking about school and future careers for Evan's liking, but he figured he was in for the long haul. Late in the day, it was time to head into the city, and Linda wanted a coffee or it would be an early night. Evan happily obliged.

Reaching the coffee shop, Evan was backing into a parking spot when he took notice of a young lady rushing toward his car. The thought that she looked familiar quickly popped into his mind, but her hair was brown, and she wore no makeup or lipstick. Evan was able to get in only a quick look before she suddenly dropped to the ground. At the same time, he heard several cracking noises but at first he didn't make the connection they were gunshots.

"Oh my God. She just collapsed. She's bleeding, Evan!" The pair quickly jumped out of the car and rushed to the young lady's aid. Evan looked at the woman and then to Linda.

"Get behind the car, Linda. She's been shot. That's what that noise was." Evan couldn't believe his eyes. This was indeed the same woman from the train station.

From there everything happened quickly. Evan pulled the woman from under her arms to the rear of the car next to his for cover. She was conscious but struggling to breathe. All she could get out was, "Where's Joe?" Evan pulled his windbreaker off and placed it under her head.

"Keep pressure on this, I'll be right back."

Evan didn't give Linda a chance to refuse, pulling her hands down onto the wound in her chest. He then ran to the coffee shop like he was under fire and yelled out to the staff inside to call for police and ambulance. He returned to Linda yelling out in fear that the girl had died.

"Her eyes rolled back ... and she went. Her eyes rolled back twice. Is she breathing? Oh my God! I think she's dead!"

Evan could see Linda wasn't handling this situation very well, so he took over and tried his best to calm Linda down. What Evan did next was unbelievable to Linda, leaving her speechless and frightened. Evan's hands glowed like heating elements and the girl suddenly come to. It was more than she could rationalize.

Once Evan was convinced the young woman was stabilized, he drew a blank look and slipped back onto his folded legs, closed his eyes, and fell over. When he opened his eyes again, he was sitting on the ground with his back against the rear side of his car. This was something he never experienced before. The amount of time that had just passed was a mystery to Evan, much to Linda's dismay.

The police quickly finished asking Linda their questions as the EMS were loading the victim into the ambulance. For her own purposes, Linda was quick to cover for Evan, saying he passed out or fainted, but clearly showing her disgust. Evan was shocked, trying to regain his focus. He could see Linda was more than upset, seemingly repulsed by him. He ran his fingers through his hair repeatedly as if he were trying to pull out the confusion. Then without reason, he looked at his blood-stained hands. As he turned them over to examine, he had a flashback to a hunting trip with his father as a teen. This only muddled things even more, leaving him perplexed over this intrusive and seemingly irrelevant memory. He would later equate it to the fact he had to rescue that girl whether Linda was present or not.

"Are you okay, Evan?" Linda growled, sounding like an angry, impatient schoolteacher.

"Yeah, I'm fine. What happened?" he asked, as the ambulance went racing out of the parking lot, its sirens blaring and lights flashing its way down the street.

"Take me to my parents, please," she demanded. Evan picked himself up off the ground without another word. They, along with any gawkers, were ordered out of the area so the police could make an attempt to find the shooter, who was long gone.

When the fog lifted, Evan quickly concluded that it was over between him and Linda. As time passed, the fact that Linda wouldn't speak to him on the drive to her parent's house, or ever again, wasn't that big a mystery to Evan. He never bothered to try and explain anything about that day to her. He let it be, and he let her go without a second thought.

12

Damage

1990

Ballistics determined it was a nine-millimetre slug that ripped through the flesh, bone, and organs of eighteen-year-old Carol Landry, also known as Misty Lane. The bullet broke a rib before bouncing around like a pinball and stopping against her spine. The second bullet was what is referred to as a through-and-through. The round entered her back and exited out her chest two inches above her right nipple and was never recovered.

The media was cleared to report the story about Carol getting shot and the ensuing court case for those involved in carrying out the attack. However, the media was barred from releasing the names of victims of violent crimes. And although the hospital had Carol's name, it wasn't their policy to release patient's names or give any information. In this case, she was listed as a Jane Doe to protect her from the person, or persons, involved in the crime.

If anyone requested any information about a girl getting shot, Detective Frank Hansen of Robbery-Homicide was notified directly. Frank kept a plain-clothed officer on the floor where Carol was recovering for added protection. It was the least he could do for what she sacrificed for him and the Crown. This was an investigation that started long before the blood-soaked parking lot where a young woman was gunned down. Frank was furious this happened in the middle of his investigation into four jewellery stores being robbed with the same M.O. The robberies always occurred at closing time and were carried out by four men with sawed-off shotguns and one finely dressed and unarmed woman. Carol Landry, as it turned out, was one of the main players along with this foursome of armed robbers. The most important reason for the protection was the fact that she just started helping Frank as a confidential informant.

Carol being alive was thanks to twenty-year-old Evan Quinn being there at the right time. He and Linda Bradshaw were the first people Frank interviewed. Talking to Evan was a breeze. Evan welcomed Frank into his small, messy, four-hundred-square-foot bachelor apartment. Several flattened pizza boxes and empty beer cases laid throughout the room. The walls were covered in Sunshine Girl posters, and the remaining floor area was covered with both clean and dirty laundry. Frank scanned the place and smiled, thinking back to his own youth. There was no judgement. They sat at a small kitchen table where Frank began the interview. It didn't take Frank long to figure Evan out.

Frank gave Evan his card and thanked him for everything and left to question Linda Bradshaw before returning to the hospital. Linda was a different story from Evan altogether. She stood in the middle of the doorway and propped the screen door open with her foot, holding the entrance door open against her back. There was no invitation inside and no niceties or manners. She referred to Evan as a guy she dated. And the rest was a summation of the events. "The girl got shot. We helped and didn't see anyone." End of story. Anything else out of Linda's mouth was, "I don't know," or "No." Frank was just dotting the *i*'s and crossing the *t*'s and didn't waste a great deal of time with her. While walking down the stairs from the porch of her home, Frank quickly looked back and shook his head.

Kid, I think you're better off, he thought to himself.

Frank headed back to his car for another trip to the hospital to pick up the bullet as evidence in the case. Following his return, Frank went directly to check in on Carol's condition and discovered the surgeon doing the same. Frank hadn't admitted this to himself at first, but before long he felt primarily responsible for what happened to Carol.

"She was lucky," Frank said as he continued to look at Carol like a concerned parent.

This one bothered him more than most. Seeing her lying in bed breathing with the aid of a ventilator, four separate IV bags, and drainage lines coming out of her abdomen and chest, left his stomach queasy and his knees weak.

"This isn't luck, Detective. This is something I've never seen in my thirty-five years in medicine. There's no way this girl should be alive, just from the blood loss alone. Not to mention everything else the bullet damaged on its way through," the doctor replied, looking out through the glass partition next to Carol's door before closing the blinds again.

He gently shook his head in disbelief, but he was pleased he could help keep her alive. She was recovering exceptionally well. The doctor towered over Frank by almost a foot, forcing the detective to look up to have a conversation with the man.

"I don't say this lightly, Detective, because I'm not a believer. Not after the number of years seeing what I've seen. But this was a miracle, plain and simple. I can't argue that. This girl should have never made it into that ambulance alive, let alone to the hospital."

"Well, doc, I guess there's a first for everything," Frank said, looking at Carol and pulling on his beard as he usually did when pondering something new or unusual.

Carol's name was a closely held secret between Frank and the doctor, but her professional name, Misty Lane, was something Frank wouldn't share with him. Completely uninterested in hearing any more from the surgeon, he reached his hand out to receive the bag with the bullet inside. This was the evidence needed and the only reason for engaging in this much conversation with the pretentious surgeon.

"I will say this, however. Her survival would have been beyond all possibilities without the help of whomever was there with her before the EMS arrived," the doctor said as he and Frank walked down the hall together until reaching the head surgeon's office.

As Frank was about to reply, the doctor walked into his office and closed the door in Frank's face.

"I just came back from interviewing him by the way." Frank said, waving the bag in front of the glass of the doctor's closed office door. Frank shook his head. "Fucking doctors," he growled, concluding with a harrumph, walking his way to the exit. "Miracle ... pff," he scoffed.

What Frank had seen in his life didn't allow for the possibility of miracles.

13

New Direction

1990

When Carol recovered, she knew her life as Misty Lane was over. After giving the police everything they needed to arrest Joe Miller and his partners for the jewellery store robberies, her life was in jeopardy. Carol was an unwilling participant in those robberies. Having played the owners of the stores in a blackmail scheme in her role as Misty, the robberies went unchallenged.

The man with the plan was Jacob's boss, Blair Dickson. He was married to the daughter of one of the store owners and knew the ins and outs of the business. Along with his father-in-law's store, Feigenbaum's Fine Jewels, Blair planned to hit three of his close business associates, to make sure it didn't look like Feigenbaum had been singled out. The story of Jacob's boss being involved in these robberies to pay off a debt from a serious gambling problem was gossip for the water fountain at work. And that's where any connection to Jacob ended. However, it was not where the story ended.

Detective Hansen had been the one who caught Carol trying to catch a train out of town. He gave her a choice to either be arrested as an accomplice in the robberies or be an informant and walk free. It was her cooperation in the investigation that led to her being shot by an enraged Joe Miller. Frank was left feeling responsible as if she was his own daughter. During her unusually quick recovery, Frank kept

Carol's safety front and centre. Whatever might be in Carol's future, Frank would assure she made it there with no more harm from Joe or any of his associates. Even though it was his job, Frank had a bad feeling from the beginning after sending Carol back into Joe's hands. And it seemed that she had been shot the only time Frank turned away from his surveillance to quickly take care of some personal needs and check in with his partner. The guilt ate at him more so on this case than any other.

Frank pulled around to the west side of the hospital where he hoped the staff's entrance would provide for a quick pickup to get Carol out under the cover of night. In the time Carol had been in recovery, Joe was trying to get one of his associates to make sure she never made it to court, ever. In his world, she committed the ultimate betrayal. It was an insult to have your old lady sell you out, and it made him look as stupid as he was. Everything Carol had done was under threat from Joe. Thanks to a couple of snitches on the inside of the West End Jail, Frank was now painfully aware of what might be coming for Carol. To complicate the situation more, Frank and his partner had only a handful of cops they could really trust outside of their precinct for help. Joe was facing heavy charges. With his record, he would have to do hard time. Time he wasn't willing to do.

On top of the four charges of armed robbery, Joe was being charged with attempted murder for shooting Carol. After his jailhouse contract was discovered, he was also facing conspiracy to commit murder charges for the second attempt on Carol's life. Joe had become toxic to everyone in his world.

Frank's twisted stomach left him without an appetite, and he had only coffee over the last twenty-four hours. Getting Carol out of the province was his first concern but a recent development in the investigation was eating at him and wouldn't stop popping up. Joe Miller had one of the city's best criminal defence attorneys, Brad Watson, working his case. When Frank traced back the payments to Joe's lawyer, he learned that Blair Dickson had paid the retainer in cash. That would be Blair's downfall and he was charged as an accessory. He lost his job and his wife. Frank concluded this case was a discovery of conspiracies on top of conspiracies.

§

Carol put on the same black wig she wore the first time she tried to catch the train out of town. This time she wore a green dress suit to match her eyes, passing on her previous choice of navy blue. Instead of watching Carol on surveillance, Frank escorted her to the train this time. A grizzled veteran, Frank was a serious-looking man, wearing a grey sports coat, blue jeans, and sporting a goatee.

"Got everything you need, kid?" the tired detective said to Carol.

She turned to him, the steps to the train directly behind her, and lunged forward, reaching her arms around Frank's thick neck. On her tiptoes, she hugged him as hard as she could. Frank was becoming emotional, something he never handled too well.

"I can't thank you enough, Frank." Carol quietly spoke into his ear, still holding on tight.

He gingerly grabbed Carol by her sides, gently pushing her away from him and looked her in the eye. "Just make sure you take care of yourself along the way, and we'll talk in a few weeks from now when you get settled."

Carol's green eyes began to well up, and Frank nodded toward the train. "Come on, kid. You better get going."

She looked at him one last time as a single tear rolled down her cheek, nodded her head, and walked onto the train. Frank stood by and watched through the window as she took her seat. He didn't move until the train left the station, heading west.

As it turned out, Joe took a deal from the Crown instead of looking at twenty-five to thirty years. This meant there would be no trial and there was no need for Carol to testify.

14

Miracles West

1994

Sunday, September 4, 1994 - 10:32 a.m.

The closer Marion Baldwin's car advanced toward the oncoming logger truck on the narrow Quarter Mile Bridge, the more she seriously considered her younger sister's nagging as good advice.

"Get over now! As far as you can and let him go by," Sandra said with conviction, loudly and repeatedly.

Marion's consideration of this advice quickly turned to panic. She slammed on the brakes at the same moment the front tire hit a deep rut in the pavement. With that overzealous push to the pedal, the brakes locked up, and the back end of the car started to slide around. Still in panic mode, her next pump of the brakes was a slip, and she hit the gas pedal, snapping the car around near ninety degrees. With tires squealing, the car smashed through the wooden rails of the bridge nose first and plummeted thirty feet into the flowing waters of the Elk River.

10:35 a.m.

Constable Evan Quinn was taking his partner and mentor, Glen Simon, to get his personal car back from the garage when the call came in.

"A car crashed through the Quarter Mile Bridge. One or more passengers in the water."

With his foot to the floor, Evan had the cruiser racing in the right direction faster than Glen had a chance to pick up the mic and respond to dispatch. "Eleven-ten. Responding."

Glen and Evan both lived a few miles outside the town of Franklin, B.C. They knew the area better than most — the little dirt roads, logging trails, and everything else surrounding their mountain valley home.

Still, the speed Evan was taking some of those sharp bends resulted with Glen yelling at the excitable young officer. "Damn it, Evan! Go as fast as you want on them straight runs, but you'll put us down the mountainside if you don't slow it down on those bends. Jesus, boy!" Glen yelled, keeping a firm grip on the handle over the passenger side door.

"Sorry, Glen. But they just said someone's in the river," Evan confidently replied to his mentor.

"Yeah. I know, Evan. We ain't gonna be any help to 'em if we're dead at the bottom of the mountain somewhere along the way, now will we?"

"Right, sorry. I guess I am a bit jumpy today," Evan said, lifting his palms off the steering wheel to glance at the speedometer. Glen looked over to his young protégé with a friendly expression.

"No worries, my excitable friend. Let's just get there. Alive preferably."

PART 2

10:31 a.m.

Marion Baldwin wasn't a seasoned driver at just twenty years of age. Her sister, Sandra, constantly reminded her of this. Getting a driver's licence in the 90s was easy. Once you wrote the exam and passed the driver's test, you were on your way, no restrictions. And perhaps her 1970 Chevelle, with its three-fifty small block rebuilt to original condition, was simply too powerful for a new driver in the mountains. Her lead foot wasn't doing her any favours in these conditions. This area had received five minutes of light rain earlier, freshly raising the oil to the surface of the road yet to be washed away.

Sandra leaned forward with both hands on the dashboard to emphasize her concern while looking across to her sister. "Like seriously, Marion, you should pull all the way over and let this guy through. Okay?"

"Oh, Sandy, don't be a back-seat driver. I know what I'm doing," Marion said with a two-fisted, white-knuckle grip on the steering wheel.

"Don't call me Sandy. You know I hate that. And I'm serious. Pull over. It's too close. We're not in a hurry. That's why we left a day early. Come on, Marion!"

The truck driver started speculating the second he saw them enter the bridge going too fast and hugging the centre line. "Jesus, man. Slow down," he said aloud, while checking his passenger-side mirror to see if he was over as far as possible without hitting anything. He made a quick back and forth from his mirror to the car in the short time he had. The instant he saw the car fishtail, he locked his rig up. In brief seconds, he could see nothing was stopping the car from busting through the old wooden rails of the bridge.

The heavier fall rains came early this year, causing the river to be deep enough it could pull a car and take it down river. For the moment, the car's rear end was bobbing in the water and slowly moving forward. The bridge itself seemed solid enough with all the exposed structural wood painted white every few years, and the asphalt brightly lined with thermoplastic white and yellow. The vertical posts were placed every six feet, but the speed of the car sheared one of them clean off.

Bill Walsh worked at Everly Trucking for years and witnessed his share of accidents in the often-treacherous mountains of the Okanagan. This, however, was rather dramatic and happening in live action right in front of him. He jumped out of his truck for a quick look at the gaping hole in the side rail and the car in the river. Running back to his rig he pulled his plaid button up off over his head and tossed it and his baseball cap in the truck. Reaching for the mic from the C.B. radio, he called for help.

"A car smashed through Quarter Mile Bridge … uh … Highway 28. It's in the water. Uh … two, uh at least two people … hurry, they need help…" His excitedly stammered words trailed off, quickly becoming inaudible.

Jumping into the river's cold rushing mountain water took Bill's breath away. As he was about to make his dive to the car, up came Sandra, choking and spitting out water, screaming that Marion was stuck in the car and the seatbelt wouldn't release.

"Swim to the bank!" Bill yelled out to Sandra, and down he went.

When Sandra reached the bank, in shock and out of breath, she watched in horror as the car broke free from whatever rocks were holding it up and it began to float downriver. There was an access area, a cut out in the brush, on the west side of the river about seventy-five to a hundred feet from where Sandra clung to the riverside. As a popular fishing spot, it had a small dirt road leading to it down off the main highway.

Sandra summoned the courage to get past her fear and began to fight her way through the dense brush along the riverside, trying to make it to the opening between the road and the river. The more the car moved, the more frantically she yelled out Marion's name. Finally, she bust through the last of the brush and into the opening, shaking from cold, fear, and adrenaline.

To her amazement and relief, she saw Bill pulling Marion out of the water and onto the rocks of the opening's small shore. Sandra dropped to her knees and began to wail at the sight of her lifeless sister. As soon as Bill caught his breath, he pulled Marion to an area of wet sand and started first aid to the best of his limited ability, trying to breathe air into her lungs. He lifted her arms between compressions but was dismayed when her head flopped to the side. When all seemed hopeless, sirens could be heard approaching in the distance. The ambulance arrived first, and two medics jumped out of the vehicle, set the stretcher aside, and ran over with their bags of equipment and a backboard. With Marion absent a heartbeat and not breathing, they carried her to the stretcher beside the ambulance and began CPR. An IV was inserted, and the defibrillator was charged.

PART 3

After it was determined that Marion was beyond saving, the medics received instructions from the doctor of the local E.R. to stop compressions. The police arrived and Glen was the first to get out of the cruiser. In his early forties, Glen was a good-sized man at five-foot-eleven and two hundred pounds. He had a serious but friendly clean-shaven face and dark brown eyes. Evan followed after he finished making the status call back to dispatch.

Evan was just finishing his second year working in the area, and his third year on the force. When he got out of the cruiser, he could see a soaking wet and exhausted Bill Walsh sitting next to Sandra Baldwin, looking dejected. The pair rested on one of three large logs that surrounded a well-used firepit, fifteen feet from the front of the ambulance. Sandra was expectedly devastated. One of the medics, Darcy Jones, was helping her while the other medic, Mike Collins, tended to Bill. It was far too much emotion for Bill to handle, so Glen helped both the medics with what he could. It was clear to Evan from the look on their faces that whoever died was family or friend.

As Glen approached Bill Walsh to determine what had just transpired at the bridge, Evan stopped short, next to the rear of the ambulance, and lingered unnoticed. Nobody felt the need to pay attention to anything else in the moment as the immediate danger had passed.

In front of Evan, a body lay on a stretcher covered with a blanket head to toe. His instincts were fighting his knowledge of procedure and decorum as a cop. He decided to look and see if he could recognize who it was. A light tug of the blanket didn't reveal enough for him to see, so he gently pulled it back far enough to see a young woman unknown to him. Evan slowly leaned to the side of the ambulance to see if anything was happening that needed his immediate attention. There was little movement, no screaming, nor any voices calling for him. He felt he was being pulled back in to look at this stranger.

Marion's head turned toward Evan, but it was translucent, floating just inches over where her real head lay. Evan saw and heard Marion's soul gently calling out to him. *Will you help me … please?*

Over Darcy Jones's shoulder, Sandra saw a flash of light the colour of the sun through the side window of the ambulance but thought nothing of it. It didn't dawn on her that the sky was overcast with a combination of light and heavy rains, which would have led her to realize any light had to be artificial.

In short time, Evan stuck his head out from the back of the ambulance and yelled out to the paramedics. "Ah, guys. Hey! I think this girl is alive. Yup, she's coughing; you better get over here," Evan said, pulling on the blanket more. At first he spoke like he was both shocked and confused but without hesitation, Evan repeated his words for action with a deep authoritative growl.

Sandra's head snapped up to attention, and she could feel a push from her stomach up through her throat. The paramedics raced to the rear of the ambulance with Sandra right behind. Evan held a frantic Sandra back while the medics jumped inside to see Marion heaving out small amounts of foam in between coughs and gasps for air. Marion fought to sit upright, which she did rather quickly, leaning over and continuing to cough and gag, fluids coming out of her mouth and nose.

The medics managed to calm Marion down enough to check her vitals and ask her name, where she lives, and the year. Standing just back from the rear of the ambulance, Sandra was quivering when she shouted out, "Oh my God! Oh my God! Marion!" She called it out repeatedly with a shower of joyful tears and giddy laughter. As soon as it was possible, Sandra pushed her way in and grabbed a hold of her sister, almost squeezing any residual water from her lungs, laughing and crying simultaneously. Marion smiled with an otherwise blank look, staring out to the cosmos or anywhere. Standing farther back, Glen and Evan both took turns looking around the group and to each other. Suddenly Evan took a few steps back, and his backside plopped against the hood of the cruiser. His legs became weak, and he put his face in his hands, fighting to stay alert. Neither of the experienced paramedics had ever witnessed such a thing.

15

Fallout

1990–1999

One of the several rest stops along Lakeview Road was directly across from the precinct. Evan stopped in there before his shift, staring at the building, his eyes not focusing on any one thing. What happened the day before was eating at him, but he wasn't quite sure how to deal with what might arise from it. It wasn't the first time this happened, but it was the first time as a cop. He knew the day might come when his ability might push him into a corner.

Finally entering the station for his upcoming shift, he passed the lead paramedic from the Baldwin recovery the day before, Mike Collins. The encounter was odd and cold from Evan's perspective. He said a cheerful hello, but the response from the medic was barely audible. And it came with a glare of dislike or disrespect.

What the hell is his problem? Evan thought but wrote it off as the guy having a bad day. The young cop's instincts kicked in, and he wondered why the medic was in the station to begin with. *They fax their shit over, so what's he doing here?*

Thinking it best to dismiss it, Evan headed for the lockers. Before he cleared the long hallway, he heard Glen call out for him.

"Hey, Evan, Chief wants to see you before we head out today."

"Do you know what he wants?" Evan asked, freezing on the spot, and squeezing his eyes shut for a long blink.

MARK J. CANNON   71

"No. Mike Collins was just in there, and then he asked for you. Go on. Go see him, and I'll see you in the locker room or out in the car."

As Evan was approaching the Chief's office, he felt a mild chill on a small area on the back of his neck, just before his muscles tensed up.

"Hey, Chief, you … uh, you called for me?" Evan sounded as unsettled as he looked.

"Come in and shut the door, Quinn," Chief Danson said sternly. His tone was serious, and that was never a good sign. Chief Ronald Danson was known for being a good-natured man, so this was disconcerting for Evan.

As Evan assumed, it was Collins who suggested to the chief that he did something to shock Marion Baldwin back to life. Once Evan gave the chief the assurances that he needed to let it go, he reminded him that Marion was alive. That was the miracle the chief seemed to be overlooking.

The chief agreed and told EMS as much, telling them their toes weren't stepped on in the slightest. For obvious reasons, it was a distressing meeting for Evan to get through, and he was grateful to have it over. He entered the change rooms and walked straight to a stall and gave up the contents of his stomach. After he rinsed his mouth out, he leaned on the sink, staring into the mirror.

Suddenly and shockingly, while he continued to look into the mirror, his sight actively changed and was now seeing the inside of the ambulance as Marion was seeing it, seeing himself, in the moment when she came to life. Then his memory and sight suddenly shifted to recall the young woman in a Toronto parking lot, fighting to stay alive after being shot. In association with that memory, another image popped up, showing a walk through the forest, kneeling, and gently running his hand over a deer's bloody fur. These images were bizarre and unwelcomed in this moment, under these circumstances, keeping Evan frozen and unable to move.

"Come on, Evan!" he said aloud, not knowing how to react to these visually definitive snapshots and replays of his life to this point as a guardian. Everything he was seeing and experiencing disappeared in the snap of a finger when he heard Glen's voice calling for him. He didn't notice Mike Collins in one of the stalls, witnessing his dead stare and strange behaviour in front of the mirror.

§

Following the incident with Marion Baldwin, things didn't go so well for Evan at work, and it continued to get worse. He was left dealing with the gossip going around his station and the EMS. There was no shortage of speculation feeding that gossip as to what happened on that day.

A few years later, that speculation increased when something similar happened with a seven-car pileup on Highway 7 South. It was a horrible scene. An entire family had perished in a completely burned-out minivan after colliding with a fuel tanker that lost control on a patch of black ice. In one of the other vehicles, the medics came upon a five-year-old boy but couldn't find a pulse after he sustained serious injuries. His grandfather had been tossed from their pickup truck and died after landing on the road next to the inferno of vehicles.

Nonetheless, they tried to resuscitate the boy, but he was declared deceased at the scene, covered with a blanket, and placed in one of the ambulances on-site. The boy's poor fortunes changed after Evan checked in on him. Once again, just like Marion Baldwin, he was miraculously alive. And like before, this happened after the paramedics had pronounced him deceased.

Evan was going through an agony following these events that was similar to what Jacob O'Connell experienced. He was becoming too exposed to people through his job, and that left him vulnerable. The amount of gossip in the community had a negative impact on Evan, leaving him morose and becoming despondent. What his peers were saying about him only added to his grief. He began to get strange looks from people he had known for years, and some for his entire life. Evan made his mind up to resign, immediately, without notice.

Before leaving the force, Evan had to fill out the reports after the accident on Highway 7. He remembered a picture taken from the wallet of the boy's grandfather, Harold Brownstone. The name on the back of the picture was Eugene. It was the boy Evan saved, only a year younger, taken just after kindergarten ended. Seeing the fear and shock on Eugene's face that day left an indelible mark on Evan. He would often wonder how difficult the trauma of losing his grandfather would be on him, and what would become of him after that event. Evan had sensations before when he met different people, but he felt a connection to Eugene. Long after that tragic day, the boy would often pop into Evan's thoughts.

16

Clarity

1999

PART 1

Evan pulled into the parking lot of the Salmon Hatch, a local watering hole a few miles outside of Franklin. It looked like an oversized general store out of the nineteenth-century Wild West, and it even had a raised façade over the entrance to give it a bigger look. This was where most of the off-duty cops, fireman, and EMS staff would normally hang out away from town. You could smell the stale beer when entering, along with the equally stale (but free) unnaturally yellow popcorn. The place wasn't exactly elegant when it came to décor, with moose and deer antlers, wagon wheels, and horseshoes mounted to the barnboard-covered walls. Glen Simon was already inside when Evan walked through the doors. He bypassed the bar of regulars he knew by heart. The new bartender was in the back loading the coolers.

When he sat down, he noticed one of the EMS crews having wings and a pitcher of lager at the table across from them. They all had the same green work pants and grey t-shirts with the department logo on them. Evan waved to them, no different than any other time. He wasn't willing to change who he was for anyone.

"Howdy, boys. How's the day treating you?" Evan said, as jovial as ever. The response seemed the standard collective rumblings of okay, all right and the like.

But then Mike Collins piped up. "So, Evan, save any more dead victims lately?"

Evan hung his head down with a slow shake and a look of exasperation. However, it wasn't his voice, but that of Glen's that responded.

"Hey, Mike. Buddy." The word buddy came in a slow, low tone, followed by a three-second stare that would intimidate most anyone. "Aren't you going to find it hard eating that big basket of wings without any teeth to chew them with?"

It didn't matter that Glen was a cop in that moment because Mike knew exactly what he was capable of. They grew up in the same town and played hockey in the same league at each level. And during one of those games, Mike made the mistake of fighting Glen. It was a painful and humiliating thrashing, which everyone knew about. Those were Mike's last words on the subject. He was one of those cowardly mouthpieces.

Glen continued to glare at Mike for a couple more seconds then looked back at Evan and smiled. "Anyway, Evan. How's my ever-curious partner doing on this fine day?" asked Glen, appearing only mildly annoyed by the interruption.

Evan had Glen join him at another table where he concentrated on keeping the conversation at a level that could be carried out without the others overhearing any detail. This was as good a time as any to break the news to his partner, seeing as Evan wouldn't be at work for their next shift. They were watching a couple of regulars playing a game of pool when Evan turned to face his mentor.

"I'm done, Glen." Evan spoke with a tone that left no confusion to what he was talking about.

"What do you mean you're done? Done with what?" Glen asked, but he knew.

"I just handed my resignation in to the Chief."

"The hell you did! I won't let you do that, Evan. Why would you do such a thing? You're a good cop, so don't let what happened stop you from doing your job. Trust me, it'll blow over. Most everything blows over in time." Glen did his best to make it seem trivial, waving his hand like he was turning the suggestion down. Evan just looked at Glen with a mild smirk and said nothing in rebuttal. Glen's face grew sad. "No changing your mind?"

"No. Sorry, Glen. Consider it the seven-year itch. But it's the job I'm divorcing and not you." Evan pushed out a small laugh before finishing what he had to say. "Listen, I appreciate everything you've done for me, really. But I'm going back to the family business in the orchards and plan to just stay quiet for a while," Evan said, wrapping up the conversation.

"That, my friend, is not such a terrible idea. And I'm sure your dad will be over the moon to have you back in the business." Glen got up to shake Evan's hand, and with a slap on the back, he offered to walk him out to the parking lot to say his goodbye there.

On the way by the bar, Evan stopped in his tracks. He was floored when he set his eyes on the new bartender he missed on his way in.

"Evan, haven't I taught you it's not polite to stare." Glen said with a smile. Evan was keenly locked in on this new woman working the bar.

"I'm sorry, I know this totally sounds cliché, but do I know you? I'm pretty sure I know you." The woman turned and walked toward Evan, continuing to dry a glass in her hand. She looked at him with a straight face, then a slight tilt of her head with squinted eyes.

"Oh my God! It is you. I wondered, but you were too far away sitting over there." The bartender walked out from behind her station and threw her arms around Evan and began to cry. Stopping and wiping her eyes, she reached her hand out and shook Evan's hand.

"Hi. I'm Carol Landry. I think you saved my life." A sudden bright, unbreakable smile came across both of their faces. Glen looked on with shock and fascination at what was unfolding for Evan in this moment.

"Listen. I have to go right now, but—" Evan didn't need to say anything further.

"Yes!" She exclaimed. "We should definitely talk. I'll see you around here I imagine?" Evan's smile seemed impossible to remove.

"Yes, you will," He said with exuberance.

As they headed for the door, Glen looked at his newly retired friend. "This might just be a sign that you made the right decision after all, young man."

And out the door they went. It didn't dawn on Evan that what she said about saving her life would definitely raise more questions. He was enamoured with this green-eyed beauty.

PART 2

The stress left Evan's body like the slow deflation of a hot-air balloon. He was shifting through his anger toward the EMS and his coworkers to the release of walking away from any more exposure and the delight in seeing the woman he had saved. All sorts of possible scenarios of being with Carol swirled about his mind. He wondered what his life might be like now that he was free from the force and free from scrutiny. But just as a nervous teen, he didn't want to appear too eager, so he chose not to return to the bar the next day to see Carol. Though, he couldn't get her out of his thoughts. Sitting in his idling truck at a stop sign in downtown Franklin the day after he resigned, a flash of memories of Carol, Marion, and the boy on the highway flew by. While he thought of Eugene often, wondering how his life would turn out, he always tried to push his memory of Marion to the bottom. Not because of her, but because of what happened to him after. Now that Carol had shown up just as he was leaving his job as a cop, he took it as an omen of better things to come.

Evan's daydreaming was rudely interrupted by the loud honk of a vehicle directly behind him. He knew he had been caught not paying attention, so he politely waved and moved on through the intersection. Three-quarters of the way along the block ahead, Evan noticed someone from the car behind was waving to him. Evan's curiosity peaked as he pulled over to see what the fuss was about. Out of a blue Chevy Impala stepped Carol, wearing a big smile as she approached Evan's truck. As he was about to get out and greet her, Carol dodged around the back of the truck and entered from the passenger side. Evan was caught off guard with such a forward move, but he was delighted, nonetheless.

"I'm on my way to work, but the bar is not the kind of place I'd choose to have a conversation with you. Especially you," Carol said, still sporting a smile that weakened Evan's knees and stirred butterflies in his stomach. "Don't you agree?" Carol piped up after a brief pause.

"Um … yeah. I mean, yes. I agree." Evan was struggling to keep cool in his excitement of having Carol sitting right beside him. She could read his difficulty in talking to her, so she ended his suffering.

"Here's my number." Carol handed Evan a torn paper from her little notepad. "What's yours?" Again, Evan stumbled his words, somewhat shocked by Carol's forwardness. "So, what are you going to do now that you're not a cop anymore? Oh, never mind. You can tell me all about it when you come to see me."

Carol's words came out quickly and with a subtle wink. But again, with his body tingling, Evan paused and looked a bit confused. "No, not at the bar, at my place. Call me. Or I'll call you. Either way, we'll get together."

Carol gently tapped the back of Evan's hand that held the piece of paper with her number on it and slid across the seat and out of the truck. She used two hands to close the door and took a couple of seconds to look at Evan's still surprised face. She gave him a smile he would never forget. Evan was dumfounded and embarrassed that he was so stuck for words. He found himself vibrating inside from the interaction.

He had three clear images of Carol. The first, the day on the train platform. The second, her bleeding to death in his arms. And the third was seeing her in the bar for the first time after all those years. They were all her, but different. He found it amazing how easily she could change her look, but they all merged into one. One he couldn't let go of. He was taken by her, completely. It didn't take Evan and Carol long to realize their attraction to one another, despite the circumstances from years ago. Although Carol wasn't left with any kind of clairvoyance from Evan saving her, as some recipients of a guardian's touch do, she found herself hopelessly attached to him. She discovered Evan to be a gentle man who wouldn't hurt her, and he wanted nothing from her other than herself, and that was refreshing to her. As their relationship developed, so did their chemistry. They made love at the drop of a hat, anytime, anywhere. While Evan was infatuated with Carol's energy and zeal for life, she was fascinated by what Evan could do. She was quick to learn that it was something to be talked about rarely, and something that required protecting. That's when she began to research stories about unexplained miracles where lives were saved against all odds.

Evan had a job waiting for him at the family business whenever he was ready to start. For now, he was choosing to take a few months to shake off the effects of his time as a cop and spend time with Carol. She was welcomed into the family with open arms and not much longer after that they were married. After a rough start for both, a life for Evan and Carol in the Okanagan was laid out in front of them for the taking, which they gladly did.

17

Inequitable

2017

PART 1

Vic Armstrong was just a few years older than Evan and was already the foreman at Quinn's Orchards before Evan resigned from the force. While Evan knew Vic from his being a big part of the family business, their interactions had been minimal. That would change soon enough. Vic and Evan got along famously, quickly becoming best friends. Although Evan was family, he worked as a labourer under Vic when he resigned from the force. Evan refused to take Vic's place as it was a hard-earned position, not to mention Vic was considered family by that point, and by everyone. Vic could have lived elsewhere, but rents weren't cheap. He chose to renovate the foreman's room in the front of the bunkhouse and call it home. His logic was that he didn't want to spend money on an apartment he would hardly ever use. With his hours, that was true.

Vic was born in 1963. Like many Indigenous children, he had been ripped from his home and brought to a Catholic group home. He was forced to attend Catholic school and church. At fourteen, he had enough abuse and took off, drifting from one town to the next, living on the streets and working mostly day labour for survival at first. He ultimately worked various construction jobs over the years on his way to a life that suited him.

When Vic arrived in the Okanagan Valley, he knew he found the place he wanted to settle down in. He met Evan's father, Gerard Quinn, on the road while hitchhiking his way through. As it turned out, he inadvertently discovered in the Quinn's those he would ultimately consider his family. Vic had never learned who his biological parents were, if he had any siblings, or where he came from. The reality was he was unforgivably housed after being taken from his family, not raised. Sadly, in those years things went from bad to worse, and worse to horrible.

Vic was only five-foot-nine, one hundred and seventy pounds, but he was a powerhouse of strength and never seemed to tire of work. A considerably handsome man, Vic had dark, black hair with eyes to match, so dark brown they appeared black. Like most people, he had a few rocky relationships along the way, but he arrived in the valley with no attachments. Several years after settling in at the orchards, those types of relationships seemed to disappear for the most part. Except for a couple of girlfriends, Vic concentrated his efforts on work and took courses on chemical handling certification, which helped in growing each year's bounty.

In the years that passed, the senior Quinn retired. Evan and Carol moved into the family home and took over the business. Evan and Vic turned their crop into cider, with and without alcohol, and ice wines, the latter being the most profitable. Vic and Evan took care of the orchards, and Carol mostly took care of the cider and wine business. Twenty long years passed working with Quinn's Orchards, seventeen of those with Evan. Vic was enjoying his life immensely. Between his job at the orchard and volunteer work with the Salvation Army and Big Brothers, Vic was always busy. But most Sundays were his alone time for rest and relaxation. On this particular Sunday, he was trying to shake off an ugly incident from the day before.

PART 2

It was Saturday afternoon when Vic stopped in to see his friend, Sam Ellison. Sam bought Franklin Cycle and turned it into Sam's Motorcycle a few years back now. He called it his retirement hobby shop after years in the restaurant and bakery business back in Toronto. Sam had been a rider for many years, so this was heaven for him. Maybe it was Vic's work ethic, but something about him reminded Sam of Jacob O'Connell. When meeting Vic shortly after taking over the store, Sam took to him almost instantly and it was mutual.

"Hey, Sam. How's life treating you today?" Vic said upon entering the store.

"I'm not in the city, and I'm not cooking for anybody. Life can't get any better now, can it?" Sam, always friendly, was quick to reply before the two shared in their usual banter.

Vic caught sight of a man who wasn't a regular, scanning the supplies in an almost suspicious manner up and down the aisle. It appeared he was doing it on purpose, like he was buying time. Sam kept the shop neat and organized with the latest in accessories, along with a good stock of motorcycles and ATVs outside facing the highway.

"How long has that been going on?" Vic quietly asked Sam, nodding his head in the direction of the mystery customer.

"About ten minutes now," Sam replied in a near whisper. He finally offered some assistance to his new customer. "Hey, buddy. Do you need help finding what you're looking for?"

"No. I'm sure I can find it," replied the stranger, sounding annoyed and condescending.

"What is it exactly you're looking for? Maybe it's something I have in the back. You rode in on a Triumph right. What is it, a '73, '74 Bonneville?" Sam asked sincerely, nothing pretentious. Vic thought the customer should be impressed, but Vic also knew Sam had two Triumphs, both rebuilt by his own hands.

"Get a good look, did you?" Instead of an answer, it was a snarky question from this unpleasant, hawkish individual.

"No. Just been working in the store, talking to my good friend here." Sam nodded toward Vic. "Listen, buddy, I don't mean to sound pushy, but people that come in my shop from around here have some manners. So, enough with the attitude already."

The man was taken aback by Sam's no bullshit, direct approach. To him, it was like Sam didn't care one way or the other if he got his business. For this customer, that's exactly the way Sam felt.

"Yeah, it's a '73 Bonneville," the customer relented. "I'm just getting some supplies, but the gears are sounding funny, so I'll give it an oil treatment. Unless you happen to have a gearbox assembly and the springs?" Again, the customer's sarcasm was clear.

"I've got that. Be right back," Sam said, directly, without the pleasantries.

The customer appeared shocked that he actually had such a rare item. Truth was Sam wasn't about to reveal he had two near-identical bikes. He could possibly use those parts himself soon enough. Even at the age of seventy, he was still an avid rider. Vic was standing at the counter throughout this exchange. His opinion of this man was poor at best, and he gave him a look to let him know. After the customer's business was concluded, he purposely brushed up against Vic on his way out.

"Careful, it's a dangerous ride around Pell's Landing."

Vic couldn't believe what he just heard. *Was it a coincidence or something else?* he wondered. It threw him off and he was stymied, unable to get the words out to challenge the stranger before he walked out. Vic chose to write it off as just another asshole born with a big mouth.

Depending on the weather, Vic often rode his bike out to Pell's Landing, close to where he first met Gerard. This was paradise to him, his place to peacefully unwind from his busy schedule. And the following day after his run-in with the stranger at Sam's, that's exactly where he went. He had his backpack with food and drink and a book to read. He would prop himself up against one of the huge boulders on the edge of the partially man-made multi-levelled cliff and take in the beauty of the area. On the warm, sunny day near the end of May, it was a perfect spot to relax from trials and tribulations. And it provided a superb location for Vic to watch one of many breathtaking sunsets.

§

It wasn't long after that sunset on Sunday that the police dispatch started receiving calls about hearing and seeing a small explosion somewhere along the cliffs at or near Pell's Landing. The residents assumed it was kids partying, which wouldn't be a shock. The police searched along the cliffside on both sides of Pell's Landing. While searching the edge of the rocky landing itself, they couldn't find anything over the seventy-to-eighty-foot drop. There still remained at least thirty feet between the sporadic brush covered shelf to the water below. Looking up from the water, a small inflatable search and rescue boat could go almost twenty feet under the shelf.

Accessing the cliffside from the water would turn into a rock scaling event. In the dark it would be highly dangerous to attempt. Two men from search and rescue were in a smaller inflatable boat searching the same span on both sides of the landing but found nothing. A further search would be done at daylight for confirmation. For the moment, they shut down the boat engine and called out repeatedly, listening for any kind of response. Even in the silence of the lake none could be heard.

PART 3

Early Monday morning, two young police officers approached the front door of the Quinn residence with their hats in hands and undeniable looks of carrying grim news. Evan was returning from the warehouse when he saw the young officers on the veranda talking to Carol.

"What's going on, boys? What's with the early morning visit? Did one of my guys get busted for something?" Evan's question sounded more of a routine annoyance than curiosity.

Just then Glen Simon, now retired, pulled in the driveway, causing Evan's thoughts to race. Not a big believer in coincidence, he felt if Glen was here at the same time, something was seriously wrong. First Evan thought maybe his brother, Ryan, who suffered with addiction issues might have overdosed. Still having some pull at the precinct, Glen didn't waste any time getting the officer's attention. Once he took over and sent the constables back to the precinct, Glen went inside with Carol and Evan.

"I'm sorry, Evan, but there's been an accident at Pell's Landing. It's Vic. I wanted to let you know instead of you hearing about it from anyone else. I'm really sorry, Evan, but Vic didn't make it," Glen said, pausing to gauge the response. Evan and Carol were stunned speechless.

"You're pretty much his only family, so the chief asked if you could come down and talk to him. Maybe you could I.D. him for the record?" Evan was staring at Glen almost expressionless, not sure how to respond or what to do. His face turned white and his knees gave out from under him, slipping backwards onto one of the kitchen chairs.

"Evan?" Carol said, shaken and concerned for her husband.

"Evan? Are you going to be okay? Do you need us to get something for you?" Glen asked, equally worried, and concerned he would pass out.

"Yeah, yeah, I'll be all right, just give me a minute."

Without raising his voice, he grabbed Carol's hand and looked Glen in the eye, then Carol. "What the hell happened to Vic, Glen? He goes to that place every Sunday to have time for himself. Hell, you know that! And he's always home after sunset. So, what the hell happened to him that he would end up dead?" Evan's voice may not have raised, but there was clearly anger behind his question. But the next query didn't come quietly. "Can you tell me that?" Evan slammed his hand down on the kitchen table. That set Glen back a step, catching him off guard.

"I'm sorry, I don't know the details yet. I'm going to see the chief now. Why don't you take some time before you ... uh ... and when you feel ready." Glen was struggling. "Look, I'll come over later and pick you up and take you in to see Vic ... Evan?" Glen wasn't talking to his young rookie anymore. This was his friend and his respectful tone showed that.

"Yeah. Sure, Glen. Thanks for coming over. I appreciate that." Glen waved his hand to push Evan's concern aside.

"This is going to be hard on all of us, but especially Evan," Carol said to Glen as he stepped out the door.

The official response issued from the coroner's office regarding Vic's death was that it was accidental. Their summary of events was that Vic had taken his motorcycle down to a popular spot to lounge farther down next to some man-made barriers of armour stone. All that was there to warn people and vehicles from going over the edge was a bright white chain that was looped from post to post with a few rail ties as curbs.

The police concluded that Vic lost control riding up or down from one level to the next. This never sat right with Evan. Whenever he saw Vic's bike, it was parked on the top level. Vic wasn't foolish enough to take a five-hundred-pound street bike down a narrow cliffside path just to park his bike closer to his favourite spot. None of this report jibed with Evan. Outside of a hypothesis that Vic accidentally popped the clutch, he couldn't figure out how the hell Vic would end up at the bottom of that cliff. There were no witnesses, nor any pieces of evidence found. Evan thought of his friend lying down there all night. He wondered if he had been alive and unable to call out for help. Evan was devastated.

18

Questionable Fate

Two weeks after Vic's funeral, Evan was still spending his spare time in the house, still grieving. He spent hours at a time sitting in the La-Z-Boy reclining chair, watching the twenty-four-hour news channel but not really watching. It was a Sunday when Carol came into the house and disturbed Evan from his routine of staring nowhere in particular.

"Evan, honey. There's a man down the road there pushing his motorbike and he seems to have a heavy load. Why don't you see if he needs some help?" Carol was delicately encouraging Evan to get out of the house. This was as good a reason as any.

"I'm sure he can figure it out, Carol." Evan's tone lacked compassion or any recognizable concern, energy, or affect.

"Okay, that's enough!" Carol snapped. "You can't just sit here hour after hour, honey. You have to get back on the horse. Would Vic let some stranger remain stranded on the side of the road with his motorcycle like that?" Carol was becoming animated now, with one hand on her hip and the other pointing out to the road like she was ordering him to go. She also knew invoking Vic's name would either rise him from his misery or lead to an argument. She hoped for the former.

"Come on, honey. Just go and see if there's anything you can do for him. Except for work, you haven't been out of the house since Vic's funeral. It's time don't you think?"

There was no verbal response from Evan, just a groan as he slowly rose from his chair to go to the bedroom and change. On his way out of the kitchen he turned to Carol.

"Happy? I'm going to go help the guy, okay?"

"Yes, dear, I think that's a wonderful gesture, I'm glad you thought of it."

Evan just gave Carol a smirk and went out the door. The truth was Evan and Carol had a wonderful marriage, and they loved each other dearly. But she needed to wake him up and stir him from his grief before it swallowed him. When the couple looked back, they thought it had to be more than circumstance that landed her in Evan's backyard. As difficult as it was, Carol forced Evan to discuss what he did to save her life those many years ago in that parking lot in Toronto. She told him what the doctors said about her survival. Evan finally gave in and admitted — to Carol only — what he was and what occurred on that fateful day. After that revelation, he shared other experiences that happened throughout his life.

About a hundred feet down the road from the Quinn's house, a man in his mid-to-late thirties was working on an old Triumph. He had a huge, overstuffed backpack strapped down to the rear of the seat with multicoloured bungee cords. A fairly clean-cut-looking man with spiky dirty-blonde hair, and a big black mark across his forehead from wiping the sweat from his brow, looked up at Evan.

"Hey, how ya doing? Triumphs, eh? They either purr like a kitten or they're choking up hairballs," the stranger said.

"Well, I don't think I've ever quite heard it said that way, but I get the gist of what you're saying. Have you figured it out yet or is it just no fuel?" Evan was hoping his effort would require nothing more than a can of gas.

"Oh no, I've got gas. I just don't seem to have any spark."

"Come on then, I've got a shop just there. It's probably a coil." Evan pointed toward his property. "I've got every tool under the sun and lots of spare parts, so I'm sure we can get it running and get you back on your way to wherever it is you're going." Evan made sure to emphasize the moving on part.

"That would be great, thank you. I really appreciate it."

As they walked down the side of the road, Evan couldn't help but notice the size of his backpack, so he surmised he was travelling to find work or on a long holiday.

"I'm Evan Quinn by the way." He extended his hand out to the stranger.

"Oh yeah, hi. I'm Nathan. Good to meet you, sir."

Before Evan let go of Nathan's hand, he looked him in the eye. "Nathan…?" Evan waited for a last name.

"Gravallos. Nathan Gravallos, sir," he said, intentionally without further elaboration.

"Well, Nathan, call me Evan." He respected this younger man's privacy, and he returned a good handshake while looking him in the eye.

"Okay Evan, glad to know ya." Nathan was polite, but his demeanour was a bit nervous, seemingly glad to have this exchange over with. Evan could be intense, not always approachable.

Normally, Evan would be swift to size up a man, and even though there was something odd about Nathan, he was so distracted in mourning that he wasn't really seeing through it. Evan concluded the possibility that it might be fortuitous that this man came along when he did, needing help with Vic's absence. This wasn't the first time Evan hired transient workers when harvest was busier than usual. Together the two had the bike running in short order, but before Nathan mounted his Triumph to head out for the road, Evan offered him the job. Nathan graciously accepted. Evan made his position and pay conditional on his experience. Nathan managed to pad his verbal resume sufficiently in response. Evan was grateful for the help, but it came with an odd sensation scratching at him that he couldn't bring to the surface.

19

Of Mice and Men

Under his new persona, Nathan picked up on the rumour of Sara's plans while he was working for Vickers Landscaping in Clarington. It was a small town. Heather Keegan taking ownership of Able Hands Construction & Design Ltd. with her daughter was a big deal in the local area because the business had been started and built up with Jacob and Sara, and Pat and Heather. Of course, the tragic news of losing Jacob and Pat in 2005 made Sara's sale big news yet again. When Nathan found out, he kept nosing around and tried to learn all he could of Sara's plans. He set his long-game plan into motion and took off for Franklin, B.C. This was his biggest challenge to date and one he felt his father would be proud of if he could execute it properly, to quote a phrase. He wanted to establish himself ahead of Sara's arrival and to score the job next to her new property, Nathan had been far more successful than he had hoped. He was bouncing off the walls with delight that his skills had brought him this far.

It would be late summer before Nathan would eventually bring his jailhouse buddy, Joe Miller, out to the Okanagan from Toronto. For their purposes, Joe would have to remain in hiding for the majority of his time until Nathan was ready for certain events to start unfolding as the year progressed. There were a series of tasks he wanted Joe to complete in a hit-and-run style. When he was done those, he would receive a bonus. For the dirty work about to be carried out, a forty thousand dollar payday was coming for Joe. Nathan and Joe had this worked out in advance because Joe would be leaving town on the run from parole restrictions and that would require money.

Before he arrived, Joe put Nathan in touch with his friend, Lenny Bonacorso, who was a drug dealer at the level Joe was back in Toronto. Joe knew that Lenny had set up in Franklin and was running supply from Calgary and throughout the resort areas on the east side of the province near Franklin. Skiers apparently enjoyed two kinds of fresh powder. Nathan seemed to have a talent for picking out men who were middle-of-the-road drug users and dealers, but always with an emotional flaw or two. And always with the intention of targeted manipulation.

Nathan discovered the fallen former police officer, Rick Jackson, through Lenny. In Rick Jackson's case, he was addicted to just about anything from the opiate family, heroin, and morphine for starters. Percocet and dilaudid were aspirin for him. But he also used speed, coke, or crystal meth if he was too loaded and needed to bring himself back from the edge, a difficult balancing act. Rick was the most addicted and useless among Nathan's crew, but he served a purpose. None of the others in the group could understand what that could possibly be, but Nathan did.

Near ten years ago when Nathan did a small stretch of time in Chilliwack, he met the Gundry brothers, Dean and Brian. The brothers weren't twins, but for the most part they looked like it. They were almost identical in body size and although their faces were somewhat different looking, they weren't far apart from appearing like fraternal twins. Joe was the odd one out, with age not treating him well in his mid-fifties. He was considerably shorter and far from handsome compared to the other men. This was an important distinction for Nathan in his plans.

Joe had a raging vengeance inside him and looked the same out of prison as he did inside. Beyond bulking up and putting on a few pounds, he was the same. Joe was a quality piece of shit, and he exuded that. He was a most undesirable man. He kept his trademark spiked hair with dyed light blonde tips. This reminded Nathan of the crew from Vickers, all looking the same in their uniforms. He developed the idea from that. He, Lenny, and the Gundrys were all similar in size, so he had all of them cut and dye their hair the same. Explaining his rationale to the men, he told them it would be hard for the O'Connells or the Quinns to say for sure who they saw if they witnessed something. It was Nathan's version of psychological warfare.

"What are you guys, the Bobbsey Twins? More like triplets. Holy! Fuck, dude. Did you take these guys to your barber? Did you all get the same dye job?"

"Yeah, we did. You got a fucking problem with that?" asked Dean Gundry, the more unstable of the brothers, while pulling out a ridiculously sized knife that was tucked down the back of his jeans. Nathan needed only to look at Dean to make him behave. Money and drugs were big motivators. It turned out that Joe could have easily passed for the Gundry's father. And they all spoke the same language.

Nathan's plan was to start terrorizing Sara when she and her kids arrived in Vancouver, just like his father did. This was his twisted version of welcoming Sara to B.C. — letting her know she hadn't escaped anything. Darkness prevails. He used contacts, gossip, and a reasonable quality of hacking skills to learn Sara's itinerary. It was part of his pathology to be that much better than his father. He would carry on with this antagonistic stalking of Sara, then he would go after the kids. His intention was to cycle this behaviour from the shadows, close, yet never seen. This was the standard practice he needed of his group until his real plan was ready. The drugs and money would keep the men within reach, ready to act when needed. Overall, Nathan was surprised at his own drive on this mission.

20

Arrival/Departures

PART 1

The O'Connells' flight arrived in Vancouver at the end of June with an excited Mary, a miserable Ben, and a tired mother. Sara had a meeting with her new employers to have everything she needed set up for her work in the Okanagan Valley. She traded in her older Suburban for a newer model and pre-arranged for it to be ready when she arrived in the city. Ben planned to tag along with Mary and tour the university she would be attending in the fall. Sara and the kids left Toronto on the red-eye and landed in Vancouver at eight-thirty a.m. after a four-and-a-half-hour flight. Since arriving in the airport, Sara had a familiar and annoying sensation return, creating an unwanted desire to keep looking over her shoulder. Without reason nor confirmation, she felt that someone was watching her. Mary was quick to pick up on her mother's discontent. As the three loaded their suitcases into the limousine, Sara's uncomfortable sensation turned into a cold chill. In that moment Mary turned to her mother.

"Did you feel that?" Mary asked, inspecting her mother's body language and expression. Sara put her hand on Mary's shoulder, gently guiding her into the car.

"It's not the first time, honey." Sara's response was calm yet direct.

Sara tried to shake it off, remaining stoic for everyone's sake. The kids were in the car. Sara had one hand on the roof of the limo and the other on the top of the door, about to join them. Just then she looked across the thoroughfare and noticed a man with unnatural-looking blonde hair. Sara quickly became convinced he was staring at her, not just the general area. He was far enough away she couldn't make out his face with any great detail, but she was fully aware he was locked in on her. Sara squinted her eyes, displaying her rising anger, but she thought it best to let it go and joined the kids in the limo to leave this asshole to his own misery.

Their first stop was at the dealership to pick up her vehicle, then on to the university. Sara looked to Mary and Ben with a forced smile. "Well guys, you ready for this?" Ben just stared out the window of the limo, and Mary looked at Sara with obvious concern.

"What is it, Mom? Did you see someone?"

Before she could answer, Ben piped up. "It's too early in the day for ghosts to be out."

"Oh, very funny, Ben. Are you going to be a jerk the entire time?" Mary growled to her brother.

"That'll be enough of that. Just enjoy this beautiful weather … without the arguing. Understood?" Mary just nodded, but Ben remained silent, defiant. "Understood?" Sara exclaimed, demanding acknowledgement. Ben turned to his mother, careful to use a civil tone.

"Yes, Mom. I got it."

"Okay then. My meeting shouldn't take too long, so I should be at the university around eleven-thirty, noon at the latest. The movers are going to be at the house early afternoon tomorrow, so enjoy the day and the hotel tonight because there's a lot of work ahead of us starting tomorrow."

When Sara dropped the kids off at the university, Ben got out of the car and turned to his mother. "He looked similar to the guy that worked for Vickers … the landscaping company, remember?" Ben said, prodding his mother.

"That one you told me about? At school?" Sara asked, sounding astonished.

"I saw you looking at him, so I looked over, but I couldn't make out the guy's face. He just resembled the guy from Vickers. The same sort of look. Didn't Vickers work for Able Hands before?" Ben asked with a hint of forcefulness.

Sara was quick to pick up that Ben was concerned for her, but he had no knowledge of who the man was nor what his mother experienced when seeing him.

"No. And he was too far away anyway. But he did seem oddly familiar." Sara was trying to make it out to be inconsequential as she couldn't confirm one way or the other.

"Mom! The guy stared right at you," Ben said, raising his voice.

"Ben, if he knew me, he would have waved to me. He could have been looking at anyone there. It's a busy place," Sara said dismissively. Ben's brows started to squeeze together with a piercing look on his face.

"See ya later, Mom."

Sara watched as Ben walked away from the car toward the university grounds. She broke a weak smile, completely aware of her children being a bit more than intuitive the older they got.

PART 2

Sara didn't pay any attention to the car the stranger was standing next to at the airport parking lot. She was too preoccupied with why he was staring at her to begin with. When she was leaving the U.B.C. West Parkade, an older silver Acura with heavily tinted windows followed her. She continued east along University Boulevard south of Kitsilano, enjoying the new car smell when the vehicle following her turned north, heading toward the Spanish Banks Beach. This was Sara's third trip to meet with the owners of Cailey & Higgins, so she was becoming reasonably familiar with the area. She thought it was probably a group of kids heading toward the beach, which made perfect sense on this beautiful summer day. Considering the amount of rain the province received each year, there was a lot of traffic on this sunny summer day. Coming along West 10th up to Burrard, she was surprised to see the same car ahead of her on the street perpendicular to her. When the car crossed the intersection with the passenger window down part way, Sara saw at least two men, but the closest man remained in the shadows.

Her stomach started to wobble, and she felt a lump in her throat. Her hands squeezed the leather steering wheel so hard her knuckles were turning white. The empty feeling in her stomach was quickly replaced with a tightness throughout her core.

"What the.... Is that the same guy?" she wondered aloud as if she were talking to an invisible friend in the car with her.

She turned her head to follow the car as it crawled through the intersection, with a look on her face that expressed more anger than fear. All of a sudden, HONK! The car behind her laid on the horn as the light in front of her turned green. She jumped so hard that her hands came off the steering wheel momentarily.

"Oh, you fucking asshole!" Sara yelled out from being startled. With the possibility of a stalker following her, which she would be sensitive to, it had put her on edge. She tried to convince herself that it was only kids fooling around in the car, but her senses spoke a different truth to her.

It was a dejecting feeling for Sara in a moment that was supposed to a new lease on life filled with optimism and hope. For the moment, darkness put a dent in her optimism. But catching her attention out of nowhere, Jacob's scent quickly floated by. Even for just that second, it provided her with a sense of calm reassurance.

All went well at the meeting with Sara's new employer, including the meeting with her liaison to the firm's new clients, Trevor Holdt. Sara may have appeared too tired to notice, but she was definitely taken with Trevor's looks and mannerisms, a true gentleman. He looked nothing like Jacob, but there was a familiarity about him she found comforting and inviting. The company Sara was designing for was called Nordic Trails, a high-end developer in Alberta and B.C. They were building a new ski resort and villa with condos throughout The Narrows mountain range, about a forty-five-minute drive from Sara's new home.

Sara, Mary, and Ben had made it to the Marriott shortly after dinner hour following a trip through Gastown to see its famous Steam Clock and surrounding cobblestone. Ben may have been fighting his mother over this move, but he was taken with the look of the area. It was beautifully unique compared to Clarington. He was impressed to constantly see mountains as a backdrop whereas back home seemed flat in comparison. As a treat and pacifier, Sara treated the kids to their own rooms, no bunking up. Ben quickly hit the pool for a swim, and Mary enjoyed a bubble bath in a huge soaker tub with a built-in entertainment centre. She was quick to photograph and post her visit in the lap of luxury to her friends on social media. Sara poured herself a tall glass of white wine and flopped on the large corner couch in front of the gas fireplace. It wasn't like home, but that was the point. After Ben finished his swim, sauna, and shower, he went to his room to call and check in with Diane back in Clarington, again.

Mary was out of the tub and comfortably wrapped by a soft, white terrycloth robe and curled up on the bed with her tablet in hand chatting with friends.

Sara and the kids fell asleep within seconds of each other, and all had the same dream, a first. Their disturbing dream ended with all of them jumping awake, startled and chilled. The knock came, and Sara opened her door to Mary followed by Ben only seconds behind, both complaining about the dream they had.

"Come on. Come in here you two. It's clear we need to talk."

Ben and Mary filed in without another word. The siblings looked at one another, not quite the same but similar to how spooked they were the day at school when they shared a vision of Shelley Randall's murder scene. To this point, it was something they hadn't shared with their mother, nor could they currently find a reason to. The three of them gathered around on the sofa and began a difficult conversation about what they just experienced. Sara did her best to convince the kids, as well as herself, that there wasn't any danger facing them in their life here, that tomorrow would start anew. Sadly, she hoped more than she believed.

PART 3

Ben seemed to get taller and heavier from spring to summer, bringing him to just under six feet, one-hundred-eighty pounds. With the emotional turmoil of the last year, including saving Daryl's life and leaving Diane behind, he struggled with his anger. With just under five months to go before he turned seventeen, Ben was changing rapidly, which left Sara highly concerned.

It was another early rise for moving day with a five- or six-hour drive to their home to meet the movers by early afternoon. It was five-thirty a.m., and Sara was more than surprised when she knocked on Ben's hotel room door to hear him respond right away. "Yup. I'm up, Mom."

Wow! I wonder what alien abducted my kid, Sara thought. Mary was already awake, so Sara turned around to head back to her room to finish getting ready. Just then the elevators across from her room sounded off a rather loud *ding*. It startled Sara, causing her to take a deep breath and put her hand to her chest. She watched the elevator doors open, but no one came out. Sara watched the doors close and turned to carry on to her room but nearly slammed into someone standing unacceptably close.

"Jesus! You scared the hell out of me!" she exclaimed.

Sara began to back up even farther, instantly having a strange feeling about this man. She wasn't sure what to think of this stranger who just stood there, silent, and expressionless. He had the same dirty-blonde hair and bad dye job over brown roots that she saw yesterday; however, too close for comfort now. A man in his early-to-mid-forties by Sara's guess. He had on a pair of beat-up green army fatigue-style shorts and t-shirt with a dirty old pair of Reebok runners and a black fanny pack. He had a scraggly goatee on his otherwise bare face but only from his lip to the chin line without a mustache. He looked like an oddly dressed modern Mennonite to Sara, having seen many back in Ontario. His eyes were grey and when Sara looked into them, she saw malicious intent, an unsettled man. He stood still, right in front of her.

"Can you get out of my way?" Sara would forego any manners in this moment.

The man still said nothing, clearly trying to intimidate her. Sara stepped to the side to go around him and he mirrored her move, continuing to block her. Sara now felt a familiar feeling of fear that would soon turn into rage. But for the moment, it was fear, and she believed he intended to hurt her or worse. Like an animal playing with its prey.

He reached out to grab Sara by the throat at the same moment the door to Ben's room flew open, and Ben burst out in a hurried, direct attack on the man. Before Sara had a chance to say anything, Ben gently pushed her out of the way. The man tried to take a swing at Ben, but Ben grabbed his fist like it was coming at him in slow motion. The man screamed out in agony as Ben took his hand and bent his wrist unnaturally backwards to the point bones were about to start snapping. All in just a few seconds, the man was down to one knee on the floor, then on both. Sara was truly frightened, seeing a look in Ben's eyes she had never seen before as they started to glow the colour of the sun.

"You shouldn't have done that. You shouldn't have come here," Ben said, sounding like a robot, keeping the man on bent knees and in agony. Ben squatted down in front of him, staring directly into his eyes, then he pushed his other hand against the man's chest over his heart. He began to push, not trying to punch or knock him over. He just kept a pressure applied that had the man frozen. Suddenly you could hear this stranger grunt and groan with little breath that sounded like a combination of pain and terror.

"Stop. Please, stop. You're—" the man pleaded with bated breath.

Ben remained calm, holding the bent wrist against the attacker's shoulder with one hand and keeping the pressure against his chest with the other.

"You shouldn't have done that. You shouldn't have come here," Ben repeated, sounding like he was in trance.

Sara was aghast, lost as to what she could say or do to stop her son from hurting this man any more. The man's face started to turn grey, like the life was coming out of him. The harder Ben pushed, the more the man weakened. His legs were folded over to the floor on one hip, ready to collapse.

"Please. Please, stop." The man was weakly and quietly pleading for his life.

To her horror, Sara could clearly see where this was leading. For all intents and purpose, Ben was killing this man. A complete over-the-top reaction for protecting his mother, an instinct for family to eliminate the threat. Sara's whole body was shaking now, as she squatted down behind the man to look Ben in the eye.

"Ben. Stop it. That's enough. You're hurting him … you're killing him, Ben, stop it!" Sara's words bounced off Ben like she wasn't there at all. He just kept pushing. "Damn it, Ben. Stop it!" Sara raised her voice to get her son's attention, but no reaction yet.

Mary's door swung open, and she stepped out into the hall and stood behind Sara.

"Ben!" Mary yelled so loud that surely the other guests could hear. "You're going to kill him, Ben, stop it!" she yelled one last time, and it pulled Ben out of his trance.

He let go, and the man fell over onto the floor face down, out cold. Ben backed up, looking at Mary and Sara like he just got caught with his hand in the cookie jar. But then he grew solemn.

"Get your bags. Now. We're going," He said calmly.

"Ben?" Sara was attempting to get Ben to acknowledge what just transpired, but he ignored her and stepped over the man, guiding Sara and Mary back to their rooms before he quickly stepped into his own room.

Mary could see her mother was completely flabbergasted. "Mom … Mom, we better go," Mary said. Sara was at a loss for words and a loss for direction. When the girls came back out into the hall, the man was gone.

"Impossible," Sara thought. Ben was already outside of his room, suitcase arms extended, ready to roll.

"Let's go," Ben said with no other commentary as he stepped across the hall and pushed the elevator's down button. Sara looked at him like he was a stranger.

Later that morning when the cleaning crew came through, they found a man in a fatigue shirt and shorts sprawled out on the floor of Ben's room. The cleaner had to shake him awake as he was still out cold, but luckily alive.

21

Ethics

The drive to the O'Connells' new home was a quiet, uncomfortable one. The tension in the air was palpable. Mary decided to take herself away from thoughts of the morning the best she could by reading anything. Out of her bag came a *New York Times* magazine she "borrowed" from the hotel. She began reading a miraculous story about the courage and strength of a young girl who had survived against enormous odds in 1939. She had lived through a brutal attack in Washington State by a monster of a man who was an escaped serial rapist and murderer. The same girl had managed to save a young deputy's life after he was stabbed and left for dead by the same escaped prisoner.

The location of the stab wounds were considered, under normal circumstances, to be fatal, so this rang a familiar bell for Mary. She came to realize there were more people like her father and brother out there in the world and not all were the same. In that sudden realization, Mary leaned back in her seat with a comforted smile and drifted off to sleep. In her dream, Mary thought it odd to find herself talking to her father as an adult as she had been only six years old when he died. The words that came from Jacob O'Connell were similar to words spoken in a university ethics class.

There was Mary's father, standing beside the same pine tree near his gravestone where he assuredly stood for Ben all those years ago, still dressed in casual attire. He looked the part of a teacher. Mary sat on a nearby bench with her legs swinging back and forth like a child being read a story, enthralled with her father's presence and every word. She was that six-year-old in size but had her adult mind.

"Mary, there's one thing Ben needs to become aware of and that's the profound effect his power has on the individual he subdues with it. That man in the hotel was brought to the brink of death."

"Oh, you saw that did you? It must have been pretty scary for him. But he was going to hurt Mom, or worse," Mary said, holding her head down for a moment, sharing in the disappointment of that occurrence.

"Yes, I saw it. I can't explain how, but I saw it. Ben was shown the eternal pain and misery he would find himself suffering if he continued on that trajectory. There's a big difference between murder and taking a life in protecting your family. But do it out of anger, for a regular person even, that would mean trouble. For him, it spells disaster. He may not remember it for a while. Memories are tricky. Some are designed for protection and some for direction. What Ben did to that man was no different than Newton's third law of motion." Just then Mary and her father spoke at the same time. "For every action in nature, there is an equal and opposite reaction." Both giggled before Jacob wrapped up. "Ben needs to understand how this will, in turn, affect him. If he pushes an individual close to the point of losing their life, with that very intention, then his could be lost as well. He needs to not just understand that. He has to believe it and live it, always knowing. You will have to tell him, Mary. And you will have to remind him, subtly."

"Yes, Dad. I will. Dad...?" Before Mary could start asking her father some of the many questions she had of him, she woke from the dream.

Mary woke with the loud horn of a passing transport truck, sitting still with her hands in her lap. She began looking back and forth between her mother and brother from the back seat. The gravity of what their family had experienced that morning, and what might be coming, began to flow into sharper focus as each mile went by.

22

Welcome Wagon

Evan and Carol took their cue from fate after meeting at the bar the day Evan resigned from the force. Their first meeting had been a traumatic event that left an indelible mark on the pair. After six months of dating, plans were in the works to get married. For a myriad of reasons, the couple settled for a modest affair. And now, nearing their twentieth anniversary, their love for one another had never waned, and they fit together quite comfortably.

Carol kept her natural auburn hair — with secretive hair dye. With dark emerald eyes, she has remained as captivating a woman as ever. In her mid-forties, she could still easily pass for ten years younger. Evan held his own, as far as his shape and looks for his age were concerned. He carried a few extra pounds, and some dignified-looking grey streaks had begun to appear above his sideburns. Being such a baby face for so many years as a rookie cop, he still had a bit of that youthful, mischievous smile, but he was mostly a serious man. As husband and wife, the couple looked completely natural together, meant to be.

The new neighbours had been in their home, next to the Quinns', for just a few weeks. After Evan hired Nathan, Carol began to gently push him to go meet the O'Connells and welcome them to the community. Evan had been running on autopilot since Vic's death not long back. He went along, begrudgingly. As they circled the driveway and turned the SUV toward the road, Carol caught Nathan peeking out from behind the curtains of the bunkhouse window. It became evident she was never that comfortable with the new guy who had taken Vic's job, but not his place — so to speak. Although she hadn't told Evan that Nathan creeped her out, she thought he would at least pick up from body language and attitude toward their new foreman. It wasn't that Evan was over the moon for the guy. He needed the help in Vic's absence and the timing of Nathan's arrival and availability was too convenient to turn down. A little too convenient upon closer examination, but oddly Evan wasn't seeing it.

§

To Ben, the melancholy teen, it seemed like an endless grey veil of rain was clinging to the earth like an oppressive wet blanket. Every morning, for the last few days, the door opened and he would be greeted by this abysmal overcast stifle. "My God, is it going to rain forever? No wonder suicide rates are so much higher here," Ben said, embellishing the angst in his exaggerated teenage mind, brooding while he stared out the kitchen window.

"Being a little dramatic there, aren't you, son?" Sara said, reading the local rag.

"Well, come on, Mom! It's rainy and grey here an awful lot, don't you think? Like, it's Saturday. Give me a break already!"

"The weather is different here; I'll give you that. It will take getting used to. But it hasn't been that bad. And anyway, I heard we're supposed to be in for a dry summer, so this will pass. Look how warm and sunny it was when we arrived. Would you rather have to shovel two feet of snow?" Sara asked, flipping the page of the newspaper at the kitchen table.

"Actually, yes! Because that would mean I'd be back home," Ben said, pushing himself away from the sink and turning to glare at his mother.

"You're not going to stop flogging that dead horse, are you?" Sara was becoming agitated with Ben's incessant complaining.

"Maybe when it starts to look like dog food," Ben said belligerently.

"Okay, Ben. That's enough of that!" Sara raised her voice but was cut short. "Oh look, someone's coming up the driveway. Why don't you go out and see who it is. It might be one of our neighbours. Maybe you should introduce yourself to them." Sara seemed pleasantly excited at the prospect of neighbours coming to say hello and introduce themselves.

"Really? It's bad enough you drag me here, now you—"

"Go out there now and introduce yourself!" Sara interrupted, pointing to the driveway. Her voice had elevated to that special level that meant "Not now, but right now!" The look on Ben's face when he came out to greet Evan and Carol was far from inviting. But the moment Ben made eye contact with Evan, his demeanour began to change. There was something about Evan. He had a fatherly authoritative way about him that affected Ben almost instantly. He managed to minimize his scowl and use a more respectful tone to receive their new neighbours.

"Hi, I'm Ben. You guys own the orchards next door," Ben said in a monotone voice, nodding toward the decals on the SUV.

"Yes, we do," Carol said to a momentary uncomfortable silence. "Well, my name is Carol, and this is my husband, Evan."

"Hello, Ben, it's nice to meet you," Evan said, holding his hand out for Ben.

"Uh, it's, uh, nice to meet you too. My mom's inside," Ben said, quickly shaking Evan's hand. For the moment, that was the limit of any congeniality Ben could muster. He managed to choke down his angst and drop some of the attitude, but it was still present.

The Quinns went inside the O'Connells' Confederation-style log home with their gift basket and spent a few hours getting to know their new neighbours. As soon as Sara laid eyes on the couple, she felt a sense of familiarity take over the room. She sensed nothing but goodness from Evan and Carol, but Sara caught herself staring at

Evan a bit too much, which Carol picked up on. Sara didn't realize it at first, but the vibe she felt from Evan was similar to what she felt with Jacob and his parents when she was younger. She knew there was something special about him. For now, she remembered her manners and invited the couple to the dining room table. The Quinn and O'Connell families definitely clicked. Before long, they were talking like old friends who hadn't seen each other in years.

After Sara invited the Quinns to come in, Ben went to his room to play video games, almost entirely unimpressed. Mary was home, so she was introduced. A short time of pleasantries ensued before the adults were eventually left on their own to get acquainted.

The fact that Sara was an architect caught Evan's attention as he wanted to design a new expansion to accommodate an increased volume of ice wine. The three of them covered all the standard topics, eventually arriving at Ben. Sara was worried he was rude to the Quinns but was pleasantly surprised to hear he was polite. Nothing else. Just polite, and that was good enough for a start.

23

Conversations

Sara contributed the marked improvement in Ben's behaviour and well-being directly to Evan's goodwill and guidance since they met. When Sara first met Evan, there was an aura she saw around him. It was identical to Jacob's when it shone. As bizarre and astronomically against all odds as it was, Sara believed there was more to Evan like there was with Jacob. Having Ben take on a full-time job with the Quinns for the summer was the perfect way for Ben to adapt to his new surroundings. He responded well in meeting his newfound responsibilities. Sara was quick to notice the changes in him, and she would often let him know how proud she was. She didn't fear Ben after the incident in the Marriott in Vancouver. She feared *for* him.

Evan had a unique way of describing where Ben was at in his development. "He's got one foot in the kiddie pool and one in the adult pool, and he's trying to balance between the two, not sure when to make the step."

It was a Saturday night on the last weekend of September. Ben was out at a friend's place in town watching movies, and Mary was on campus in Vancouver. Sara filled this alone time by inviting Carol and Evan over for dinner. The meal was mostly prepared, except for the chicken that Sara left for Evan to barbecue. With the weather still warm out, Sara easily persuaded them to the back deck with some cold beer and conversation. In the short time since they met, they got along like life-long friends. Evan was first to pick up on Sara's demeanor, appearing somewhat demure and distracted. "What's on your mind, Sara? Looks like something's bothering you. Or maybe you're just tired."

"Oh, nice one, honey! Nice way to compliment the woman." Carol looked over to Sara shaking her head. "Men. What can you do?" Carol asked, with a scolding look to her husband.

"What?" Evan raised his arms in the air, a beer in one hand and a pair of tongs in the other.

Things turned quiet for a moment, and Evan lowered the lid on the barbecue. He walked over to join the girls and sat directly across from Sara. "It's Ben, isn't it?" he asked, taking a swig of his beer. Carol looked at Evan with her head tilted, showing a look of curiosity.

"You picked up on that, didn't you? But then you pick up on a lot when it comes to Ben, don't you?" Sara replied, calm and direct. Carol quietly sat back in her deck chair, not sure what direction this conversation would take. "It's because you're the same as him, aren't you?" Sara bravely asked, looking to Evan with an honest and pleasant expression on her face.

"Well, aren't all guys the same?" Carol interjected nervously.

"It's okay, Carol, she knows," Evan said, looking over to Carol.

"Well, I didn't say anything," Carol said, holding her hand to her chest and her two fingers up in scout's honour pose.

"It's okay, sweetheart. She didn't need to hear it from either one of us. Isn't that right, Sara?" Evan said, rising from his seat to deal with the burning chicken on the barbecue.

"I think it's a warning system. Call me crazy, but many of us can see a white aura around certain people, right? Well, Evan's aura is white with another layer on the perimeter that's the colour of the sun just as it's falling — a dark yellow, almost orange. But I only saw it when you first came in, standing behind Ben," Sara said, looking at the pair to judge their reaction to what she claimed. Carol leaned farther back into her seat, like she was suddenly enjoying a movie. Sara impatiently waited for the response. Evan was facing the barbecue, turning over the chicken.

"So, that's when you realized?" he asked, still not turning to face her.

"The moment I met you, I knew." Sara looked at Carol and smiled, which in turn allowed Carol to finally breathe easy.

"Oh my God! So, it is true. Ben's the same?" Carol's excitement could barely be contained. "I'm sorry, Sara. It's just ... what are the odds?"

All at once, everyone agreed that it wasn't just coincidence that Sara landed there.

"That's one of the things I need to talk to you about. That and Ben," Sara said, lowering her head into her hands. Evan walked back over to sit down and grasped Sara's hands in his, gently squeezing.

"Don't worry, dear. Carol's just excited to have someone to talk to about this. We rarely discuss it. More like she brings it up, and I tell her I don't want to talk about it. But I knew that Ben was like me when I shook his hand. I can't explain it. But we also know what it can invite. Actually, it's already here," Evan said, thinking of Vic, but still made no connections as to who could be responsible for his death. Sara burst out into tears. In between her sobs, she managed to squeak a few words out.

"It's ... it's after Ben, and Mary too. It killed my husband. I think it's here." Sara could barely finish what she was trying to get out.

"We know, honey. We know," Carol said, reaching over to join all of their hands together. Sara sat straight up, pulled her hands away to wipe her tears, and looked back and forth between Carol and Evan.

"What do you mean, you know? You mean, you know about something being here to hurt us? Because you couldn't have known about Jacob." Sara's tone shifted to one of suspicion. Evan sat up and motioned to Carol.

"Go ahead. You've started it, you might as well finish it."

As the evening went on, Sara found out that Carol first learned about Jacob from an online search that revealed the shooting in the Clarington news. Originally, Carol had been researching for stories about people being saved by unexplained miracles. What she learned about Jacob and Sara was coincidental, as learning of the term, guardians, came later. The story of Sara surviving being hit by a car thanks to Jacob saving her life, was what led Carol to more information about them. It never dawned on Sara that anything from her life back then could be discovered online, nor why.

24

Real Time

PART 1

Sara always worried about her kids. But she couldn't really be considered a typical mother with typical kids. The dreams she was having more difficulty getting over lately were the ones about Ben. She tried her best to stop thinking about what happened in that hotel hallway because it caused her intense flashbacks of the day Jacob died. Learning Ben could take a life so easily was distressing, knowing the results of that action.

In the dream she had on this night, that's exactly what Ben did. And just like his father, he paid the ultimate price for taking a life.

Sara was screaming as loud as she could for Ben to release the stranger in the hallway, but he wouldn't let go. Just before Ben collapsed dead from what he did, Sara was startled awake, her forehead covered in beads of perspiration, and screaming, "No! God, no."

She struggled to calm her breathing after fearfully shouting out upon waking. From his room, Ben didn't hear the sound of such desperation in his mother's voice, and Sara was glad he didn't. However, she knew she couldn't keep putting off a much-needed conversation with Ben about that day in the Marriott, among other things.

However, her night's sleep was over with. It was shortly after six-thirty now, and the sun started to reveal its strength as Sara took another sip of her tea, continuing to stare at a blue spruce in the yard. She felt her eyelids becoming heavy when she was startled, seeing Mary standing in front of the tree. Sara shook her head to clear the fog before looking back out. But now, Mary's image was gone. Sara wasn't sure if she had started to nod off into a dream or if she just had a vision of her daughter. Either way, a shot of adrenaline left her wide awake. She grabbed her phone to text Mary, more concerned about her well-being than waking her up. Not long after, Mary replied that she was fine. A mother's curiosity served and satisfied. For now.

§

On the Thursday before the Thanksgiving long weekend, Sara experienced a cascade of chills that bolted her upright. She couldn't believe what she just saw was so clear. She was still seeing it in shocking detail as each second passed, leaving her appalled and horrified for her daughter. Sara was frozen momentarily, unable to get the image out of her head. She had seen Mary running for her life through the halls of a near-empty campus.

Mary's flight to the valley wasn't set to arrive until the following morning. Most of the students and faculty would leave by noon the day before the long weekend. Mary loved her choice to pursue a career as a journalist, and it showed in her work ethic at school and in her resulting grades. It wasn't a surprise that she would be hard at work while seventy-five percent of the university's population were either en route or already at their respective homes.

Sara felt as though she had been pinned down and forced to watch as the man who was chasing Mary caught up to her and knocked her down. Mary hit her pursuer in the face with the spine of one of her books, which stunned him enough for her to break free. This is what Sara saw just before she snapped out of her dream while she napped on the loveseat of her second-floor office.

Now fully upright, Sara became panicked. Her eyes were wide open, but she couldn't see out the window to the tall cedars at the rear of the property. All she could see was an ugly blonde-haired man catch up to Mary again, then get on top of her. It was him, the man from the hotel, but Mary never saw him standing behind her mother that day, and in effect, standing behind him. So, when Mary first saw the man in the university, she didn't recognize the level of danger, outside of her senses telling her something was off about the guy.

Sara was seeing everything through Mary's eyes, as she had years ago during a daytime dream about Jacob, while it was happening to them. The more Sara's abilities as a seer increased, the more intense her visions became, often leaving her weakened and distraught. It was a constant struggle to interpret images and sensations to determine what was real or not. Her vision finally returned to normal, and she ran downstairs. After her mad panic for her keys, Sara managed to calm herself enough to make a practical decision in the moment to help her daughter.

"911. How may I direct your call?"

"Vancouver police for the Simon Fraser University." Sara's voice was panicky and high pitched but clear and loud.

"One moment." The operator switched Sara over to police dispatch.

"Don't put me on—" Sara didn't get a chance to scream in frustration before another operator quickly took her call.

"My daughter is being assaulted at the university library. Right now! She just called me, and then the phone went silent. You need to get—"

"What's your daughter's name, ma'am?" the operator calmly interrupted her.

"Look, we don't have time for this—"

"The police have already been dispatched, ma'am, but I still need her information. Did she tell you who was assaulting her? I'll need her name and description, please."

Sara's shoulders dropped as she took a deep breath and let it out with a moan. "Thank God! You got the information out that fast?" Sara asked, in astonishment and with a little doubt.

"We type as you talk, ma'am, so the information is transferred to the police the second it comes in. So, may I have your daughter's name and description and your information, please?"

Sara was silent for a moment, taking in another deep breath and fighting back tears.

PART 2

By the time the police received the call, Mary was already out by the west entrance with a young officer. Her maroon-coloured sweater was ripped at the neckline and her hair was a bit of a mess. Even though she was naturally shaken from the experience, she hadn't shed a tear. The shock from the trauma hadn't registered yet. Strong like her mother, and alike in almost every way, her fear quickly turned to rage. This may have saved her life.

"I cut him," Mary said, making a slicing motion with her hand past her eyebrow.

"Sorry, Miss. What was that?" Young Constable Price could see Mary's hands shaking from the adrenaline.

"I cut him just above his eyebrow. With, um, one of my books. I hit him hard two different times. What a total creep! He knocked me down and…. Anyway, it split him open, and it started bleeding."

She picked up the book and made a swinging motion for a replay of how she hit the man. The constable couldn't help but smile, reaching out to take the book from Mary. He turned the spine of the book toward himself so he could see.

"Ethics in journalism. Who knew ethics could be such an effective weapon?" the young officer joked, sharing a small laugh with Mary and setting her a little more at ease.

The officer pointed with his pen to her sweater. "I see your sweater is torn. We may need to take it for evidence if it comes to that. Not right now though, you can leave it on."

Mary simply smirked as she pulled at the collar trying to assess the damage.

"Let's get you in the ambulance, and we can finish up the interview at the hospital. We have a basic description of the guy out over the radio."

The constable spoke into his shoulder-mounted radio mic and suddenly the wailing from the approaching ambulance stopped. Within seconds, the vehicle carrying the EMTs turned the corner, coming into view as it drove up to where Mary and the officer were standing.

She was initially reluctant to go to the hospital. As the shock of what happened started to subside, the pain and trauma began to register, and she made her way to the awaiting ambulance. Officer Raymond Price was a six-foot-four, two-hundred-thirty-pound buff specimen of a man. He was born in Canada, but his father was from Trinidad and his mother from England. His skin was a light brown colour. All of which caught Mary's attention. Even though he had a soft voice, Mary sort of giggled to herself because he sounded a bit nerdy. He was well spoken, but a bit nasally. He had his hair cropped at the sides and mesmerizing dominant golden brown–hazel eyes. Although an imposing man in full uniform, he had a gentle demeanour. He was also at least ten years her senior, but that was irrelevant to Mary, taking a shine to him instantly.

When the constable arrived at the hospital, he carried in a plastic bag containing a blue sweatshirt with the R.C.M.P. logo on the chest. "Compliments of the R.C.M.P. University Detachment," he said sheepishly. "Sorry, I only have a large size."

Mary thought her stares were becoming obvious, so as a deflection, she reached for the shirt but knocked over her glass of water in the process. Price calmly walked over to the paper towel dispenser, pulled a half-dozen sheets out and bent down to wipe up the small spill. When he turned around, he caught Mary checking him out. A quick smile came and went.

Nice. Far too young for me, though, Price thought, wishing he were ten years younger.

"So, Mary. Is it all right if I call you Mary?" A nod came in response. "Okay, Mary. Are you sure you're up to talking about this?" He purposely paused for a few seconds to gauge her reaction.

Mary managed to describe the events and her attacker in fair detail considering the circumstances. Although there were a couple of moments she needed to pause and compose herself, Mary was a solid witness for the most part. She refused to be seen as a victim. Especially by herself.

"When you're finished with the sketch artist, we'll get his picture out there. The sooner, the better. That's if we can't get some video of him on the grounds." Officer Price's tone was all business again. "I'll be honest, time is crucial in catching these types. We'll check your sweater to see if any of his blood got on it. If there is, maybe there's a match in the database."

Mary looked up at the handsome officer with bashful green eyes and a smile she was failing to keep turned off for the entirety of their interaction and seemingly unable to say anything else. Price returned a quick smile and slapped his thighs as he rose from his seat.

"Okay, then," he said, jumping to his feet. "I'll be right back with our sketch artist. And thanks, Mary. This is a brave thing you're doing."

He reached his arm out. When he shook Mary's hand, it all but disappeared inside his. This level of shyness was not typical for Mary, and again, an ever-widening schoolgirl smile shone across her face.

His hands are so soft. Gentle too, she thought. *I wonder what pub he drinks at? Did I shake his hand too long? I definitely stared at him too long.* Mary was thankful for the distraction after such a dreadful event.

Mary's moment of attraction to constable Price fell to the wayside as the trauma of what happened earlier in the day came to the forefront. The more she continued describing her assaulter for the sketch artist, the more the event, and its psychological effects, replayed in her mind.

A few hours later, Mary went to the airport to catch a charter flight into Kelowna, no matter the cost. Anxious and emotional, Sara waited to greet her daughter. They burst into uncontrollable tears, daughter running into her mother's arms. Mary squeezed Sara like she would never let go. Mary's sobs were dwindling.

"You're going to be okay, honey. You're safe now. I saw it happen and called the police. You did everything right, Mary. Don't question yourself, at all."

"But I didn't see it coming, Mom. Nothing! Wait, you called the police?" Mary lowered her head, shaking it in disbelief. "What would have…"

Mary was horrified at the thought of not getting away, or of the university police not being so close when it happened.

25

A Dark Search

It was a miserable fall night. The darkness seemed to encapsulate Evan's mood, inarticulately and dispassionately. He drove headstrong through the dark matter of night with one thought and several agendas steering the way. Earlier in the day, he called and booked himself a street-facing room in the King Edward Hotel for three nights. It was not a nice place in a not-so-nice area that became risky after dusk, and that's exactly where Evan wanted to start looking. This was the genesis, or drop-off-point, on the moral slide toward a life on Hastings Street. Either way was lubricated from this point onward for new arrivals. His agenda, driven by anger and revenge, was built from years of dealing with an addicted brother, Vic's passing, and Mary's recent attack at the university. When he emerged from the winding mountain roads and had only straight highway ahead of him, his stomach started churning again, thinking of the last time he saw his brother, Ryan.

The most important reason for driving was it gave him the time he needed to calm himself down as opposed to flying and arriving just as angry as when he left. Evan's sister, Rose, had pressured him to go to Vancouver to look for their little brother, Ryan. It was unusual that Rose had received text messages from Ryan. He hadn't been in contact with anyone for a long while, and he always used someone else's phone. This was his own pay-as-you-go phone, quite out of the ordinary. His last, rather impersonal text said he was going into rehab, but he left no name for the facility. Then his phone service was cut off.

Evan was going to meet with Price to pick up Mary's file and enquire where the greatest likelihood of finding Ryan would be, or at least where to start.

Evan carried a small duffel bag into the hotel. He quickly washed up and then headed for Price's detachment at the university. The young constable invited Evan inside the precinct, showing respect to a former police officer. He was more than willing to give a copy of the report and printouts of the suspect's likeness to someone like Evan over just anybody. A little white lie, that Mary was his niece, eased Evan's way to attain the information he needed to hunt down Mary's attacker.

Before Evan left, Price let him know what an exceptional young woman Mary was. "A strong and determined girl," Price said. "For cameras being everywhere throughout the university, all we got was his height and clothes. It's in there," Price said with disappointment as he handed the file over.

"Sort of tells you he knows what he's doing. Scary."

"You got that right, Mr. Quinn! This likeness went out throughout the lower mainland and even on the island. You never know," Price said, with a shrug of his shoulders.

"Good work, Constable. Thank you kindly," Evan said, nodding his head and shaking Price's hand. Just before Evan crossed the entrance doors to go back out to his truck, Price gave a last piece of advice, but in jest.

"Don't shoot him if you find him before us, eh?"

Evan kind of choked a little and threw a passing salute on his way out.

With a few copies of the composite in hand, Evan started by checking out pubs in a small radius of the university before heading back to his room for the night. He was tired from the long drive and in need of a shower. Sitting on the edge of the bed, a wet towel wrapped around his neck atop his shoulders, Evan pulled out a thermos and poured himself a stiff triple of Glenfiddich to sip on. He carefully scanned the report on Mary's attack, making sure every detail was firmly planted in his head. Like a psychologist, Evan could see much more than what was written in the report, all pointing to different possibilities. What time of day? Where was the attack? Where did he exit? Where did the last camera spot him? And then, of course, Mary's statement. Looking down at his duffle bag between his legs, Evan could see his handgun exposed but still snapped into its holster. First, he giggled about Price's comment. "You better hope I don't find you. You son of a bitch!" Evan growled out, glaring at the composite sketch, taking another sip.

Evan's quest to find the unidentified suspect in Mary's attack was fruitless. He wouldn't have shot him dead, for obvious reasons, but he wouldn't hesitate to put one in his leg or shoulder to stop him. As expected, his search for Ryan brought him to the east end, in and around Vancouver's infamous Hastings Street. He ran into a few people who said they knew Ryan. Each round of questions came with a handout, until Evan finally ran into a dead end. The closest he came to a lead was from an old roommate, Maury Babich. Maury said he saw Ryan being picked up a few times in a small, red pickup. That tip didn't register for Evan other than to think it was the imagination of another drug addict in need of another fix.

Evan felt a tightness throughout his abdomen and chest, but it was more from sadness from what he had been seeing on the streets of the city. It made him wonder what had happened to his brother. Evan believed if not for the bad skiing accident breaking both his legs, and the subsequent surgeries and pain medications to help him through, Ryan would have never gone on such a dark search.

26

Vengeance

PART 1

Over the months Ben had been working for the Quinns, he was made to feel as though he was part of the family. On this cold November night, it was just after nine p.m. when Ben got out of the store after stocking all the coolers and display shelves. The neon open sign was off, and the store was locked up for the night. It was Friday night, and Carol was cleaning up the end-of-week receipts in the office at the back of the building. Ben said goodbye for the night. More cathartic than an interest in art, Sara was taking painting classes again, and she would be done at ten o'clock. Her plan was to swing by, pick Ben up with pizza in hand, and head straight home.

"Goodnight, Carol. Do you need anything else from me?" Ben asked, hoping the answer would be no. But that's not what he's made of, he had to offer. "I can stick around until you're done if you want."

"No thanks, Ben. I've another hour to go, give or take. You go and enjoy your pizza. Say hi to your Mom, and I'll see you in the morning. Thanks, Ben."

Ben went out the back door, down the alley beside the old, converted warehouse and onto the front street. Always the cool one, Ben wasn't big on umbrellas, even with these heavy winter rains, so he made a quick jog to the pizza place. He ordered their pizza and went to pay, but his bank card was with his phone, which he discovered he had accidently left at work.

"I'll be right back. Damn!" He cursed himself and out the door he went, in a full run back to the store.

By the time Ben was halfway there, the rain became a torrential downpour. His run came to a stop when he reached the back of the store, which had access from the original loading dock. A flat overhang roof provided Ben with cover, preventing him from getting any more soaked than he already was. He looked out to the rear lot and saw what he thought was Carol leaning over the driver's side front seat of her SUV looking for something. The light was on in the car, but the steam on the windshield made it impossible to make out if it really was Carol.

An incredible and completely unfamiliar feeling came over Ben. He felt like his body was being pulled off the loading dock. He was seeing flashes in his peripheral vision that he couldn't quite make out, but they hurt his head and he felt a sharp pain in his eyes. Quite out of the ordinary, the muscles in his back spasmed so hard that he arched backwards as though he was being forcibly stood up into an unnaturally upright position. His stomach began to rumble as he humped his back over, feeling horrible, needle-like pains jabbing throughout his chest. All of this happened within seconds and culminated in a sense of dread, snapping his body back to attention.

What the hell is happening to me? Frightened, Ben wondered what could possibly be happening to his body and mind. He put his hand up to his forehead to block out the glare from the overhead light.

"Carol!" he yelled out while swiftly jumping the five-foot distance from the top of the loading dock onto the asphalt below.

Back into the rain, he was in motion, which was better than what he had been feeling moments ago. The movement in the car stopped when he yelled out again, but Carol didn't produce herself to answer his call. Ben's fear was building, but he was determined to make sure Carol was all right. He felt his legs becoming weak and wobbly as they did in some of his bad dreams in which running away from his attackers became increasingly difficult or impossible.

"Carol?" he yelled again as he reached the car, demanding a reply.

Just then, cowboy boots fell from up inside the car to the ground. A man wearing a long, dark raincoat came around the driver's side door. In one motion, he turned and hit Ben with a metal baton across his forehead. Ben fell to his knees and instinctively covered his head with his hands while trying to look up at who hit him. It was impossible. His forehead was split open, and blood poured out from the wound, mixed with rain, and washed down into his eyes and mouth. The blood and heavy rains stung his eyes, making it impossible to make out anything other than a dark figure.

"Don't matter, kid. I got her," he heard the man say, faintly. Ben couldn't understand anything. He felt like his head was cracked open. With a sense of vertigo and seeing stars, he fought his way back up to his feet, thankful at this point that the attacker had fled.

"Carol? Carol, are you all right?" Ben was shouting out to her while holding his head with one eye shut. When he got around the open door, he saw Carol on her back, sprawled out across the entire front seat. Her jeans were unbuttoned, and her zipper was down, but all Ben could see was blood. Her blood. The buttons were torn off her blouse, and the clips to her bra were broken from being ripped apart. The blood flowed dark from her chest and over her stomach.

"Oh God! Oh no! Carol, what happened?" Ben cried out, trying to pull her upright in the seat, but she was completely limp and lifeless. Ben looked down to see his arms and hands drenched in her blood. She was unresponsive. He screamed her name over and over in complete panic when suddenly her phone's ringtone went off, illuminating a text message on the screen from the floor of the passenger side. When Ben saw it light up, he reached down and pulled it out of her bag, quickly calling 911. He set the phone down on speaker mode. In a panicked voice, he did his best to tell the operator what was happening while he held his sweatshirt over Carol's wounds.

After Ben desperately yelled to the operator to send an ambulance to the back of the store, all sound suddenly stopped except for the noise of rain pouring down and bouncing off the roof of the Rover. Ben was silent and nothing else was said. Suddenly, loud feedback screeched through Carol's phone, cracking its glass face, and breaking the silence in the cocoon of the truck.

"You're going to be all right, Carol. Hang in there," Ben said, holding Carol's hand. With his other hand, he peeled back the sweater to see her wounds were barely bleeding. Carol opened her eyes briefly and lifted her head slightly. She looked up to Ben and a weak but calm smile came to her face for a second before her head flopped back onto the seat.

"Thank you for coming back," Carol whispered, and she was out. Ben looked at her, astonished that she could get a word out.

PART 2

The deluge of rain that fell on the roof of Carol's SUV was so intense that it sounded like a muffled drumroll that wouldn't stop. Ben's grip on Carol's hand loosened and his eyes rolled back in his head. He lost all control as his mind shut down and his body slumped over. Sliding down the driver's seat and onto the pavement, his head was wedged between the floor and the open door of the Rover. The shock from this kind of scene and the hit to his head resulted in Ben passing out.

When he came to, Ben was confused to find himself on a stretcher side-by-side with Carol. He watched one of the paramedics tend to her in the back of the ambulance in preparation to race away to the hospital. He felt a large bandage wrapped around his head when he lifted it to look to the back doors. He was still dizzy and a bit out of focus when his mother came around the corner of the ambulance and into sight. When Sara began to pour out the questions of a terrified mother, Ben couldn't hear a thing. He perceived his mother as moving in slow motion.

He looked out beyond her to see a man standing in the distance of the lot. He didn't have the appearance of some imposing or frightening figure. He was somehow a comfort to Ben. Even though he hadn't seen him since childhood, he quickly realized it was his father. Ben squinted to focus in on him but was confused. He watched his mother talking, but he could hear only this man in the distance.

"It's okay, Ben. You're both going to be okay. You did a fine job, son." Ben thought it odd that his father was perfectly dry without a single drop of rain falling on him as he stood under one of the light standards in the parking lot. All of Ben's senses returned, along with a piercing, loud shrill that penetrated his head like he was being stabbed in the ear with an icepick. The man in the distance slowly faded out of sight. After Sara told Ben she would see him at the hospital, the doors of the ambulance were shut. That was all he heard from his mother as the entire interaction was less than a minute.

A few members of the police force were in and around Carol's vehicle. Some were pointing flashlights, looking on the ground for any evidence or a weapon. They went through the motions even though they knew there was little to no chance of finding anything the rain hadn't washed away. Either way, not knowing if she was stabbed in the car or somewhere else, they had to treat it as the crime scene. After getting various samples of blood for DNA tests and dusting for fingerprints, the police found nothing that pointed to the attacker.

Not long after Evan got the call, he came flying into the hospital parking lot, the wheels on his truck screeching to a halt. As he ran in through the automatic doors of the emergency department, he saw Sara was there to greet him.

"She's stable, Evan. Ben was there to help her," Sara said, taking Evan by the hand to the nurse's station.

"Mr. Quinn, your wife's in surgery. You can't see her now, but they had her stabilized when she came in. That's all I can tell you right now," the nurse told him. Her words were a comfort, but she could see Evan was shaking and walking circles around Sara, repeatedly holding his hand up to his forehead. The nurse managed to get his attention and motioned for him to come over. She reached across the desk to firmly grasp his hand. "She's going to be just fine, Evan. Maybe you should sit down. Sara, can you take him to sit down, please? I'll come and find both of you to let you know when you can see her and when Ben's ready, okay?"

Evan let out a sigh and thanked the nurse. Realizing he hadn't said anything, he enquired about Ben. "I'm sorry, Sara. What happened to Ben? They didn't say anything about Ben on the phone."

"Oh, he's got a nasty bump on the head and he'll need some stitches, but he's going to be okay. Thank God!" Sitting next to Evan, Sara could see the emergency room triage beds across the hall. With the door open, only the privacy curtains could be seen. All the while Sara anxiously waited for one to open and reveal her son. "I should have seen this coming. I've been getting bad feelings all week. I'm sorry, Evan. After what just happened with Mary, you'd think I would be more in tune than this, for Christ's sake!" Sara's face became red, and she grabbed Evan's hand, squeezing it.

"You've got nothing to be sorry about, dear. You're not alone in that. We can't always see it, and we can't change our lives because of these blackguard sons-of-bitches!" Evan declared. Sara's jaw dropped. She turned around in her seat to look Evan in the eye.

"Where did you hear that name? You even said it like…" Sara was caught off guard by that word coming out, having only ever heard it from her now-deceased mother-in-law, Irene O'Connell.

27

Ignorance Is Ageless

PART 1

Sitting in the police station parking lot, Ben thanked Evan for the ride in. He tried again to apologize for not getting to Carol sooner and for not being able to describe their attacker. Evan wouldn't hear of it. He was grateful they were both alive. And he knew Carol being alive was due to Ben's actions.

"Give Carol my best. Uhhh … yeah. See ya soon." Ben slowly slid out of his seat, feeling the throb in his head from the night before and from the painkillers he took that morning. Evan was glad to drop Ben off on his way back to the hospital to be at Carol's side, but he was impatient, nonetheless.

"You sure you're up for this, Ben? It can wait for another day," Evan said, leaning over the seat, looking up at him in admiration.

Ben gently tapped his sore head with his fingertip. "I'm okay. Just a killer headache and a bit loopy from those painkillers."

"You be careful with those. They can be addictive. Believe me, I know. Text me right away if there's any kind of a problem, okay?" Evan said, pulling himself back into his seat and glancing to his watch.

"For sure. I'll text you if need be. And no worries about the pills. I don't like the feeling, and they make me nauseous. I had to take a

Gravol with them." Ben said, standing straight up at attention. "Thanks again, Evan," he said, giving a single wave as he walked into the precinct. Evan watched Ben cross the threshold to the station with a gentle shake of his head. Without question, Evan was impressed with Ben.

Ben was clearly a little loopy from the pills and lack of sleep. The constable at reception gave Ben a strange and unwelcoming look. Ben was quick to conclude it was from his association with Evan, having heard some of the stories passed on from Carol. Being as protective as he was with the people he loved and cared for, Ben didn't appreciate the attitude. He wouldn't tolerate any disrespect to his neighbour, friend, and mentor. Even though Ben was taught to respect his elders, he was a firm believer that respect given is respect earned. Just because somebody was older than him, that person wasn't always entitled to an outpouring of respect. The constable looked like a holdover from the seventies, with a clean-shaven face and a thick black mustache Ben thought was cheesy. The officer was a huge man and looked like he was about to burst through his uniform.

"Ben O'Connell," Ben said calmly, in deep monotone, not feeling very animated. The constable rudely ignored him and continued to type into the computer. "I'm supposed to give a statement, you know. About last night." Ben gently rubbed his temple and mildly shook his head in disbelief and anger. *There's no way this clown doesn't know what happened. This isn't that big a town*, Ben thought to himself.

"Sign-in sheet," the constable piped up, using his pen as a pointer to indicate a clipboard at the far end of the counter, just below the sign indicating so.

"For real!" Looking back to the officer, Ben spit out his disgust with him. He had already given a short statement to the police at the hospital. This was a formality and, in Ben's eyes, a favour to them. He signed the sheet and slid the clipboard across the countertop, slamming it against the aluminum window frame separating the public from the police. He stared at the constable and waited for something, anything, to happen. Ben believed the unfriendly cop should not be allowed to deal with the public.

"Take a seat." Again, he used his pen to point to the chairs behind Ben.

"Fuckin' Nazi," Ben grumbled under his breath as he turned around.

"Sorry. What was that?" The constable demanded with indignation.

Ben just stared at him with a crooked smile and returned an equally defiant silence. Even in his discomfort, Ben had a sense of humour. *If I had a pen, I'd point it at you to show you who the fucking Nazi is. You stupid prick, extra-sized asshole!* Ben would have loved to be able to say that aloud.

Forty-five minutes later, Constable Stevens came out from inside the precinct and summoned the officer at reception. Ben could see the pair talking like two kids in the hall at high school, looking out at Ben and then back to each other, sharing dirt on the new kid. Stevens stepped out into the entryway and sauntered across the hall toward Ben. His face was buried in a file.

After a few uncomfortable moments standing in front of Ben without a word or acknowledgement, Stevens slowly lifted his head. "You have a problem with being here, Mr. O'Connell?" the officer asked, glaring. Stevens turned away and walked back to the door, expecting Ben to say no and follow directly behind him. When Stevens turned around, he saw Ben still sitting with an undeniable look of scorn.

"Yeah, this is going to be a pass, captain. I'll be back with my mom or Evan," Ben said, knowing about the animosity that led to Evan's retirement. Thanks to Mary's fine reporting.

After sending a text to Evan to come pick him up, Ben rose from his seat and walked out of the precinct. If his mother came, he would feel obligated to stay and make a statement. As it turned out, Ben was feeling less than stellar and far from agreeable. The negative attitude from the police toward Ben had left him feeling it would be more trouble than it was worth to stay.

PART 2

Earlier, Carol was sound asleep when Evan arrived at the hospital. He kissed her on the forehead and whispered, "I'll be right back, sweetheart." His old mentor and friend, Glen Simon, was there in the waiting room. Glen was an intellectual who chose the simple life of being a cop in a small town. He also chose not to rise in the ranks beyond becoming a sergeant. There he sat, one leg folded over the other, a book in one hand, and the other habitually pulling on his mustache and beard, grown in retirement. They greeted each other just as Evan received Ben's text. "You busy?" Evan asked Glen.

"No, why?"

"Want to take a drive with me just up to the station to pick up Ben? He's supposed to be giving them an official statement, but they're giving him some grief by the sounds of it," Evan said, putting his phone back in his pocket, looking annoyed.

"They're like children, I swear to God! They just don't know how to let things go. It'll be my pleasure, Evan. Lead the way, Greenhorn," Glen said, pointing his imaginary gun at Evan before pulling on his grey and white beard again.

The two drove back to the station, Glen griping about Evan's lead foot as he had many years ago. The pair laughed about it and talked about how it should be Evan who was angry with the police and not the other way around. When Evan pulled into the parking lot of the precinct, Ben was standing by the roadside ready to go. Evan made a U-turn and grabbed Ben on the way out.

"Any more on the description come to you?" Evan asked Ben after he hopped into the truck.

"No, sorry, Evan. The guy is different looking. I can sort of see him, but he's hard to describe. Know what I mean? Sorry."

Evan assured Ben he had nothing to be sorry about and that his memory would clear up in time. Before Evan pulled out onto the road, he believed he saw Nathan in the passenger side of an older, beat up, faded-red Ford Ranger driving by the detachment in the opposite direction. He squinted his eyes and leaned forward to strain a look down the road, but the small pickup had gone around the next bend of the mountain road.

"What's the matter, see someone you know?" Glen asked, looking down the road with him.

"No, nothing."

On the way back to the hospital, Evan had several things on his mind, but at the top was Carol. The thought of Nathan shuffled down to the bottom of the list. Evan was proud that Ben had the wherewithal to get himself out of what he perceived to be a hostile situation at the station. And personally, he was pleased that Ben would turn to him in a moment of need. Indeed, Evan had unofficially adopted Ben and would protect him and the O'Connells with his own life.

What happened to Carol would remain unsolved for the near future as far as the police were concerned. Once she was alert and feeling better, Carol began a difficult process of explaining to Evan that the man who shot her all those years ago when Evan saved her life was the same man who attacked her in her vehicle. It was Joe Miller.

Carol was quite surprised with Evan's response to the news. "Whatever you do, don't tell the police! If he knows the police are on to him, he will either run or come back to finish the job. He's going to know you're still alive," he said, holding Carol's hand, remaining supportive. Carol looked back to Evan and nodded.

"Okay," she said, in an easy calm breath.

Lying on the side of the bed next to Carol while she fell back asleep, Evan looked up to the white ceiling tiles and fought off the image of killing Joe Miller. He wanted to take the same knife he used to stab Carol and bury it to the hilt in Joe Miller's chest. The method didn't really matter though. Vengeance did.

28

Haunted

Not having the chance to see his attacker and defend himself, Ben was left disappointed that he couldn't at least identify the man who had done so much damage. Sometime later at dinner with the O'Connells, Carol and Evan would clear that up for Ben and take that weight off his shoulders. The event certainly struck a chord with Sara, leaving her little choice but to enlist Mary's help to have a difficult and long overdue conversation with Ben. It was instigated by a poorly conceived and off-handed comment Ben made about killing Joe before he had a chance to hurt Carol. After what happened to Carol and Ben behind the wine store, Mary needed to talk to her brother about his new-found power, for one. With the knowledge Sara shared with Mary about Jacob's death, and Mary's dream about Ben's power, she was chosen to talk with him. Sara concluded that it was Mary's voice that shook Ben loose from his trance at the hotel, so she was considered the obvious and wisest choice.

Mary knew it was critical to convince Ben that his ability to take a life is a reminder of how fragile life is, including his own. If he were to use it to incapacitate someone if need be, he would need to restrain the urge to kill in the act of protecting his family. Most importantly, the end result would be the same as his father's.

Mary told Ben about her dream and conveyed to him that this seemingly antithetical power was partly there to protect him from his own temper. A temper his father shared but not to the level Ben's could rise to, or at least not as fast. The conversation ended when Ben was finally told how his father had died. This was a difficult pill for Ben to swallow, always told a different story before. For him, it was simply a lie.

The house grew quiet for a while when Ben stepped out onto the rear deck to consider what he just heard. When Ben returned, Carol showed him a picture of Joe Miller that she requested from retired Detective Frank Hansen. It was much better than a driver's licence photo. Frank still felt the responsibility to protect Carol in every way possible to his abilities.

Ben was stunned, looking at the photo, repeating himself. "That's him. That's the piece of shit!"

The last topic of conversation was an uncomfortable one for Sara, and she avoided it for most of the night. She didn't want Ben to feel he had a label on him, or for him to believe his life had become preordained for a specific task. After dinner was over, Mary dove right into the file Carol brought with her, trying to absorb everything she could related to unexplained miracles or guardians — ever the journalist.

Carol finally had the opportunity to talk to Sara about the night Ben saved her life. Once again, she emphasized the unbelievable odds that they would arrive here as neighbours. These were extraordinary topics of conversation that didn't stop and continued through dinner and into the rest of the night. But now was the time to get to the heart of the matter. The four congregated to the living room and joined an already enthralled Mary, face deep in the file. Having the right atmosphere would allow the conversation to keep flowing, so Ben lit a fire. This was a task he turned into a fine art since living in his new home, where it commonly gets cold at night in the mountains, frigid in winter months.

There was one moment of heightened awareness and tension when Mary spoke about her attack. "I'm pretty sure I saw the guy who attacked me in Franklin, but I couldn't say for absolute because he went by too fast."

"So, you're in journalistical school, eh?! Do they teach ya all how to red and writ real goood?" Ben said with a southern US drawl. "I couldn't say for absolute!? Fine grammar, sis." Ben couldn't help but take advantage of the rare opportunity to tease his sister.

"Oh, you know what I mean. I'm not in class, so give me a break, pinhead!" Mary's retort came with a laugh shared among everyone.

With the brief moment of humour out of the way, the conversation turned to the dark presence that seemed to be attached to both families. Evan turned back into a cop for a moment, questioning Mary on every detail of the car, the time of day, where she saw him, and what direction he was going in. Unfortunately, Mary was concentrating more on whether it was really him more than she was on those details. At the first lull in the conversation, Carol didn't hesitate to offer up Joe Miller's name as the man who tried to kill her that night behind the store.

"Look, everyone. We're going to have time to talk about all of this stuff. So for now, let's concentrate on what we need to watch out for. After what happened with Ben at the police station, come to me if you see or hear anything. Don't bring it to them. Everyone clear on that?" Evan scanned the room, the lines on his forehead growing, indicating his demand for compliance.

29

Charmed

With Ben somewhat calmer after being informed about his responsibilities as they relate to his recently discovered additional and deadly powers, Sara could go out of town for work with less worry. On her last trip, she enjoyed a lunch meeting with Trevor Holdt, the liaison between her company and their primary client, Nordic Trails. Today was no different, with the meeting taking place at one of the villas designed by Cailey & Higgins. The project was still under construction, and Sara was taking over. Trevor was the consummate gentleman, opening the door of his pickup truck for Sara and pulling out her chair inside the restaurant.

"You know, Trevor, this isn't a date, so you don't need to do all this," Sara said as she adjusted herself in her chair, breaking the ice.

"Apologies, Sara. It's an old habit. It does get me into trouble occasionally. But I was told by the owner of my company to take care of you and make sure you have everything you need. And I am a mediator, salesman, and liaison slash rep for Nordic. So, here we are."

With the flow of conversation pouring from Trevor, Sara wasn't quite sure how to take him. "Well, there's no denying you're a salesman," she quipped.

"Again, apologies. I seem to have some nervous energy today. Shall we order?" Trevor asked, scanning the restaurant. Sara let out a quiet giggle, acknowledging his nervous demeanor.

"Sure. Whenever you're ready," she said, checking her phone with her own butterflies developing. After Trevor grabbed the attention of one of the waiters, he handed Sara a wine list from the centrepiece of the table.

"It's a little early in the day for wine, don't you think?" Sara asked, looking at Trevor with an inquisitive yet harmless smile. Trevor laughed out in response, agreeing with Sara. He pointed to the names on the bottom of the list, telling her much of the wine list came from Canada, and the ice wine and cider coolers were provided by Quinn's Orchards.

"See, these people are just outside of Franklin. That's where you moved to, right?" Sara became blushed, realizing Trevor wasn't considering ordering drinks and simply pointing out where the suppliers are from.

"The day we moved in we drove right by the place. They're our next-door neighbours and truly wonderful people. We've become such good friends." Sara's disposition was genuinely happy throughout lunch.

She felt an awkward guilt for enjoying herself in the company of a man. In the years since Jacob died, she hadn't so much as gone out for coffee with another man. Not that she didn't look, but she simply hadn't discovered anyone who interested her. Sara had buried herself in her work and focused her energy on being a good mother to Mary and Ben. In this moment, she wasn't sure how to feel about her reaction to Trevor. There was no denying the fact that she was enjoying his company.

"Next door, hmm, I can see a drinking problem developing on the horizon for a certain Sara O'Connell," Trevor said, sharing bouts of laughter with her.

They had a pleasant lunch together. So much so, they hardly talked about business. They were supposed to go over the design for a second chalet in a mountain plateau called The Pass higher up through The Narrows. He had all the necessary contact information for the development manager, the plans department, and council members. When they left the restaurant, Trevor once again apologized for babbling on. Sara assured him it was just as well as she was tired from a long couple of days in preparation. They would have more time the next day to work on the project. She was looking forward to taking a tour of the different developments before checking in at the hotel for an early night.

When Trevor drove Sara back to her vehicle, her own nervous energy was starting to become apparent. In the middle of thanking Trevor for everything, her cellphone rang causing her stomach to jump. She saw on the display that it was Mary calling. Sara answered the phone and told Mary to hold for a moment.

"Thanks again, Trevor," Sara said with a wave as she put the phone between her ear and shoulder, fumbling through her purse for her keys.

"Ooh. Trevor, eh?" Mary enjoyed teasing her mother. "What's new with Trevor, Mom? Dish, dish. Come on! Is he a dime?" Mary sounded like a preteen, poking fun at Sara, trying to get more information about the mystery man.

"Stop that. I'm at work," Sara said quietly, climbing into her Suburban.

"Sure, you are. Ah huh. I bet. Are you working in a hotel room?" Mary continued poking her mother and loving it.

"Okay, okay. You can stop anytime now."

There was a brief silence before they both burst out in laughter that sounded more like teens giggling than mother and daughter. Even though it was Sara's choice, Mary was thrilled at the prospect of her mother meeting someone after so many years alone. It wouldn't be the first time Mary pushed her mother to get out and meet someone.

30

Hard Truths

2018

PART 1

It started out as a beautiful day of warm temperatures and sunny skies, a welcomed friend for an otherwise cold, damp winter. The sun coming through the bedroom window penetrated Ben's chest, resulting in aberrant energy. A P.A. day gave him the day off from school, which was an opportunity for Ben to make some extra cash for an upcoming weekend in Whistler. He would be snowboarding with some friends and his new girlfriend, Kim Preston. That definitely motivated him. The trip meant he would have time with Kim, and the possibility of uncomplicated sex was hanging in the balance. As for any normal red-blooded kid his age, the possibility of sex would be front and centre, as it was from the moment he woke.

Unexpectedly, other thoughts began to intrude on his fantasies of time with Kim. "Damn it! Why am I thinking about everyone else? And the forklift at work, and stacking the friggin' barrels? Get out of my head for Christ's sake. Ah, the hell with it!"

He yanked the covers off and looked down disappointedly at his now-flaccid penis. "You can forget it now, Skippy."

He swung his legs around and slightly stomped them onto the fuzzy place rug that lay in front of his bed. He rubbed his hands up and down over his face, rubbing the sleep away and then stopped to focus in on a picture of Kim. "Two weeks, sweetheart. Two weeks," Ben said, standing up to shuffle off to the washroom to empty his bladder.

When Sara heard the floor squeaking above her, she walked over to the bottom of the stairs and looked up at the loft-style hall through the spindles, trying to catch sight of who was awake. "Ben? Ben, honey, is that you?" she asked quietly.

"Who else would it be, Mom? Mary's not here," Ben said, sticking his head out of the upstairs washroom, peering down the stairs.

"Yes, she is. She came home late last night, so keep quiet please. She's very tired."

Ben walked by the opening of the stairwell and simply nodded to his mother that he would keep the noise down.

"Must be nice to be able to afford a charter flight every time you want to come home for a weekend," he complained under his breath.

Eventually Ben went downstairs and greeted his mother good morning and gobbled down a bowl of cereal. Respecting his sister's need for rest, he headed for the main floor shower. Ben's consideration of Mary put a smile on Sara's face as she went about her business. All seemed normal for a while until she heard a loud thump against the wall of the bathroom. She ran to the door, but Ben was quick to assure her he was fine. He had just lost his footing in the shower.

When Ben closed his eyes and dipped under the shower head to soak his hair, he was met with a parade of congregating visual effects. This is what originally pushed him backwards, slamming into the wall. It wasn't exactly similar to the vision he shared with his sister; but it knocked him off balance, literally and figuratively.

He saw far more in this vision than he had back home in the high school hallway. He could see Evan, Carol, Mary, and Sara in different scenarios and in different states of fright. Apart from Mary, they were all running through the woods. Evan was clearly chasing someone, but Ben couldn't focus on who it was as he dealt with the onslaught of images. After regaining his balance, he put his hand to his chest, looking down to see his heart pounding so hard it was forcing his sternum to rise and fall more than normal. The images disappeared as quickly as they came, but they left Ben rattled.

After he was dressed and ready for the day ahead, he headed for the kitchen like nothing in the morning was askew. As he was approaching the archway between the dining room and kitchen, he caught the end of a conversation between Sara and Mary.

"So, when are you going to tell him?" Mary asked.

"I think I'll tell him tonight. There's no time now—"

"Tell me what?" Ben interrupted.

"We'll talk about it later. And you shouldn't eavesdrop," Sara said, giving Ben a look that told him to leave it be. Ben looked over to Mary who was sipping her tea.

"Forget it, pinhead!" she exclaimed. Without saying another word, Mary walked away and into the living room. Ben looked back to his mother, but she only raised her eyebrows.

"Have your breakfast, Ben. Oh, Evan called. He won't need you until ten today," she said, snapping open one of the flyers that came with the newspaper.

"Ah, thanks, but I just had breakfast before I hopped in the shower. Did you pull on a blunt when you got up this morning, Mom?" Ben asked, receiving "the look" once more.

PART 2

After Jacob's passing, Sara's time had been taken up by her children and her business, the latter intruding the most. She worked hard to provide for her children's futures but work also provided distraction from the pain of losing her husband. Ultimately, Sara arrived at the conclusion that she had been missing out on too much, and she wanted that to change. She stopped and observed her kids long enough to realize that when she wasn't looking, they leaped from being children to becoming young adults. But in Ben's case, there were also moments that reminded her how much further a journey into manhood it was for him. She also realized they both had a heavy weight on them because of what they knew and what they had experienced. Maybe that why Ben's maturity was in flux as it was in this moment. He was about to take a slip backwards.

"This is a pretty fucked up family if you really think about it," Ben blurted out, in his sloppy attempt to restart the conversation that had begun with the Quinns at their most recent dinner.

"Ben!" Sara gasped, slamming her hand on the kitchen table. "Don't talk like that. You know how I hate to hear you talk like that." Sara returned her attention back to the local flyers.

"Sorry, Mom. It was a slip of the tongue. But you know what I mean," Ben said quietly. But Sara wasn't interested in having this conversation. She was clearly distracted.

"Your sister needs to go in town to get some things at the drugstore. There's a list of things we need at the grocery store on the countertop. You can pick them up before you go to work, please."

Sara sounded tired, but her tone was a familiar one to Ben. Without argument or further comment, Ben picked up the list and joined his sister when she was ready. As he walked to his side of the car, the sun disappeared behind a large cloud bank, and the rain started to fall.

"Figures," Ben moaned about the weather again. "What's with Mom?" he asked Mary just after the car started.

"Just stop and think about that question, Ben. Who is she? Who was she married to? What was he, and what are we? Getting the picture, or do you need me to draw it for you *and* spell it out?" Mary's retort wasn't harsh, but she made her point.

Mary quickly took advantage of Ben's quiet reflection. "There's another thing. You know Trevor, the guy mom works with once in a while?"

"Yeah. What of it?" Ben grumbled.

"Well, she's been seeing him. And I think she's having a hard time telling you. So when she does, you better be supportive. No bull, all right?" Mary said, sticking her finger into her brother's ribs.

"Yeah, I know. I've heard her talking to him and then she'll shut the door. Or if I ask her who's texting so late, she just says it's work emails." Ben paused and looked out his window. "I'm not an idiot, you know," he said coolly.

Mary's reply was notably subdued. "Well, that's good then. I can send back the 'I'm with the Idiot' t-shirts with the bright yellow arrow." Mary burst out laughing. "I'm sorry. Just kidding. Anyway, I'm glad to hear that. And I think you should tell her you know."

"Uh, no thanks, I'll pass. I'll leave that up to her. I'd probably end up saying it the wrong way. Like I said, I'm not an idiot." After short delay, Ben's words started the pair laughing and the mood lightened.

§

While driving through Franklin's mix of old western-style architecture and modern aluminum and glass, Ben realized he had finally adapted to his new surroundings. The day turned dreary and seemed to give brother and sister a case of the humdrums. Near the mall where the grocery and drugstores were located, Mary and Ben were idling at the traffic light waiting for their turn to go. The light changed, and Mary drove forward but made the mistake of not checking for cross-bound traffic. The sound of the impact was a loud crashing together of metal and glass as the Suburban was T-boned on the passenger side by an older four-door sedan. Absent were the sounds of brakes screeching before impact, providing no warning at all.

"What the— You stupid— Oh shit!" Ben yelled out, his fast-rising temper quickly settling down. Fortunately, logic took over and he turned to his sister.

"Are you all right?" Ben asked, reaching over to grab Mary's arm and examine her for any cuts from the glass. The car had been coming at a good speed and the impact was hard enough that Mary's head snapped sideways and broke the driver's side glass.

"I'm okay. Are you hurt?" Mary asked, putting the truck in park.

"Yeah, I'm good," Ben replied, covered in broken glass.

"Look, Ben. He's an old man. I think there's something wrong with him. We better check."

The two passenger doors were trashed from the impact, leaving Ben no choice but to get out the driver's side after Mary. A small crowd had started to gather around the accident scene. One considerate person took it upon herself to direct traffic around the intersection.

Ben leaned over to look in the driver's side window and rapped his knuckles on the glass. No response. Then he loudly slapped his hand up against the glass, but the old man wasn't moving. His head slowly tipped over, landing against the frame of the car door. It was clear he was knocked out or worse. Ben gingerly opened the door and caught the man as he slid farther out the door and down into Ben's arms. He pushed the man back up straight in his seat, but he flopped over onto the steering wheel. Not sure what to do, Ben pulled him up again and released his seatbelt, then lowered his limp body into his arms.

Ben had his weight in his arms, so he slid him out of his seat and onto the pavement. A bit panicked, Ben looked all around him, worried someone might come over and help, interfering with his attempt to save the man if need be. One man did come to offer his assistance, but Ben just shook his head, indicating the old man was gone. Timid and turning white, the stranger wasted no time in backing away. Mary grabbed her umbrella and phone from the car and called 911.

"Mary, what do I do? He's got no pulse. I think he had a stroke or something. Or a heart attack. I don't know!"

Mary shrugged her shoulders and shook her head. "I don't think there's anything you're supposed to do, Ben. Just keep holding him. Don't let him pass alone."

Ben looked up to Mary when she said that and took a deep breath and placed his hand on the side of the man's head. Mary noticed a few people had turned their attention to Ben and the old man. "Ben! Ben!" Mary grunted out, trying not to be overheard.

She walked over and stood between Ben and the spectators to cut off their view.

"Don't! You can't, Ben. Let him go. He wants to go."

PART 3

Ben took his hand away from the side of the man's cheek and temple. A barely noticeable smile slid across the man's face just before his body went limp, his life slipping away. Ben started gently crying, letting the rain fall on them both. He couldn't understand his emotions, but he didn't try to fight the tears away. Mary crouched down and curled up close, holding the umbrella in an attempt to cover the three of them.

"Don't worry about it, Mary. We're already soaked," Ben said, as though the man he was holding was still with them and not gone somewhere beyond. "How do you know he wants to go?"

"Trust me," Mary said compassionately. Ben turned back to Mary, wanting to know more. "He's okay, Ben," Mary sighed. "It's freaking me out though. I can see him. He's standing right there," she whispered, nodding her head toward the rear of the sedan.

Mary could feel the sensation of a cool draft rushing over her body, a most unusual chill. With the umbrella in one hand, she rested her other arm on Ben's shoulder and waited while the old man's body gave in, allowing his soul to move on.

The rain continued steadily, and Ben remained motionless. The elderly man's upper body was propped up in Ben's lap as they waited. Ben's knees were folded and his pantlegs soaked up water from the pavement. Mary kept standing up then crouching back down while waiting for the ambulance to arrive. She kept moving the umbrella back into position in a failing attempt to keep the three of them dry.

"Is he going?" Ben asked his sister.

"Yes. I think his wife's here," Mary replied, looking to the other side of the car.

Ben lifted his head. "What?" He forced the question out of his throat, attempting to keep his voice down. "Okay, you're just screwing with me now. That's messed up, Mary. Even for you," Ben said, indignant. Mary kneeled and looked Ben in the eye.

"I'm not lying, Ben. I wouldn't do that. Not like this. And you know that."

"You mean—"

"Yes, that's what I mean. He's joining her now. They're right there. It's totally freaking me out," Mary said, nodding in the old couple's direction. "Jesus, Ben! This is scaring me. I've never seen—" Mary couldn't finish. She had a look of astonishment and fear. "I can sort of see through them. They're fading in and out. Oh my God, Ben."

Mary leaned up against her brother for a moment. When she stood up, the elderly couple looked back at her and smiled. A comfortable and calming feeling came over Mary. As the couple began to turn to walk away, the man turned back in stride.

"Thank you, Ben," he said before resuming his walk.

Mary looked down at her brother still holding this man's body. "He said, 'thank you.'" Ben's head dropped in emotional exhaustion.

How am I supposed to respond to that? You're welcome? Wow. I'm glad you're with your wife, sir, he thought to himself.

Ben was genuinely sorry for this man. And he felt terribly guilty for becoming angry when the accident first happened, wanting to hit whoever it was driving. It was a brilliant reminder for him to keep his temper in check. Mary turned back to watch the elderly couple fade away as they walked down the sidewalk, hand in hand. She was shocked, saddened, and happy all at once. She had never seen or experienced anything like this before. It was a profound moment for her. Ben may have been disappointed that he wasn't able to see the couple as Mary did, but he believed Mary completely. He wasn't about to lay the man down on the wet pavement just so he could stand up and possibly see them.

The ambulance arrived, and the medics quickly moved the man from Ben's lap and went through their procedures, securing the elderly gentleman for transport. Damp and sore from his legs being bent over beneath his weight, Ben slowly walked over to grab his phone from the Suburban. On the way, Ben passed one of the medics, who he thought was kind of old to be doing that kind of work. Ben nodded a hello to the man. What Ben received in return wasn't quite as pleasant, however.

"What's the matter, kid? Didn't Quinn show you how to resurrect the dead?" the medic quietly asked an astonished Ben.

Ben recalled what Mary had told him about Mike Collins being such a loudmouth asshole, and the role he played in Evan's decision to resign from the force. When Ben looked at Mike, his eyes began to glow ever so slightly for a few seconds, but Mike was the only one to see it.

"So you're the fucking asshole with the big mouth. I heard about you," Ben said. He slowly approached Mike, showing nothing but rising anger without an ounce of fear. All Ben did was stare at Mike, but he hadn't realized his eyes had glowed.

"Ben!" Mary yelled at her brother to stop. She could see the fear forming on Mike's face as he backed up to get as far away from Ben as possible.

Ben gave Mike one more piercing glare before backing off. The look he gave Mike told him exactly how much he should fear him, which he did. Mike wasn't about to try and convince anyone else about he saw. Not now.

Considering they had witnessed a man die, Ben and Mary weren't terribly rattled by the events of the morning. It had been a frightening event that turned into something beautiful. What happened was something the average person wouldn't be able to rationalize or believe with their own eyes.

On their way home afterwards, Mary looked over to Ben. "So Mom should find this interesting." They burst out laughing.

31

Salvation

PART 1

Even though Sara and Trevor kept their relationship quiet in the beginning, that didn't stop a genuine attraction from blossoming into something more serious. Things are considerably different in the romance department when a person is in their fifties, a fact that wasn't lost on the couple. They came to a quick and heartfelt conclusion that life is short and finding someone you're attracted to and compatible with is rare, and not something to casually disregard. With the blessing of Mary and Ben, and high marks from Carol about her choice, Sara went away for the weekend with her new beau.

Trevor walked into the quaint, loft-style cottage with an armful of firewood to load the box adjacent the fireplace for the night. The emanation of wood burning battled the smell of musk that penetrated the older cottage from years of off-season closures. Resting on an antique French maple end table, a faux-Tiffany lamp highlighted a line of smoke developing above it. The thick, yellow smoke began to swirl like an asp slithering into position before striking its prey. Noticing this, Trevor quickly tended to the fireplace damper and adjusted its air intake accordingly. The handle was hot, burning his fingers. He quickly yanked his hand back, licking his fingertips and blowing on them. Just then, he caught the movement of a man outside as he shifted out of sight behind the red maple tree in the front yard.

The evening sky, full of bright stars, fought off a falling horizon for ownership of the night. It was a cold, crisp winter night, and the moon was full. Its light exposed most outdoor movement. Trevor did his best not to react and played on like he hadn't seen a thing, keeping his body language as relaxed as possible. The living room and small kitchenette had been built in an open-concept design, and Trevor knew that Sara could be seen as clearly as he.

"I'm just going to go out for one last load of firewood to make sure we have enough for the night," he said to Sara, with his back turned to the apparent peeping Tom. Trevor's words came out slow and robotic, which Sara quickly picked up on. She did her best not to overreact or stare out past Trevor to the front of the cabin. The ominous atmosphere of the moment raised the hairs on Sara's neck and arms, a familiar and bewildering feeling.

In the kitchen, Sara managed to keep a relaxed pose as she continued slicing and chopping away at the vegetables for tonight's meal. Trevor had indicated where she should move by motioning with his eyes toward the side door past the small dining area. Sara waited for Trevor to go back out the door before she grabbed a stack of dishes and turned to the dining area. Once she was out of view of the front window, she set the plates down on the table with shaky hands. Then, she deftly pulled a butcher's knife from her back pocket. Squeezing it, she turned the sharp edge up and looked at it.

This is nuts! God damn it! When is this shit going to stop? Maybe he's just seeing things. Please tell me he's seeing things, Sara thought to herself before dismissing her wishes, recalling the attack on Ben and Carol barely a few months back. She didn't know what to think. Her entire body began to vibrate as she hesitantly tiptoed toward the side door. Once there she was startled to see Trevor standing outside clearly visible from the exterior light.

"We had a peeping Tom. He's gone. Man, can he run. Whoever he is he won't be back. I think I scared him well enough. Are you all right?" Trevor could see Sara shaking as she placed the butcher knife on the stack of dishes once inside.

"I am now. We've had enough of this in our life. I don't want to have to use that to put an end to it. You know what I mean?" Sara said, motioning to the knife.

"Yes, I do, honey. Nothing like that is going to happen."

Trevor wrapped his arms around Sara, comforting her as best he could.

PART 2

The grip of winter was lingering, and the howl of the wind was continually changing its pitch as its unforgiving force pushed through the tall trees of the mountainside. The treetops indicated the wind's direction was from the west as they battled to maintain their upright position against the unrelenting gusts. The density of the trees thinned out closer to the valley's basin, offering little resistance or interference to the winds as they built up speed. In short time, the temperatures fell dramatically to bitter levels of cold. An hour or so earlier in mid-afternoon, Trevor and Sara's casual nature walk was accompanied by cold but reasonable temperatures and a moderate breeze. Now the increasing wind chill tore at Sara's exposed skin.

However, when they started out, they hadn't been running for their lives from some unknown madman with a rifle and an itchy trigger finger. But now Sara was experiencing a horrible, burning pain. Trying to cover her cheeks with her hands only increased the pain to the skin over her fingers and wrists as she raced against the wind and away from a psychopath. All thoughts of the romantic weekend were gone and were replaced with nothing other than thoughts of survival.

Tears stained Sara's frozen cheeks, which were turning white with frostbite. An image of Trevor on his side screaming for her to run away drove those tears. The blood on the snow heightened her awareness of the brutality of the scene, and the image repeatedly played out in her mind as she fled. She had refused to leave Trevor when he was first shot, but then a second round ricocheted off the frozen topsoil next to his wounded body.

She raised her hand to her forehead to block some of the daylight. Focusing up and across the mountainside, she could barely make out someone aiming a rifle down at them. They were too far for her to see who it was, but she thought she could make out the blue, yellow, and red coat similar to the one she had seen on a man earlier in the day. She had become suspicious of the man when they were about to leave the villa. He had kept his distance while following Sara and Trevor, making his presence appear coincidental. After the peeper from the night before, Sara found herself becoming leery of most anyone. It was an awful reckoning for Sara, and she questioned whether she should have spoken of her suspicions earlier, perhaps staving off this tragedy. But for now, she would have to put such thoughts away and focus on the immediate goal of surviving.

After getting shot, Trevor pleaded with Sara to go for help, knowing it would get her away from this danger. "Go, Sara! Get out of here! Now! Please. Sara, go! Go and get help." Trevor had pointed, yelling, begging, and pleading with her to run to safety. Every grunt of his voice came with a wince of pain after a bullet pierced his lung. He pointed to a ranch a fair distance away in the valley. Patches of blonde and green wild grass could be seen as the elevation decreased.

"I can't, Trevor. Look at you."

A third shot hit the tree next to them, snapping one of the branches. It detached from the tree, swinging by a thin layer of bark. The noise caused Sara to crouch down for cover.

"Trevor," she said, kneeling next to his shaking body, her face expressing every emotion. The sight of Trevor's pain tore Sara up.

"Please, Sara. Go. Go and get help, Sara, sweetheart." Trevor squeezed her hand with a half-smile and purse of his lips.

Sara began to cry. She knew he was forcing her to leave because of the inevitable. She feared he would be dead before she could find anyone, let alone by the time she could return with help. The look in his eyes told her he was well aware of that reality and had accepted it as a likely outcome. A fourth shot hit a patch of snow less than three feet away.

"Go!" Trevor screamed with all he had left, loud enough to shake Sara.

She looked up the mountain, gritted her teeth, and cried in pure rage. When she looked back to Trevor, he had passed out from the pain. Sara screamed out and reached down to check his pulse. It was there. Sara gasped, thankful that he was still alive.

With her peril evident, she finally bolted south toward the ranch, praying she could find help. She tried to gain as much ground as she could, dodging through the tall trees and various small spruce trees as she negotiated the mountainside. During that run, she kept thinking of Mary and Ben. They were the only reason she was willing to leave Trevor. Other thoughts raced through her mind, including an ever-increasing fear that a bullet would cut into her back. She prayed the shooter would think Trevor dead and leave him be. The shame she was feeling for leaving him became oppressive. The only comfort was knowing they would both assuredly be dead if she stayed. She couldn't know the torturous game being played out was to maim or kill Trevor in a warped revenge designed for Sara, to leave her suffering with that loss once again. How could she possibly know her life wasn't supposed to be in jeopardy? She wouldn't learn until much later that the man shooting at her was the peeping Tom from the cottage. For all she knew, it could have been someone with a grudge against Trevor alone.

Sara stretched the sleeves of her wool sweater as far as possible over her hands for some protection, but it might as well have been paper for the little good it did. She knew she was nearing her end, out of breath and energy. Her faith in survival was dwindling. She believed whoever was trailing her was coming at a daunting and relentless pace now. She felt his presence as ice-cold hands pulling her shoulders back to slow her pace even more, similar to her nightmares.

When she felt all hope was fading, she was amazed to spot Jacob standing there not far off in the distance. He stood calmly in front of an old cattle fenceline next to a stunted and spindly pine that looked like a giant bonsai tree. Sara couldn't muster the strength to have an internal debate about if she were delusional or not, as Jacob's face provided instant comfort and a sense of security from all she was experiencing. She felt that she ran twice the speed to the fenceline, skirting the few remaining trees, ducking every time she heard another shot ring out. For the moment, she believed the death that was surely coming for her had been abated.

She stopped briefly and bent over, panting. She held onto her thighs with her hands as her back, on fire with pain, rose and fell as she heaved, stealing each breath. For a moment, she wondered if she was already dying and about to join Jacob. She waited for that moment of warmth to grab her.

As she stood straight and moved forward, she could see Jacob's body wasn't holding form as he faded in and out of sight the closer she came to him.

"Come on, Sara. This way. You can make it. You're going to make it. You have to. Mary and Ben need you," he called to her. He turned and pointed in the direction of the ranch ahead.

Her pursuer was picking up his pace, coming down the last hilltop of the many smaller rises and plateaus along the way. As the terrain became less rocky, with more breaks in the melting snow, he started to lose sight of Sara's tracks. He started yelling out profanities in anger because it was slowing him down. He was having difficulty picking up her trail with the distance between patches of snow increasing. Out of breath and tiring, he finally caught up to her trail, seeing her tracks just over the fenceline. He was shocked when he looked farther into the field, seeing her footprints getting farther and farther apart in their stride until they were no longer visible.

"Impossible!" he grunted out as he exhaled his foul breath, fogging in the cold air.

PART 3

In Dean Gundry's desire to catch up with Sara, he left a motionless Trevor lying in the snow. He believed he was dead, which wasn't far from reality. He thought that with Trevor down, it was mission accomplished as instructed. But Dean could never control his rapacious appetite enough to stay on task, no matter the reward or consequence. The harder he ran chasing Sara, the more he started losing his focus, straining his eyes to see if he could spot her in the distance. He was getting an erection at the thought of catching her and imagined what he would do to her, which was strictly out of bounds by his director.

The sun decided to show up now, a brief appearance nearing the horizon beyond the treetops over the west range. It was that time of day, nearing dusk, when it became more difficult by the minute to make anything out at that distance with any detail, beyond its basic shape. He couldn't comprehend how the impressions of Sara's footprints became so much farther apart in the open field. He began to wonder if she backtracked and hid behind some of the trees farther back. The smaller spruce trees, with their branches growing from the ground up, would provide good cover to hide.

While catching his breath, he put his hand up to block the falling horizon and scanned the open field for Sara. Dean discovered what he believed to be her tracks making a hard right turn before disappearing. He was far from a seasoned hunter and wasn't skilled in tracking anything in the woods. Beyond her visible tracks in the snow, he would easily lose her. Pulling the gun up to his shoulder to look through the rifle's scope, he could see a dark figure in the distance, but it wasn't getting farther away. It was coming toward him.

Moving the scope from his eye, he squinted, trying to make out what was coming. The dark blip of a figure split in two. Within seconds, it divided again to three, then four. In rapid motion, he put the scope back to his eye. He could clearly see six grey and white wolves running full out and coming straight toward him. He realized they were locked in on him. He was their target.

His first reaction was panic, a sudden urge to run, but his arrogance took over and he chose to start shooting. This was typical behaviour for Dean Gundry. He was a mean-to-the-bone son-of-a-bitch by anyone's standards. He used crack and crystal meth, and it showed on his extremely scarred and pot-marked face. He had a red and purple nose from drinking. He would kill almost anyone for a thousand dollars. Five hundred if he were strung out enough. Although Nathan's associates were occasionally difficult to control, he was exactly the kind of person Nathan wanted in his circle — beholden to him, the supplier.

By the time he put a new round in the chamber, got on one knee, and took aim through the scope of his rifle, he was shocked by the ground the wolves had covered. His first shot knocked one of them down, dead. This brought a smile across his face. The second shot, a miss. Fumbling as he loaded a new magazine, he fired a third shot. A second miss. As he pulled the scope from his eye to stand up and start shooting wildly, they were on him.

Arms and legs flailing, Dean franticly tried to fight off the five remaining wolves. He shot one and managed to hit another in the head with the butt of his rifle, but that was as far as that went. In his mind, he couldn't equate the distance from where he first spotted the wolves to how quickly they were on him now, pulling his body to the ground. One part of his brain was screaming out, *Why*. The rest of his brain was in a pure agonizing hell of anger and rage. Those emotions were quickly taken over by fear, pain, and helplessness. Reaching to his hip to pull out his knife, he lost all control of his hand as the pressure of the wolf's jaws crushed his wrist. He tried to pull his hand back, but it was torn clean off, and the blood streamed up like a fountain into the cold afternoon air. His throat was torn out, and his limbs were ripped apart in jagged chunks. As he was rapidly shaken, pulled, and torn apart in multiple directions, it was an ugly scene of blood and down feathers flying. He finally succumbed to his fate.

Dean Gundry lay on his back, his throat gurgling the last volumes of steaming blood and body fluids.

As the wolves turned his flesh into food, Jacob O'Connell stood next to the small pine tree by the fence-line, expressionless. Jacob casually looked away to watch goose down from Dean's jacket float across the snow. Some got caught on pieces of wild grass in the field while others rose higher in the air. When Jacob looked back to the field, Sara was being helped onto the porch and into the warmth of one of the smaller ranches in the area. He smiled.

PART 4

It was extremely difficult and painful for Sara to get out of her cold, wet clothes, but it was necessary before hypothermia took her. Her shivering body was reddish pink from the waist down. She had spots of unnatural white on her face and hands. The only words Sara shivered out before she collapsed were "Trevor," "Jacob," and "Help."

The two women who helped Sara, tended to her immediate needs while they waited for the police and ambulance to arrive. Surprisingly, when they searched through Sara's clothes to find a phone in hope to contact her family, her pockets were empty. Nonetheless, before the emergency services arrived, the couple who owned the ranch did their best to care for Sara's frostbitten face, hands, and feet. Phillis, or Phil as most knew her, had been a nurse for years before moving west with her partner, Velma. They both worked at the same hospital, but Velma worked in administration. It was their dream to live in the country, raise a few animals, grow enough food to be self-sustained, and make some extra money. They did quite well at sixty-five. Velma was shorter than Phil with rounded features, brown hair, and blue-green eyes. She had a commanding voice.

"How's our mystery guest? Or I guess I should say patient, eh?" Velma asked, placing the firewood into the large wooden box next to the fireplace.

When Velma spoke the word "there," it came out like "dare." She never lost her heavy French-Canadian accent. Even twenty years of living in Ontario with Phil couldn't dull that accent. It's what endeared Velma to Phil in the first place. Phil was taller with black hair, brown eyes, and a pleasant and approachable face.

"She's out of it. She keeps mumbling 'Trevor's up' and 'Jacob' and 'the tree.' Maybe she got separated from a group, lost her way."

From her chair at the kitchen table, Phil looked back to Sara on their couch then poured a cup of coffee for Velma and herself.

"Do you think there's someone else out there? Trevor and Jacob could be family. It kind of sounded like there's someone out there by what she was trying to say. Don't ya think, eh?" Velma asked Phil, genuinely concerned.

"I think so because she kept looking out there when sayin' their names before she dropped," Velma added.

"Yeah, but her eyes were going everywhere before she passed out," Phil said, always a nurse.

"Well, I'll still send 'em out there. Get 'em to go up the break row cross field. If there's anybody there, they'll find them, eh? I'm still dressed. Think I should run the four-wheeler out. Try to catch a trail. See if I can spot anything," Velma said, intently.

"That's a nice thought, honey, but you heard those wolves out there. That's too close for comfort. You don't want to get too close if they're fighting over a carcass."

"I suppose you're right. We'll wait for the police," Velma said, throwing her parka over the back of her chair. She gave Phil a kiss, sat down at the table, and wrapped her hands around her fresh cup of coffee. "It's gettin' bitter cold out there with that wind, eh." Velma said, settling into her seat. Phil just smiled, reaching over to hold Velma's hand as they took turns looking over at Sara.

The police were the first to arrive with two officers in one car. Based on Velma's directions, they raced their Chevy Yukon across a field cut to the fenceline. The police didn't need any further direction as they came upon Dean's body. The younger of the two officer's vomited at the sight of Dean's ravaged body and the smell of what remained. Based on what Velma told them, there might be two men, maybe farther up the mountainside. The officers quickly discovered two sets of tracks going up the hill. Picking up the blood-soaked rifle that lay next to Dean, they marched on up the mountainside, finally coming across Trevor. He was carried to the truck in a canvas gurney and transferred into the ambulance, where he and Sara were taken away. The coroner would come to take Dean's corpse back. Dean's cause of death wouldn't be a struggle to determine.

32

Rage and Reason

PART 1

Ben couldn't stop his legs from shaking the entire time he was sitting in the Franklin General Hospital's waiting room outside emergency. Irony was abound between the Quinns and O'Connells with everyone taking their turn either in the hospital bed or the waiting room. Ben sat with his legs spread apart, his arms resting on his thighs, and stared down at the polished, terrazzo floor through the puddles of melted snow from his boots. Sitting in his seat, Ben's muscles were getting harder, more tense by the minute, and he clenched his fists so tightly they hurt. The anger building in him was palpable for anyone to see and could be felt exuding from him. He could taste his rage like a vampire's desire to savour human blood.

Ben went from sadness to anger on a very thin wire of emotional instability. He knew his mother's feelings for Trevor were deepening into something that would likely be long term. As surprising as it was to Ben, both he and Mary had come to like the man in no time. Seeing his mother in such rough shape was difficult enough, but her tears for Trevor only intensified Ben's feelings of helplessness.

Trevor remained in a coma after somehow surviving his gunshot wound and his injuries from a long exposure in the harsh cold before being rescued. Ben was every bit the compassionate and empathetic young man his father was, so his heart was swelling in pain for his mother. Not knowing how to deal with such intense emotions, his default was anger and to focus on who did this. He believed he had taken up the role of protector, a position once held by his father.

Ben's thoughts turned to Mary and the day she was attacked at the university. He wasn't one to easily fall for conspiracy theories, but Ben started to have a gut feeling these events were tied to one person who was pulling the strings.

Why else have these things happened in the order they have? he wondered.

He considered Carol's attack far more than coincidence. Ben slid his cellphone from his jacket, remaining still as he calmly made his call.

"Hi, Evan. Any news on who that nutcase was? Was there anyone else involved in this? Whoever they are, they're not gonna make it to the courthouse!" Ben's words quickly rattled out in a steady stream of increasingly uncontrollable anger.

Evan could hear the shake in Ben's voice, knowing full well Ben would be a mess over this. "How's your mother doing?" Evan stopped there, intentionally trying to steer Ben away from getting any more stirred up, directing him back toward control.

"They told me she's okay. They said they need to wrap her up and get her warm. I wasn't able to talk to her for very long before they pulled me away, but she seems to be more upset about Trevor than herself," Ben said, calmer now and lowering his voice. "I've never seen her hurt or this upset before, Evan. I was only a kid, but she seemed to hold it together better at my dad's funeral than she is right now."

Evan was quick to realize the events over the last year were more than Ben should have to deal with. "Well, Ben, you're right. You were a kid, and perceptions are skewed at that age. Your mom was in rough shape for years about your dad. But I think she is allowing herself to love again. She's going to need you for the next while Ben, so keep your cool, okay? I'll be here for anything I can help you with, all the way. I'll see you soon."

Evan's fatherly demeanour had a calming effect on Ben. But in that moment, Ben was only appeasing Evan by appearing to remain calm. Inside, he was anything but. The phone went back in his pocket, and he focused back on the puddle of water under his feet. He was turning into a solid young man at an early age. He was loyal to his family and friends. He wouldn't move from his chair until the nurse give him the all clear signal. He returned to his thoughts about Mary's attacker, wondering if the unidentifiable dead man on the outside of that rancher's property line was the same man. Either way, he thought how justifiable it was that the man suffered a horribly painful and terrifying death for what he did.

PART 2

Standing outside of Sara's room, the nurse warned Ben to go easy, that his mother just survived a traumatic event. She added, it would be a difficult recovery ahead and it could take a week or even a year, that there's no way to know. Ben was told that Sara was loaded with painkillers and a sedative, so she would be out soon. Ben leaned over and hugged his mother as best he could while she lay in bed. What started as a whimper for Ben quickly progressed to a full cry, eventually ending in gasps and sniffles.

After Ben composed himself, he instinctively inquired as to what had happened but then decided to let it go. He simply said, "Never mind about that now. Is there anything I can do for you and Trevor? Is there anyone I should call for him?"

"No. Thank you, sweetie. The police have taken care ... they took the ... they have the information..." Sara could say no more without taking a drink.

Her lips were sticking together from the morphine and lorazepam, and the balm on her lips and tongue had turned white and pasty. Her hands and feet were bandaged from the frostbite and heavy layers of white cream had been applied to her cheeks and forehead. Ben had to reach over with a cup of water and let her sip from the straw. Seeing his mother in this condition was a first for him and more than he could handle. He began to weep again. Sara tried to comfort Ben.

"My hands aren't useless, honey. I can hold the cup to drink." She gently tapped the back of Ben's head when he rested it against her hip from his chair, trying to fight off any more tears. "It's okay, Ben. It's going to be okay." A familiar phrase to them both.

By the time he lifted his head, his mother was out. The medication had taken control of a body awash in pain and drained of physical and emotional strength. He stood up, wiped his eyes and nose, leaned in, and kissed the side of his mother's head. Leaving the room, it was all he could do to walk through the emergency room exit without sobbing. Once he moved through the automatic entrance doors to breathe the outside air, he leaned over thinking he might vomit. Like his mother, his fear and sorrow were quick to turn to anger. Before he was in a full rage again, he felt a gentle touch on his back. Ben reacted like he was under attack, snapping around with looks to kill. But it was Evan, and he continued to hold his hand on Ben's shoulder.

"Are you all right, son?" Evan asked sincerely.

"Sorry, Evan. Yeah, I'm okay. Thanks for coming." Ben's voice was still a little shaky, and Evan could see he was crying.

"I got a call from Mary. She is taking a charter in late tonight, and we're going to pick her up. You ready to go for a ride?" Evan asked, attempting to lighten Ben's sorrow and hopefully reduce the anger building inside of him.

"Fuck! I'm so pissed off. Way past jarred. It's too bad that guy is dead because I would've killed him myself. Fucking piece of shit! This has me shook," Ben said, still clearly unstable.

"I don't want to hear you talk like that. You know you can't do that so why say those things? You are better than that, Ben. You're meant for better things than to be mean and violent. You can't let those urges overtake you," Evan paused for a moment. You'll figure it out," he said with a smile of confidence.

"I do, and then I go back again. I'll do better," Ben said with a nod of his head as he got in the truck.

33

Wild Ride

PART 1

"Damn it. I don't like this weather," Evan said, looking up at a black sky through the top of the windshield in his truck.

"Why's that?" Ben asked as he was dialing his phone to check his mother's status at the hospital. "Shit! There's too many clouds, no signal. Sorry, what's the matter with the weather?" Ben asked again, the glow of his phone disappearing as he slid it back into his coat pocket.

"Clouds blowing in from the northwest. We're supposed to get snow, but that looks like we could get dumped on," Evan said, periodically looking up to the sky.

"Well, we got four-wheel drive. We should be okay," Ben retorted, naively.

"Four-wheel drive doesn't stop you from an idiot who doesn't know how to drive coming the other way, panicking once they see snow." Evan was beginning to sound agitated. "It's not just a black sky. There's a darkness out there. It's around us."

Ben looked at Evan with a raised brow, finding it unusual to hear Evan talking like this. Ben was starting to feel uncomfortable after that comment, and a fear for his mother began to return. He worried about what would happen to his mother, or even Mary, if he and Evan somehow became stranded or got in trouble, unable to reach them.

Evan was about to distract Ben from some of that fear. "Oh, I forgot, I picked up a bunch of security cameras, or monitors I guess they're called, to put up at both our places. But you have to hook it up so we can all see them. On the phones, laptops, and um ... book reader ... uh..."

Ben couldn't take it anymore. "Tablet, Evan. They're called tablets," Ben informed him with a chuckle, which turned into a good laugh for both of them.

"Okay, smartass. We can get Glen Simon's grandson, Greg, to help us install them. I'm glad you and Greg are friends. He's a good kid. A lot like you, except for ... you know."

"Yeah, I know. And yeah, he's got juice," Ben said but then looked over to Evan. "Yeah, he's a good guy."

"I got it, Ben. I'm not a hundred. Yet!" Evan smiled.

The drive became quiet for a time. Much to Evan's dismay, the snow arrived in big, wet, heavy flakes the closer to the airport they got. They pulled over at a rest stop, and Ben got his first lesson in putting chains on tires before they resumed. The highway near the airport began to expand for various on and off ramps to different access points around the airport's hangers and warehouses. Along the way, there were cars off to the side of the road. Tow trucks were everywhere responding to accidents and stranded vehicles. To Evan's relief, Mary was outside and waving them down when they arrived. After a quick hug, Mary and Ben already had a significant amount of snow covering the tops of their heads and coats. It was an emotional reunion with thoughts of their mother.

Evan, still strapped into his seat, was caught off guard as Mary lunged from the back seat to throw her wet arms around him. She squeezed him hard and kissed the side of his cheek. "Thank you so much, Evan! My God! What would we have done if you weren't here?" She sat back and composed herself. "You too, Ben. Thanks for coming to get me."

"It's all good, sis." It was all Ben could squeeze out for the moment. Evan, remaining the brave elder as ever, was choked up by Mary's display of affection.

"I'm just glad your mom is okay, and you were able to get a flight out so quick. I'm glad you're here. We're glad you're here, and your mom will be too," Evan said to sounds of sniffling followed by a brief silence.

"There's a careless truck driver. Smashed right into that guardrail. Looks like his trip is ruined," Evan said, trying to break the uncomfortable silence with some mundane conversation. He wasn't very good at dealing with the many emotions surrounding him.

"There's a darkness out there tonight," Mary said. Ben and Evan looked at one another. Evan's raised eyebrow seemed to say, "I told you so."

"Yeah. Yeah, it is. Well, let's just get back to Mom, okay," Ben said quietly.

Driving up the last steep rise of the mountain on the outskirts of Franklin, a car went whizzing by them in the passing lane. It quickly disappeared and was out of sight by the time Evan reached the top of the crest of the hill.

"What an idiot! In this kind of weather?" he complained.

"Be careful, Evan," Mary blurted out, fearing something was about to happen.

"Relax, sis. Evan knows what he's doing."

Coming around the next bend, they discovered the same car had driven off the road. The tracks in the snow went in a straight line, and with the car landing head on against the side of the same rest stop Evan stopped at earlier to put chains on. The car was barely damaged. A bit farther ahead, in front of the rest stop, the snow showed tracks from another vehicle that recently pulled out and onto to the road ahead of them. What they were seeing felt wrong to Evan, but he felt a responsibility to check on the people in the car.

"Mary, try to get through to 911 if you can, and please stay in the truck. Ben, let's go," Evan said.

He pulled out two pairs of gloves from the centre console. The car was still running, and Evan quickly concluded that the small amount of damage and the lack of braking marks indicated that it had been crashed intentionally. Ben and Evan stood just off the edge of the highway and looked inside the car. There was no one to be found. Even looked behind him, pointing the flashlight down. He discovered footprints going part way down the road toward the rest stop before disappearing.

"Ben, get in the truck."

"What? Where the hell are they?" Ben inquired, completely confused.

"Get in the truck, Ben. Now!" Even repeated with urgency.

Evan grabbed Ben by the scruff of the neck and started pulling him. He let go of Ben once he picked up his pace. Evan didn't wait to put his seatbelt on before slamming the truck in gear and pulling away as fast as the truck could go. They were just getting into their lane when they were blinded by a set of high beams coming straight on. Evan put his hand up to block out the glare but was instantly sideswiped. They were hit toward the rear of the truck and pushed ninety degrees to his left. After fishtailing a few times, Evan regained control. With the kids in the truck, he was taking no chances and sped away, straight to the police station.

"What the fuck was that?" Ben yelled out in shock.

"It's a dark night, Ben. We have to get to Mom," Mary said, with a chilling calm.

Ben looked back to his sister and was upset to see the size of her eyes, wide open and almost completely black. He spun his head back around, looked forward, and said nothing else for rest of the drive to the police station.

PART 2

Evan pulled into the parking lot of his old precinct. He left his battered pickup next to the entrance, still idling, and pulled out a notepad from the centre console.

"Ben, can you take some pictures of the truck with your phone, please?" Evan asked, with total control and calmness, even though his hands were shaking. Standing outside the truck, Ben and Evan heard an unpleasant and familiar voice.

"Evan? What the hell are you doing out on a night like this?" Constable Stevens growled as he came out of the station.

Evan didn't answer as he moved out of the way for Stevens to see the damage for himself. Once the officer saw the damage to the truck, and a clearly frightened Mary in the back seat, he chose his next words carefully, knowing Evan.

"Oh no! What happened here?"

The damage was obviously fresh for Stevens to see, but he reeked of insincerity. "Come on in and let's get a report started. And bring your neighbours so they can keep warm." With a minimal sense of professionalism, Stevens forced the words out.

"It was a '90 to '92 Dodge Ram dually. Here, everything's there. We have to get to the hospital now. You fill out the report," Evan snapped, handing Stevens the piece of paper with all the pertinent information on it. "I almost forgot. There's what looks to be maybe a 2010 Toyota sedan slammed into the east side of the first rest stop west of here. But there was no one in or around the car. And it's still running."

Before they pulled out, Ben gave Stevens a scrap of paper with the cloud address where the pictures he took of the truck were. He did it without saying a word. Evan dropped the truck into drive and spit snow and bits of gravel as he left the parking lot. Stevens stood still, dumbfounded at how Evan had just treated him, and how Ben continued to stare him down until they were out of sight.

"Fucking prick!" Ben said with impunity. He felt he was entitled to at least say that.

"I gather that's the guy who gave you a hard time, Ben?" Mary asked.

"Yup, that was him. And blotto at the desk was just as much an asshole," Ben said, slightly turning his head toward Evan, unsure how he would react.

"You're right about that! Empty vessels both of them," Evan declared. Ben smiled, noting that Evan was still cool at certain times.

"So, did you recognize that truck, Evan?" Ben asked, unable to hide his temper.

"No, I didn't. But something tells me there's a chance we'll see it again. In the meantime, keep your cool. Got it?" Evan was speaking directly to Ben. "Everything is changing, guys. Not to scare you, but reality … it seems any one of us can be a target now. We all have to stay aware that somebody is pushing this."

Evan wanted to say more, but he could see Mary's face in the rear-view telling him she was scared enough and probably already well-aware. Arriving at the hospital, Evan asked Ben and Mary not to mention the accident to Sara just yet. They both replied they hadn't intended to, relieving Evan.

34

Atrophy

Sara's physical recovery may have been quick, but what happened to her and Trevor on that mountainside would linger for a time to come. Fortunately, there was a good reason for the sudden improvement in her mental health. Two weeks had passed, and her man had finally come out of his coma. After several surgeries to repair the damage from the bullet, the first few days were touch and go for Trevor. The shot hit him on the side of his chest near the shoulder, and the bullet cut through a rib before continuing on a downward trajectory through his lung, stomach, and intestines. The most serious problem occurred when the bullet broke apart into razor-sharp shrapnel, perforating his descending colon. They almost lost him from internal bleeding and bacteria seeping into his body causing sepsis.

It would take Trevor time and physiotherapy before he would have his muscles back in shape after those surgeries. The doctors could contribute Trevor's survival only to the fact that his body remained cold enough that it slowed down his heart to such a minimal pace that it slowed his bleeding. That's what the emergency room doctor, the surgeon, and Trevor's family doctor all concluded at the time. And not one of them believed their own words because miracles were on the other side of science and logic's door. The truth was that if anyone with a trained eye looked where Trevor lay after being shot, they would think he suffered exsanguination. Even though he didn't lose every last drop of his blood, by rights he should be dead.

Stubborn and determined, Sara returned to work a little over a week after the incident, against doctor's orders. Her need to clear her mind from the constant replay of what had happened was reason enough. Now that Trevor was awake and beginning to progress with physiotherapy, Sara cut her work schedule to help him as much as possible. She was slowly falling in love with Trevor. That was something she believed would never happen again in her lifetime. But even though she loved Trevor, it wasn't the same as it was with Jacob, it never is. However, Sara believed that was a good thing. She didn't allow those feelings to interfere with her commitment to Trevor as she believed him a good man. He had his scars and demons like anyone else but nothing over the top. And he loved Sara ferociously and damn near died trying to protect her. After the first shots hit a tree before striking the ground, the direction it came from became clear. Trevor had instinctively put his body in front of Sara before trying to get her behind a tree for cover. The expression of current times is "life partner," but Sara and Trevor thought it foolish. And even though calling each other boyfriend and girlfriend sounded corny at their age, they considered it better than the former. They wholeheartedly agreed on "my equal half." "Better half" was used sarcastically when in the doghouse.

Trevor cared deeply for Mary and Ben, and he admired Jacob for the man he discovered him to be. And he believed himself not far off the mark. In the beginning, Trevor had no idea about what was going on within the O'Connell family nor with Sara's good friends, the Quinns. When Sara came to him in the hospital the first few times after he woke, he was pained trying to explain what he experienced on that mountainside. At first he couldn't bring himself to speak of it, worrying Sara would think him insane.

She will probably think I lost too much blood or oxygen, and I fried part of my brain, he repeated to himself.

A few days before being released, Trevor was building up the nerve to finally talk to her when she unexpectedly walked in. When he visited Sara's home, Trevor saw a few pictures of Jacob, so he knew very well what he looked like. Revisiting the memory of what happened the day he was shot, the details had become more vivid with each passing day. He would put his head back on the pillows of his bed, simply close his eyes, and watch it happen all over again. Wanted or not.

His eyes were open, seeing his breath rising in the cold air, each breath more shallow than the last. His eyes watered over, blurring his vision. Slowly they opened and closed in a fight to stay awake. He felt like he was blinking in slow motion. It went on like this for a number of seconds as he watched Sara diminishing in size as she ran away toward the fenceline of the rancher's field. Oh, God. She's gonna make it. All else was secondary to Trevor after that.

When Sara sat with Trevor to share a coffee and conversation, she wasn't surprised at all when Trevor explained everything he saw, including Jacob. Some parts of the gory scene with Gundry and the wolves were difficult to remove from his thoughts, but they would eventually wane to an occasional unwanted memory.

35

Insight

Evan could see in Ben an anger and confusion that he himself suffered with for many years when he was younger. It was driven from a completely different source and was delicate to understand or address. His anger first came from the fallout after saving Marion Baldwin. Then it was the young boy in that horrific crash on the highway. More than anything that has happened in his life, including saving Carol all those years ago, those two events exposed him the most. Ben's demeanour hadn't changed much since the day he sat in the waiting room of the hospital waiting for news about his mother. Evan felt it prudent to have a talk with him that was based on shared experiences. Hopefully, a shared philosophy could develop between them.

Spring was humming along well now, nearing the end of April. So, on this unusually warm and sunny day, he chose to bring Ben to his shop to find some common ground.

Ben assumed he was going to be asked to help Evan with some of his personal chores, one tedious task or another. As it turned out, he was pleasantly surprised when Evan pulled the tarp off a couple of older motorcycles. Ben's eyes locked in on the Harley-Davidson Hardtail. He ran his hand across the dusty seat.

"Forget it! Not only is that not for consideration, but your mother would also kill me where I stand. Pull this Enduro out and bring it out into the middle of the shop where we can work on it," Evan said to an increasingly jubilant fellow guardian.

"What's this for, Evan? I never see you ride. Did you say *we*?" Ben asked, excited at the prospect of working on the bike with Evan.

"I might take it up again when work lightens up, but the crosser is beyond my years. It's for you, Ben. It's a good bike to start out on, and I'll help you get it into running shape. You know, give you some lessons. And it's an Enduro, so you can ride it off road or on. You'll need a licence for that, but I can help you get one when the time comes," Evan said with a smile after seeing Ben's reaction.

Ben had ridden his friend's bikes in the past, but Sara would never let him own one after a nasty wipeout. At least not until he was older, but that time had arrived. Although he hadn't thought about riding in some time, his excitement was genuine.

"Come to think of it, your mother is going to kill me for this either way. But holding you back from this kind of stuff just isn't realistic anymore. Mother or not," Evan said to Ben, seeing his smile getting wider but stuck for words. "Say a kind word about me at my funeral after your mother sees this." Evan saw Ben was focused in on the bike and little else. "Well, young man. What do you think?"

"For real? You're giving me this bike? Wow, Evan! I don't know what … wow! Sick! It's lit for sure. Thank you!"

"If all that means you like it, then you are most welcome. You can ride with Greg now. I had some good times on this bike. Some good wipeouts too! And a concussion or two along the way … I think," Evan said, raising some laughter.

With that moment behind them, Evan and Ben spent the next few hours getting the bike cleaned up and ready to ride again. As the afternoon was coming to a close, they were getting ready to put the bikes away, still needing some parts. Suddenly Nathan walked into the shop to grab a quart of oil for one of the farm's tractors.

"Hey, guys. How's it going?" he said in passing.

Clearly not caring if he received a response or not, he turned about face with the oil in hand and walked back out the door. He was gone too fast for anything other than an "okay" from either one of them. Evan turned to look at Ben and was shocked to see his eyes beginning to lightly glow a familiar colour. Ben was locked in on Nathan as he walked out of the shop continuing his way back to the orchards.

"Ben?" Evan said, with a look of confusion on his face. "Ben, are you all right? You look like you saw a ghost."

"There's something messed up about that guy," Ben said, as his eyes returned to their normal brown.

"Who, Nathan? He's all right. Not much on social graces, or a personality for that matter, but he's a hard worker. You won't have a problem with him," Evan said, trying calm both Ben and himself, making out like nothing happened. "Ben, we need to have a talk about some things. There are a few areas we need to cover, so let's grab a drink and sit on the deck."

With the bikes safely stowed away under their canvas cover, the pair went to have an uncomfortable conversation. Outside of the obvious things a young man can use guidance for, Evan had to focus in on Ben's anger. Especially now that he just witnessed how his anger for Nathan caused his eyes to glow. This was an exposure Ben needed to avoid at all costs. It was clear to Evan that Ben's temper would remain the wildcard in all of this. No matter, Ben still needed to be prepared for what and who might be coming, and Evan would be there to help him. There's no possible denial that someone was in pursuit of their families and anyone close to them. It was clear that whoever it was, they were in for the long game, and it appeared the finale might not be too far away.

Evan let Ben know that people like them can go their whole life without ever using their power. Some never know they have it. Then there are the ones who seem to have it fall all around them. What was difficult for Ben to wrap his head around was that no matter how, when, or where that power was used, something evil can easily pick up on it. Like how his father was found out, then shadowed and haunted, or hunted, and finally his family attacked.

It was a story as old as time, with a thousand different scenarios, yet entirely new to Ben. And some of it was unbelievable. What they were dealing with produced varying degrees of strengths and abilities, but always with the same responsibilities. Help when you can and be quiet about it. Keep it to yourself. Stay safe and aware of everyone in your orbit.

Evan could see Ben was having difficulty absorbing everything they just discussed. And he hadn't yet touched on Ben's ability to kill with minimal effort. Evan was left swirling in a pool of confusion and doubt, as was Sara. He couldn't understand this frightening ability, especially when it was such a dangerous enticement for a guardian, or anyone for that matter, unless it could be harnessed. When that realization hit Evan, he found a direction he could take Ben.

36

Depravity

While Ben enjoyed his time with Evan, the man he had come to loathe was heading off for a meeting with friends of his own. Associated misfits really. The reality for Nathan was that he saw them as minions providing services, a means to an end. Nathan had become skilled in the dark arts. One of those skills he developed was the ability to seek out and entice weak-minded individuals lacking any morals of note and who were easy to be led.

One of the connections he made was thanks to Joe Miller, who had been in hiding ever since the attack on Carol. Joe couldn't believe she survived. And as difficult as it was for Joe to not complete his revenge on Carol, Nathan convinced him to concentrate on their plans ahead for his best satisfaction. This was more to keep Joe out of sight, so he could do the things Nathan needed from him. Nathan wanted Joe for his final act. Joe going after Carol was unscripted and a high risk to his plans.

Even though Joe developed a nasty addiction to meth while staying locked up in a cabin, he couldn't just go and buy from Lenny when he wanted a fix. Lenny was a dealer, but not the kind to bring an endless stream of traffic to his door that could draw unwanted attention. He was a little higher up the food chain, and Joe had fallen near the bottom. Nathan, being who he was, kept a tight leash on his sycophant underlings. Sycophants because Nathan held the keys to control their addiction and the endless chasing of the dragon. In Nathan's mind, it was prudent to keep everyone else in his congregation separate from one another, other than the Gundry brothers, of course. His fervent belief was that if there was a consolidation of minds, they might turn against him. He also knew how easily an addict might kill someone to get a fix. With that knowledge, he was careful not to tease his supply too much.

Before leaving the orchard for his meeting, Nathan watched Evan and Ben's unintended interpretation of a father and son bonding moment and found it repulsive, hastening his departure. His first stop, Lenny's. There he would make his purchases for his next visit with Rick Jackson. Rick had developed a beneficial antipathy for Evan, after Evan busted him for drunk driving when he was home on vacation years back. The police might have worked with their employee over a drunk driving charge, but the coke Glen found put an end to Rick's career as a cop. His drug-addled mind over-developed the image of Evan's face from that night. Being in the academy at the same time, Rick asked Evan not to charge him with the coke, but under orders, Evan had no choice. Whatever plan Nathan had to bring harm to Evan, or anyone connected to him, Rick was all in. Nathan had to ensure Rick's mouth stayed shut. The threat of being cut off could accomplish that. Rick dealt small amounts so he could pay for his own supply, but he often came up short. That's when Nathan added him to the payroll, in a manner of speaking.

Brian Gundry was always a question mark for Nathan. Now that his brother had died on a mountainside alone, he would be an even bigger concern. The police confirmed Dean's DNA from his brother Brian's years-old sexual assault charge in Calgary. This suddenly put Brian on the radar as a possible partner in the attack on Trevor and Sara. However, it would take some time before Brian's photo was ever associated to the composite from Mary's assault. The brothers had been arrested and served time together a number of times. And like Joe, Brian was now forced to lay low or go into hiding altogether. Both

Brian and Dean were hard drinking men whose drug use only fuelled their constant internal rage at everyone and everything. After his brother's death, Brian was drinking more now and using crystal meth as fuel to stay awake during his binges. It was a dangerous cycle, and one that Brian wasn't likely to come out of in the near future.

He was paid half of his fee to go after Sara at the hotel and later Mary at school. Because he didn't hurt and scare Sara, or rape and beat Mary, he never received the balance of his money. Nathan considered taking Joe with him to see Brian in Vancouver and kill him. Nathan reconsidered after concluding Brian's strength and paranoia would cause more difficulty and noise than it was worth. After Nathan delivered Joe's supplies of food, beer, and drugs to the cabin, his final trip was to see Brian and pay him the remaining $10,000 dollars. Half was for Dean shooting Trevor, which in Brian's mind was still due. The other half was the balance for attacking Mary. Brian concluded it wasn't his fault the cops interrupted and for that risk, he wanted all of his money. It wasn't like Nathan couldn't afford it, which by his calculation was irrelevant. Principle or not, he knew he had to pay, concluding the first option to kill Brian was too risky. Nathan knew he couldn't afford to have his immediate plans interrupted by a blow up with someone as unstable as Brian.

37

Interminable

PART 1

After two weeks straight of dry, sunny weather, the smell of rain hitting a thirsty earth was pulling Ben back to a specific time in his childhood and the few memories he had of his father. He just loved it when they would go for the occasional walk down the lane from the house together to see Mary off to school. As a kid, Ben loved the smell of fresh rain, and it permeated directly into his memory banks to stay.

He sat atop his father's shoulders waving goodbye to his sister as the school bus drove out of sight. The tall oaks and walnuts, barely sprouting their leaves, stood tall in contrast to some of the full leaves of smaller maples, coffee bean trees, and sumacs. The lane back up the hill seemed so very long to Ben, just as the house looked like a mansion on the hill.

"I get to take the bus next year, Dad!" claimed an excited four-year-old Ben. He pulled on his father's forehead and yanked his neck back so he could look him in the eye. He felt like a giant so high up from the ground.

"Yes, you will, Ben. Your first year in grade one, and you'll get to ride with your sister. Come on, let's go! We're getting wet," Jacob said,

lifting Ben off his shoulders, piggybacking him while he jogged up the
hill back to the farmhouse. Ben giggled all the way up the hill, bouncing
about on his father's back.

Standing outside in the fresh rain, Ben was pushing hard to place the happiness of that memory in front of the pain of terrible news. Diane Westbrook and a school acquaintance, Andrea Barker, had been brutally murdered. It happened in the middle of the night on the same day, with the same M.O.

What Ben knew about Shelley Randall's murder was limited to rumours and a vision he shared with his sister in their high school hallway. The general consensus was that Shelley was killed by some stranger passing through town, never to be caught. Sadly, there was nothing else to add.

Mary expressed her sadness about the helplessness of the situation. She was in an extremely difficult time with tests at university, and it prevented her from travelling back home for the funeral.

The news coincided with Nathan being away on holidays in Vancouver, which at this point meant nothing to Ben, nor anyone else for that matter. However, Evan did ask Nathan to cut his vacation short and return to work. Ben thought he would be leaving Evan short-handed when he flew back home for the funeral. Even under these circumstances, it bothered Ben. Evan made it clear he would expect nothing less than for Ben to be on that flight with his mother the next day. Although he and Diane had split over the distance between them, Ben still cared deeply for her and was distraught over the news.

With a wait in Calgary for a connecting flight, Sara took Ben to lunch. She asked him a delicate question with complete sincerity. "This may sound like a stupid question, honey, but what are you feeling right now, other than sadness?"

"Other than sadness, I'm feeling guilty. But more than anything, I'm really angry. And my gut is telling me the same person who killed Shelley is the one who killed Diane and Andrea. And I can't believe this shit keeps happening in our lives. We're cursed, not blessed," Ben said, his mouth twisted, chewing the inside of his lip, and his leg shaking rapidly from nervous energy.

This caught Sara off guard. The conversation she had with Paul Kelley the night before was of the exact same sentiment. "Listen, Ben. We are not cursed. We need to rid ourselves of something that's come at us. This isn't on you, Mary, or anyone. And where did that assumption about Shelley come from? That was a long time ago. What made you think of that?" Sara asked, unable to disguise her discontent.

"Some of my friends. They told me how the cops found her."

With that, Ben couldn't stop the tears that came on. He bent over in his seat, putting his head in his hands, and he broke down. There wasn't much Sara could do to comfort him other than lead him out of the restaurant.

PART 2

Dennis Harquil was one of several friends Ben left behind in high school. Ben's return to town under such tragic circumstances left him emotionally depleted. Not a big drinker, Ben took up Dennis's offer to spend the night. When he hit the rec-room sofa, he was out. Where his dreams would take him would be an omen.

Ben found himself standing at the edge of Pell's Landing looking out to the lake below. There were high waves rolling over with such velocity they were creating whitecaps. It puzzled Ben that it was a smaller lake and there wasn't even the slightest breeze that could justify such dramatic motion in the water. He then looked down to the bottom of the cliffside with no shoreline. His balance quickly became unstable, so he promptly spread his legs and anchored himself to the earth. Hypnotically he watched those large waves smashing over and over against the exposed rock of the ledge below. And there, several feet back in from the water, he could see Vic Armstrong. The bottom half of his body lay under his motorcycle in an ugly, contorted, and broken shape. Ben leaned over to see better when Vic's eyes suddenly popped wide open, scaring him enough to jump back, almost falling over backwards. When Ben resumed his position, he looked back over to see Vic began to speak without his mouth moving, yet Ben could clearly hear him.

"Watch out for him, Ben. He's evil."

Ben snapped his back straight and stepped away from the edge. He could feel his heart palpitating like a syncopated drumbeat. He drew in a deep breath like he was about to complete a deep dive, while fighting off the urge to vomit. Catching something out of the corner of his eye, Ben wrenched his body around to his left. And completely surprising, he discovered his father standing next to Evan, both looking directly into his eyes. Seeing Evan made sense to him, but his father was an unexpected presence. They nodded their heads toward an urn Ben didn't even realize he held in his hands, and they spoke in concert. "Let him out, Ben." Then Evan said, "He needs to be seen." Then his father again. "He needs to be heard."

Ben was confused and unsure what to do, looking down at the urn then back to Evan and his father. With trepidation he slowly started to open the urn, then stopped. "Are you sure about this? Shouldn't you do this, Evan?" Ben asked, expressing his dread and confusion. "You have to do it, Ben. He needs to come out. He needs to speak to you. He needs to tell you something." They repeated their comments in the same rotation.

Ben turned the urn upside down and attempted to dump the contents onto the ground. But a wind suddenly blew in from behind him with a force that leaned his torso over on a forty-five degree angle. As he slowly straightened back up, Ben was amazed as right before his eyes the ashes rose up, spinning like a cyclone until they suddenly took form. Vic's body started to appear. Most incredible to Ben was the sight of Vic stepping outside of the cyclone while it kept spinning. Ben was flabbergasted, looking at Vic standing in front of him, appearing solid and real. When Ben turned back for some kind of response from Evan and Jacob, they were gone.

"Figures," Ben said, unafraid of showing his displeasure.

He looked back to Vic. His mouth still not moving, Ben could hear his words. "He's coming for you, for all of you. Watch out for him, Ben. He's not who he says he is." Vic showed no signs of emotion, nor facial expressions of any kind. Ben was still confused and found himself becoming more irritated than spooked. He wanted clear, concise answers.

"Who's not who he says he is?" Vic looked to the ground briefly, then raised his head again, looking Ben in the eye.

"The answer's in his name." Vic stepped backwards into the cyclone. In a blink of an eye, its form blew up into a ball of dust that the wind carried away in a rapidly upward direction, out over the lake until it disappeared completely.

"Oh, for fuck's sake! You could have told me his name. And next time, move your fucking mouth. That's just creepy dude!"

Ben sat up on the sofa and with a raised voice called out, "What's his fucking name?" Now that Ben was awake, his thoughts turned to his mother, sister, and the Quinns. He wanted to get back home. The home he had called "the new place" for so long was now just "home." He couldn't wait to get on the flight, and to a sense of normalcy, his normalcy. But he didn't leave town without stopping to say goodbye to Diane at her gravesite.

PART 3

Ben and Sara boarded the plane back to B.C. It was an unusually quiet flight. Sara chose to let herself drift off to sleep, and Ben stared out the window to the dark skies, depleted. Even though he had a heavy heart for Diane and the families of each girl lost, he couldn't escape the dream he had. A father he's only known for the first five years of his life was drawing his focus to that most unusual subconscious theatre. Evan was a comforting figure, yet Vic was new to him. Ben had only seen pictures of Vic. He also knew that Vic was Evan's best friend.

The dream shook him, and inside he was frightened for himself and those he cared about. The foreboding of what might happen was at a boiling point and it tore at what little control he had over his emotions.

Ben's apprehension about returning to work on the upcoming weekend was becoming apparent to Sara on the drive home from the airport. In the darkness of the mountain roads, Ben suddenly felt he could open up to his mother about how these events were tearing at him. Regardless of who and what he was, Ben was balancing the difficult transition from a boy to a man. He kept the dream, and the fear that came from it, out of the conversation. He talked of his guilt about not waiting for Diane. Even though it was a mutual decision to call it off because of the distance they couldn't close, he still felt he should have found a way to wait. Sara was quick to reassure Ben the feelings he was having were entirely natural, but truthfully unfounded. She agreed with him that it would take time to quell that feeling of guilt.

"It is easier said than done," Sara said. "All of us are getting together soon to talk about many of the things that need addressing. That includes Evan and Carol. And Trevor. And you're going to be there this time," Sara said with an air of confidence.

"Trevor knows all about it, about us?"

"Yes. He knows all about it," Sara said, glancing over to Ben, then back to the road.

"Hmm," Ben mumbled. Sara took that as acceptance for Trevor coming into their family circle. She was happy about that. Approximately fifteen miles from home, Sara pulled into a gas station to fill up. The large Chevron had a canopy over four bays for pumping gas and a new convenience store. At the self-serve pumps, Ben finished topping up the car and paid for the gas while Sara used one of the restrooms.

A car pulled into the far end of the station just as Sara walked around to the passenger side of the Suburban, letting Ben drive the last stretch. She opened the door and casually looked ahead between the door frame and the windshield. She caught sight of a car that just pulled in. It was the only other car in the parking lot except for the vehicle belonging to the attendant inside. She paused for several seconds, glaring at it, trying to make out the person inside. It was impossible due to the glare off the tinted glass of the four-door Acura. She slowly slid herself onto the seat, staring the whole time. After getting in, she left the door open a moment, keeping her eyes locked in on the mystery car.

"Ah, Mom. Mom? Mom!" Ben barely raised his voice an octave, but it worked and snapped his mother out of her apparent trance. "Do you know them? Is it someone from work?" Ben asked his mother as she slowly pulled the car door shut, locked it, and put her seatbelt on.

"No. Let's go," she said coolly. Once they were on the road Sara leaned back in her seat and rubbed her eyes a few times. "I'm going to rest for a bit," she said with an almost artificial yawn. Ben turned down the music and looked to his mother to see if she was all right. Sara began to wonder to herself. *Was that them? Couldn't be. God, I hope not. What are they? How could they have found us? Oh, this is ridiculous.* Sara was fruitlessly trying to convince herself it wasn't the same car who followed her out of the university the day they arrived in Vancouver.

38

A Dark Veil

In the time Nathan had worked for Evan, he never went back to Sam's Motorcycle. There was never an occasion when Vic's new replacement was a part of any conversations Evan had with anybody outside his home life. Evan never noticed that Nathan always spent his free time away from Quinn's Orchards. The timing of his first appearance didn't register as anything out of the ordinary for Evan, nor did he consider any examination of it necessary. His grief was the major factor that contributed to his lack of scrutiny of his new employee, but Nathan's increasing ability to manipulate direction and perception played the biggest part. Nathan studied his father's murder books like a dedicated Christian, or Mormon preacher-in-training would a bible. Nathan also studied another bible, except it was the antithesis of all things good. With unusual talent, he was able to tap into Evan's grief and keep his attention focused elsewhere — always away from him. And it was the same after Evan's grief lightened and his focus turned toward Ben and the rest of the O'Connell family.

While Sara knew of Dylan Matthews through Paul Kelley's suspicions of the man after Shelley Randall's murder, she had never seen a picture of him. There was never a need. Some twelve years later, with Dylan's name changed to Nathan, and his look so considerably altered to hide his identity, she likely wouldn't recognize him.

Back in Clarington, Ben had been drawn to look his way once, but he saw him only at a distance while he worked at the school over a year ago. He gave no consideration to who Nathan was, nor did he have any need or desire to know. Both Mary and Ben had a view of Nathan through a dream but had seen only his arm. Despite Mary's and Ben's subconscious instincts to look in his direction, they weren't there long enough to get a closer look.

There was nobody in this circle who knew who Nathan really was. Evan, Carol, and Ben were the only ones to have any interaction with Nathan. As Ben's immediate boss, Nathan created an ever-increasing friction between them, so Ben did his best to keep his interactions with him to a minimum. It was Ben's reaction to Nathan in the garage that gave Evan his first look at those dark clouds. It didn't mean anything to him at that time, thinking Ben was just unhappy from Nathan pushing him around like most bosses do. But as time went on, Ben's reaction started to pick away at Evan's subconscious, slowly and intently trying to penetrate the light of day. All of the events over the preceding months had Evan's guard up to a heightened level of sensitivity. But inexplicably, he still wasn't pulled in the right direction to look at Nathan with enough scrutiny.

§

Most of the summer had passed with little occurring in the O'Connells' and Quinns' lives, which was fine by Evan. Life started to seem almost normal again, with the business moving in a positive direction. Everyone remained healthy without any intrusions of a dark nature.

With Ben still on full-time at Quinn's, and the harvest not until fall, it was as good a time as any for Nathan to take the rest of his vacation. This time around, Nathan wouldn't be going to the airport. Instead he borrowed his friend's mid-sized pickup and was heading for one of the many remote islands off the west coast of Vancouver's mainland. That was the story anyway.

The morning of his departure, Nathan had a list of duties for Ben to perform while he was away and was walking Ben through the instructions. When Ben asked Nathan where he was going and what he was doing, Nathan became incensed, causing Ben's temper to flare.

"Hey! You don't have to be an extra asshole all the time! I was just asking!" Ben exclaimed, with attitude and language inappropriate to the moment.

"If I could, I would fire your spoiled ass. But you've got your nose shoved so far up Evan's ass, you can't see daylight, you little prick!" Nathan shot back at Ben. He mistakenly did so while getting within inches of Ben's face. Ben instantly snapped and grabbed Nathan by the neck, ready to swing. Fortunately, Evan came into the warehouse and put a stop to what was about to turn into bloody violence.

"You have to teach this kid some manners, Evan. Holy shit! And take a chill pill, Ben," Nathan said, straightening out his shirt.

"Fuck you! You fucking ass—"

"That's enough, Ben!" Evan loudly interrupted. "Nathan, you can just head out. I'll fill Ben in on what he needs to do. And you can both have some time to cool off because I don't want to see this shit ever happen again. And I don't care how it started. I'm too old for this kind of bullshit, got it?" Evan growled to both.

Nathan managed to keep his cool. Considering the age difference, he should have known better.

"Ben, go and get the bins that need fixing and start bringing them to the far end of the warehouse," Evan directed, wanting to get him away from the heat of the moment. "You got everything you need, Nathan?" Evan played the peacemaker with the insinuation he should head off for his vacation now.

"Yeah, I'm good to go. See you on the following Monday. Thanks, Evan. And sorry this happened, but the kid's got a hell of a temper. Anyway, see ya soon," Nathan said, tossing his work gloves down on the bench near the warehouse door.

"I'll see you when you get back. Have a good one." Evan pulled out minimal niceties to see his foreman off, but it seemed forced.

Fifteen minutes later, a familiar mid-sized red Ford Ranger pulled in the driveway. Evan happened to catch Nathan throw his bag into the back of the truck and wait for the driver to move over so he could take the wheel. Evan looked on, momentarily confused, thinking the interaction odd, but he walked away, letting the thought float from his mind.

Ben had gone the long way around the warehouse to get the flatbed truck so he could fetch the bins for repair. He spotted Nathan as he was pulling out the gravel laneway. The two locked eyes, but Nathan was knocked off his guard when he saw Ben's eyes begin to glow with his glare. Nathan almost hit the Quinn's Orchards sign on the way out of the property but straightened the wheel out in time and drove away bewildered.

39

Sins of the Father

It was a warm, late summer night, and the sky was a depressive, dark sepia. To Evan, it looked like dark chocolate milk trying to envelop every object that could be seen. He giggled to himself briefly, thinking of the movie *The Blob*. He pulled the long, cloth-covered vertical blinds apart and raised his hand above his eyes, trying to focus in on any movement he could find outside. He let go of the blinds and pulled his shoulders back far enough to crack several vertebrae along his neck. His body shook off the night's ugly discomfort and pain of arthritis. He would continue to pace the eight-foot stretch of floor between the patio door and his La-Z-Boy chair every twenty to thirty minutes, with no thoughts in mind. He plopped himself back into his favourite leather recliner, snatched up the remote, and laid his cheek into his cupped hand. Evan was surfing the seemingly endless channels on a Saturday night, when he suddenly stopped on one of forty or so news stations, without reason. The station he stopped on was based in Vancouver.

"Vancouver police are asking for the public's help with any tips regarding the homicide of a Michelle Matthews, fifty-nine, from Adams Ave North in the lower mainland. The night before last, Wednesday, August 23rd, around one-thirty a.m., a man wearing what appeared to be army-style camouflage shorts and an orange hooded sweatshirt was seen in the vicinity shortly before the homicide occurred. Anyone with any information…"

Evan sat staring at the screen, eyes squinting, and wondered why the name Michelle Matthews seemed familiar to him, it shouldn't have. As far as he could remember, he had never met anyone with that name. For the rest of the night, it gnawed at him. He found himself racking his brain to figure out if he'd ever known anyone who wore the type of clothes the suspect did, but to no avail. Evan wasn't OCD, but it continued to bother him for some time. Once again, he walked to the patio door and stepped out onto the deck, looking at his shop with no intentions of any kind.

Nathan is back Monday. I'm going to have to get some work done around here, he thought to himself. When he turned around to go back inside for the night, Evan suddenly had an empty feeling in his stomach, something about the murder he just heard about didn't feel right. "Vancouver. Hmm," he mumbled to himself.

Back in the house, he went to the fridge to grab a beer, Evan stopped at the kitchen island and picked up his phone to call Glen. "Hi, you've reached Glen Simon. Leave a message." The voicemail message was direct and to the point. Just like Glen.

"Glen, it's Evan. Hey any news on that Gundry asshole? I'm just wondering. Let me know if you hear anything. Thanks. Talk to you later. Oh, almost forgot, say hi to the wife."

In a way, Evan was relieved he hadn't disturbed Glen this time of night. He was, however, growing impatient to find out if Brian Gundry had been spotted. He needed something, anything, to provide some direction. He would love to have the chance to question Brian about Sara and Trevor. The connection to Mary's attack hadn't been made yet.

§

On Wednesday, August the 23rd, at eleven-forty-five p.m., Michelle Matthews heard someone knocking at her door. It was faint, but it was enough to stir her from her light sleep. For this gentle and solitary woman, it was most unusual and troubling that anyone would be knocking on her door at this time of night. Her only son, Dylan, had left home many years ago. When she slowly pulled aside the sheers covering the window of her entrance door, she didn't recognize the man with messy, dirty-blonde hair standing on the other side. He was probably twenty pounds heavier since she last saw him, and his eyes were older and scary looking to her.

After receiving notice from his biological father's estate attorney, Dylan became angry and bitter when he found out what he had been told about his father was a lie. By the time he left for Clarington to claim his inheritance, Michelle had taken all the abuse she could handle from him. This lovely woman, scarred by Jonathon Vargas's attack, had never married after having Dylan. She remained loyal to the Catholic religion far more than the Catholic Church had been to her. The church was her only source of activity outside of her home, other than trips to work or doctor's appointments.

She let the sheer slide back into place, taking a deep breath and wondering for a split second if that was actually her son. Perhaps she hoped it wasn't.

"I don't know you. What do you want? I have my hand on the phone to call the police," she said, her voice shaking with fear.

"Mom, it's me, Nat—" His voice was calm as he corrected his name in time. "Dylan. Your son."

She pulled the sheer back again and flipped the bright outdoor light on, near blinding Dylan. Michelle had no idea he had changed his name to Nathan, and she didn't pick up on his near flub. She had the sheer pulled halfway across the window to focus in on her surprise visitor.

"What are you doing here this time of night? I haven't seen or heard from you in more than ten years," she said, keeping the door between them locked.

"I'm in town on vacation from my job. Are you going to let me in, Mom?" Dylan asked ever so gently, playing the long-lost son come home. Michelle stood still for a moment, staring into Dylan's eyes before finally succumbing to motherly guilt.

Dylan stepped inside the entryway, waiting for his mother to lock the door. She closed the sheer and turned around. The last thing she would ever see was Dylan striking her with a blackjack as he split her head open and knocked her to the ground unconscious.

When the police found her, she was tied face down on her bed with multiple stab wounds, identical to the wounds on Shelley Randall's body. Different from the crime scene at Shelley's house, the word "WHORE" was spelled out in block letters above the headboard with her own blood. The crucifix she had on the wall above her bed was turned upside down directly over the obscenity. It would be some time before the police would make the connection to Shelley's murder — duplicate crimes happening three-thousand miles apart.

Nobody in the world deserved such evil, malice, and cruelty as what Jonathon Vargas and his bloodline rained down upon their victims. Michelle Matthews was no different. She would ultimately fall to what Vargas created when her own son carried out the savagery he learned from his deceased father and false god.

40

Lethal

The plan to expand the warehouse at Quinn's Orchards had been in the works for quite a while. The drawings Sara created for Evan were recently, and easily, approved. For some inexplicable reason, Evan never mentioned to Nathan the date that he wanted to start the addition to the rear of the existing warehouse; so naturally, he had no idea construction would be starting. Nathan had been on vacation, so he wasn't around for Evan to tell him about beginning. Nathan's near-physical confrontation with Ben the day he left for vacation had soured Evan on his foreman to a degree. Evan started feeling uncomfortable whenever Nathan entered his thoughts, troubling him. He wasn't acknowledging the fact that he didn't share this information with Nathan, which would normally be expected as he's the lead hand for the business. In the time since Nathan's return, few words passed between him and Evan, which was not entirely out of the ordinary. However, their few encounters had been noticeably cold.

On Monday morning, a truck from a concrete company pulled onto the property, drove to the far end of the warehouse, and dropped off the materials needed for the job to begin. Evan's employees were around to overhear and witness Nathan's inappropriate barking demeanor with his boss.

"What's up with these guys?" Nathan asked Evan, nodding in the direction of the truck. His tone sounded as though he was scolding a child.

"The addition to the warehouse is going to start Thursday," Evan said, looking at the emails on his phone and not at Nathan.

"Well, fuck! It would have been nice to get some heads-up about that!" Nathan growled. Evan slowly lifted his head up from his phone, expressing his displeasure.

"I thought I mentioned it to you before. And what's with the swearing?" Nathan was still acting appalled that he hadn't been included in the decision, or so it appeared to Evan. "Don't forget, Nathan, I don't need to advise you on every decision I make in regard to the business. With everything that's happened around here over the last year, I've been distracted. So, I've told you. Now you know. And I don't appreciate the tone either. You work for me, remember?" Evan's attitude and behaviour were significantly different from anything Nathan has ever experienced from him before. He was more than angry — he was indignant and forceful.

"Yeah. I do," Nathan sniped in response, then spun around and shuffled away.

§

Mary had her head buried in her laptop as usual, but this time the research she was doing wasn't for a school paper. Sara looked in on her, sitting on the sofa with knees bent and feet pressed against the edge of the coffee table. Sara noticed she wasn't typing furiously as she normally would be. She was just locked in on the screen. Sara didn't pry.

"I'm off to see—"

"Carol. I know, Mom," Mary interrupted her mother, not taking her eyes off the screen.

"Wow! Am I becoming that predictable?" Sara asked her seemingly uninterested daughter.

"Well, let's see," Mary said, finally turning her attention to her mother. "No makeup, no perfume, and those stretchy pants mean no Trevor. You don't need to be an investigative journalist to figure that one out, Mom." Mary gave her mother a crooked smile and returned to the work at hand. Sara spun about to leave.

"Smartass!" Sara was almost at the door but paused, cocked her head to listen.

She waited and finally, Mary griped, "I heard that." Sara smiled and headed out.

After the news about Ben's and Evan's encounters with Nathan, Mary decided to dig into his background. She spent the night researching what she could online and calling every source she had for information on Nathan Gravallos. Her searches were fruitless, so she gave herself a respite for the rest of the night.

§

Wednesday morning, Mary and Ben were woken up by their mother blasting out a horribly disturbing scream. They both went running to her bedroom. Ben ran so fast he slammed into the door face first, not turning the knob fast enough. Once they realized their mother was fine, that it was only a nightmare and not an intruder attacking her, Mary slumped onto her mother's bed, and Ben bent over rubbing his nose.

Only a few words were spoken between the three before Mary broke out laughing at Ben's almost slapstick misfortune. "Pretty fast there, speedy. What a pinhead!"

Mary managed to squeeze out the insults in between bouts of laughter. Sara was caught off guard by it all and ordered the kids out of the room so she could go shower and wake up properly.

Before Ben left for work, Mary stopped him by the door. "Hey, be careful today. I'm checking into Nathan's background to see what kind of trouble he's been in, but I haven't found anything yet. Still, watch out for him," she said with genuine concern.

"So, you haven't found anything, and I'm supposed to be careful because … you didn't find anything out about the guy? Okay, sis. See ya," Ben said playfully as he opened the door.

"Just be careful anyway … pinhead," Mary said with a smile, returning to her laptop and her quest to dig up dirt on Nathan.

A couple of hours would go by before she finally discovered his name change followed by his criminal record. What jumped to the forefront for Mary was how Evan didn't know, being a cop once. And if he did know, why he would hire him or keep him on. Something was off about this. Suddenly her intuitions about Nathan, and her sensation of something dark whenever they approached the Quinn property, made sense.

She just hoped she had gotten through to her brother to at least pay attention to his surroundings during the day. If she made him pause and think about her words, that was all she could ask for. And that relieved her. To a degree.

PART 2

Not long before morning break, Nathan ordered Ben to sweep the warehouse floor. That was a task that would take Ben a good twenty minutes. When he reached the aging oak barrels of wine, stacked four high, he suddenly felt a pressure on his back like a hard wind, even though the warehouse doors weren't open. In his peripheral vision, he caught sight of two barrels about to land on him. His movements were so fast, he couldn't believe he managed to get clear in time. The weight from just one of those fifty-gallon barrels would have critically injured him, if not fatally. One of the barrel's caps popped off, sounding like a shotgun blast. The wooden lid split open and sprayed wine all over the warehouse floor. Ben was on his backside, leaning on his elbows, and looking at the mess of wine everywhere, trying to absorb what happened. A deep breath followed with a long sigh said it all. Ben caught some movement on the top level behind the next set of barrels. Whoever it was could have easily gone up the back stairs and slipped down without being seen during the excitement. A couple of workers came running in from the breakroom when they heard the noise. At that point Ben was on his feet rubbing the dirt off his elbows and backside.

From the far end of the warehouse, Nathan came toward Ben, trying to make out like he was upset over someone's screw-up. "Who the fuck is responsible for this?" Nathan demanded.

The pallet jack was off to the side nowhere near the barrels, but that column had been purposely tilted. Without a great deal of thought, Ben knew it wasn't an accident. He would consider it possible that it could have been one of the other workers, but he knew better. With a right cross and an uppercut, Ben knocked Nathan on his ass. It was a quick and ferociously violent punch. As soon as Nathan shook his head to bring himself around, Ben leapt on him. Nathan could only raise his arms to try and prevent any damage from the flurry of punches coming at him.

Ben felt himself being lifted off the ground backwards. When he got to his feet, Evan was holding the neck of his overalls in one hand. He grabbed Ben by the scruff and gave him a shake. "Outside and cool off!"

Evan waited while Ben left, along with the other workers, before addressing Nathan. "I expected more from you. Especially after the last time this happened. Pack your shit and get off my property. You're lucky I don't have you charged. Those barrels couldn't fall on their own. They were either loaded on a tilt or leveraged off from the top. Don't bother trying to explain. I'll have your last cheque waiting for you at the post office. Don't come back here. Ever!" Evan stood his ground while Nathan brushed himself off.

"Whatever." This was all Nathan offered, clearly okay with being let go. He huffed and headed to the foreman's room to get his things packed. Evan grabbed a couple bottles of water from the breakroom fridge and walked outside to talk to Ben and calm him down.

"Are you going to be all right?" Evan asked Ben, placing his hand atop his shoulder and giving a firm grip of reassurance.

"Yeah, I'm fine. Much better now that I finally got to crack that ratchet piece of shit. I didn't knock those barrels over, Evan. I didn't even use the forklift or the pallet jack today," Ben said, motioning toward the bunkhouse. Surprising to both Evan and Ben, they suddenly heard Nathan's motorcycle start up. Out the laneway he went wearing a backpack with a large roll across the seat behind him.

"Did he quit?" Ben excitedly asked.

"No. I fired his ass. I should have done it sooner. I haven't seen that bike for a year now." Evan was shaking his head a little longer than usual. "Damn! He's going to need to come back for the rest of his shit," Evan said, dejected.

Ben couldn't help but smirk. "Well, there goes … what is it you call them? A blackguard? Whatever, he's gone. Fucking prick!"

"Tell me how you really feel, Ben," Evan said, injecting some humour to break the anger that was building up in Ben again.

"What?" Ben didn't catch the older reference.

"Never mind. Yeah, the word is blackguard. But it's pronounced together. Not like two words. And it's basically an insult for someone mean and dark-spirited. Or evil if you want to go that far. Do you really think Nathan is that bad?" Evan asked, clearly upset but not arriving at the conclusion he should be just yet.

Ben's eyes popped open wide. He raised his brows and looked at Evan, seeing him for the first time as out of touch with the obvious. Ben shrugged his shoulders, backing down and choosing not to say anything else to make Evan feel poorly. He respected him too much to do that, but he was impatiently waiting for the penny to drop.

PART 3

Evan appeared to be in a haze as he focused on the orchards across the road. He was quietly reflective, watching the dust that Nathan tore up with his hasty departure settle on the driveway. On both sides of the road running north and south past the property and out to the main highway, a person can see acres of apple trees of various species. For the moment, Evan's face had a glaze of uncertainty to it.

"Come on, Ben. Let's go into the bunkhouse and see how much crap he left behind. The load he had on the bike certainly won't do it." Evan tapped Ben on the back of his shoulder and started walking slowly in the direction of the bunkhouse, Nathan's spell beginning to break.

"Don't you think it's funny how fast he loaded up and left?" Ben asked Evan, but he received no reply just yet. When the door opened into the once bright one-bedroom apartment Vic had renovated, they found a dark and dismal pit. After the low-wattage lights were flipped on, Evan opened the front-facing window curtains for extra light.

"What is that smell? That's just rude. It smells like a rat died in here," Ben said while squeezing his nostrils closed.

"It does smell bad in here." Evan agreed with Ben on that. When they turned at the same time to look at the west wall, they were shocked and momentarily silenced. There were all sorts of pictures of demons in hell that any biker would be proud to have tattooed on his or her body. There was a cheesy painting of a trident all aflame and, adjacent to that, a picture of Salman Rushdie holding *The Satanic Verses* or to Nathan, the devil's bible. But what really upset Evan was the ten-inch crucifix, with Jesus affixed to it, upside down between the other two items, like a centrepiece. Evan took three quick steps, almost floating in the air, and ripped the crucifix off the wall.

Evan broke the silence. "Sick son of a bitch! If I had known this … I would…"

Suddenly Ben could see the proverbial light come on for Evan. He was mortified, holding his hand to his forehead, gobsmacked. He lowered his hand over his eyes for a second. "I can't believe I missed this," Evan said, quietly berating himself while looking at the crucifix in his hand. Ben lowered his head as well, afraid to look at Evan straight on for fear that it might embarrass him. He waited until Evan asked him a direct question before he would interrupt this moment of reckoning.

"And you saw this all along?" Evan asked, turning to look Ben in the eye.

"No. Not all along. Not all this either. This is sick, but not in a good way." Ben was trying to be generous to his father figure, but he was only placating him, which didn't help anything.

"Well, the girls saw it, and Carol tried to warn me. But I just … I just didn't hear them. What the hell is wrong with me?" Evan asked rhetorically.

Ben felt the need to assuage Evan's disturbed state of mind. "There's nothing wrong with you. But looking at this, he probably found a way to confuse and distract you. I don't know. Maybe?" Ben was trying to claw his way back, realizing what he said could be equally upsetting. He realized there was nothing in this moment that would help, so he kept any further thoughts to himself.

"You're pretty sharp for a seventeen-year-old," Evan responded, complimenting Ben. "Look around. There's nothing here. He's been planning this and moved his stuff when Carol and I weren't around." Evan's thoughts were becoming quite clear and logical now. Ben walked over to the wall and pulled the pictures down, crumpled them into a ball, and threw them in the garbage can. Evan looked at Ben.

"Thank you, Ben." He lowered his head again.

"You don't need to thank me, Evan, I didn't do anything. Maybe we should burn this stuff," Ben said, picking up the small tin trash can.

Evan nodded his head, looking at the wall now that the pictures and crucifix were down. "That's a message. He did that on purpose." Evan stopped there, not wanting Ben to become any more angry or paranoid than he might be already. "I have some calls to make, Ben. Are you good to go back to work? Because you can put in a little extra time tonight and over the next while if you'd like."

"Oh, yeah, I'm okay. He didn't lay a hand on me. Couldn't. And for extra work, that's whack. Yes, I mean. I'll help with the extra work for sure," Ben said as he turned around and headed back toward the warehouse, leaving Evan to his thoughts.

Ben picked up his phone to send his sister a quick text.

{Wow sis, U were right! Nathan tried to dump some barrels on me today & Evan fired his ass!!! Tell u more 2nite}

Mary didn't want to try to fill Ben in on everything she had just learned about Nathan through endless text messages, so she gave her sisterly advice and planned to tell Ben at home later tonight when they could speak face to face.

{That's crazy!! U should probably take rest of day off}

{No. Gotta help Evan, we R behind. Cya ltr}

As Evan has requested at work, Ben's cellphone went into his backpack and he happily returned to work.

Part of Evan's property spans across the west mountain ridgeline and ends at Highway 2. Even though it was still daylight, some of the orchards along the west line were in shadow as the sun crested the treetops along that ridge.

Ben had put in an extra three hours. Just after eight p.m., he was at the north end of the warehouse where the addition was about to begin, pushing the huge metal sliding doors closed from the outside. He closed the left door panel and pushed the slide bolt into the hole in the floor. As he tried to pull the other door closed, it caught on a bent piece of metal flashing outside, so Ben went outside to push it back in. He put his back against a large pile of wooden pallets and used them for support, pushing the heavy gauge-flashing back into place with the heel of his work boot.

He successfully pushed it back into shape. As Ben stood up straight, intending to go back into the warehouse, he was shot. Hit from behind, the bullet clipped the top of his shoulder just above the clavicle and collar bones, spinning him around and landing face down on the ground. Ben attempted to pick himself up until an incredible pain between his shoulder and neck started to register with a burning sensation that was foreign to him. The pain became so intense, he almost passed out after nearly vomiting where he lay.

41

Scramble

Ben held himself up with his hip pushed against the kitchen island and his right hand in the shape of a fist pushed down on the granite top for support. His body was weak from shock and fear. The only thing holding him up at this point was adrenaline. Ben's mind was racing as he thought of everyone he loved, more concerned with their safety than his own.

Making it home from the Quinn's property was an unbelievable challenge. He had heard multiple shots that just missed him, both at the warehouse and during his run. Now that he was home, he needed to reach out for help. His first call was to Evan. Earlier, Evan left the orchards to seek counsel in Glen Simon. Ben was aware of this. His first instinct was to call his mother or sister, but calm and logic came over him, an unexpected moment among a natural panic. He was thankful his mother and sister hadn't returned home yet. Vibrating and scared, he chose to wait for Evan to arrive and hope his sister and mother stayed away from home and away from danger.

Using tea towels from the kitchen to put pressure on the wound helped. He was lucky that the bullet had missed bone and didn't tear apart any major arteries. Regardless, the wound was still pouring out a good amount of blood due to his increased heartrate. Ben dragged a chair up to the kitchen island where he could watch both the side and front doors, holding a butcher knife for protection. He was still shaking from shock. He replayed his flight, dodging through the maze of pallets and running along the trails, constantly looking behind him. He was amazed the succession of shots fired had just missed him.

He could recall getting hit and hearing the shot barely a half-second later. It was the same with the other shots that hit the pallets with a snap, splintering pieces of wood. As he had learned from Evan, this told him the shooter had to be a distance away, making it harder to follow an unpredictably moving target. Even though three or four shots came close together, it was an eternity in Ben's mind.

Time slowed to a crawl. His senses were heightened, and he was picking up on everything, knowing which direction to run and when to move. He couldn't grasp what was causing some of the reactions he was having, and the world seemed to be muffled. He could hear his heart beating and his own breath, but he couldn't hear the crunching of twigs and leaves underfoot.

Finally inside the house and sitting at the island, his body began to warm, shaking off the chills and reducing the vibration throughout his core. Ben had become hypersensitive to all external sound and motion. Now the odd creaks and groans of the house sounded like they were coming through a loudspeaker in the room. His head lurched from door to window to door, but he saw nothing. There was no longer any sight of whoever was chasing him and no further shots were fired after he ducked into the woods. Ben was sure it was Nathan, but he hadn't considered there could be someone assisting him. He could hear the amplified sound of the battery-operated clock that hung on the wall behind him in the kitchen. Every second that ticked by felt like a minute.

The familiar sound of Evan's truck coming closer and coming to stop outside was a relief to Ben. Feet stomping across the porch made it clear to him that it was Evan who had arrived. Ben scurried to the door, his body suddenly feeling weaker and shaking. He looked out the entrance door and was relieved to see Evan. Understandably, Ben struggled to keep his emotions in check once he felt safer.

"Come, Ben. You better sit down before you fall down. Let me have a look at that shoulder." Ben cringed and took a couple of deep breaths as Evan gently peeled back the tea towel that served as a field dressing under his shirt, front and back. "Uh, yeah. He put a bit of a hole in you. But you need to keep pressure on the front more than the back." Evan intentionally downplayed it to make it sound like a small battle wound that he could be proud of.

"How bad is it?" Ben asked. He looked up at Evan like a wounded pup. Evan purposely talked in a nonchalant manner to keep Ben calm.

"It looks like it missed any part of the bone. Yeah, you're going to have a nice scar there to show the girls. They'll all be like, 'Oh my God. Are you okay? Is there anything I can do to help you? Can I make you a sandwich or anything special?'" The pair laughed. Ben was surprised to see an ambulance pulling in. "Yeah, I called them right after our call ended. Looks like I beat them here. Shocker there," Evan said to a weak-looking Ben.

PART 2

Ben woke to the sound of his sister's voice blurting something out in discovery but trying to keep her voice down. "Oh my God! That's what he's done! I don't believe it! What a freak ... and a total creep!" Mary exclaimed.

"Don't believe what?" said a raspy and dopey Ben, groaning in pain as he lifted his head off his pillow. Mary could see Ben was having difficulty swallowing, so she filled his cup with ice water so he could soothe his parched throat.

"Why am I so fucking sore?" Ben moaned.

"How do you expect to be feeling after being shot ... pinhead? You had surgery. That's why you're sore. Jesus, Ben, you scared the hell out of me. And Mom is beside herself. Evan told us what happened. It was a long night with hardly any sleep, thanks to you."

Mary kept things light between them, but Ben could see the concern. "I'm kidding, of course. Sorry, I didn't mean to wake you like that. It's just … well … hang on a sec. So anyway, Evan actually has the cops looking for Nathan, but look what I found out."

Mary sat on the edge of Ben's hospital bed, proudly showing him her notebook. Ben made a slow stretch, squinting his eyes trying to discern what was on the page between the scribbling, stroke marks, and dozens of combinations of Nathan's name. At the bottom of the sheet he could see "Jonathon Allan Vargas" in big, bold letters. Below that, "Nathan Jona Gravallos" was written with lines between the letters of the two names. At the top left of the page, the name "Dylan Matthews" was circled.

"What is all this stuff, sis?" Ben asked, slowly sipping water.

"After what's been going on with Nathan and you guys, I figured I would check him out, remember?" Mary was excited to share her conclusions.

"Of course, you did," Ben said, with a big smile as he flopped his head back onto his pillow. "Always the investigative journalist," Ben teased.

"Look, his real name is Dylan Matthews. But look at the name we knew him as and look at his father's name. See! I showed Mom and that's when she talked about Vargas's son, Dylan Matthews," Mary said, darkening the lines between the two names.

"You're saying he used his father's name to make up a fake name for himself?" Ben asked, exasperated at how far this man would go using this level of subterfuge.

"It gets worse," Mary said, folding the page over to reveal the notes she made as she went through Dylan's criminal record. "When Evan heard about his real name, he really got upset. I guess he talked to Glen Simon, and he told him Nathan's mother is Michelle Matthews. From Vancouver. She was murdered while Nathan was on vacation there. 'On one of the islands' or so he said. Yeah, right!" Mary said sarcastically, with air quotes.

"He killed his own mother?" Ben asked, with disgust and shock.

"Apparently. Evan told me this morning. I guess he already knew about this Matthews lady being killed, so—" Ben started pulling the tape around his IV off. "Stop, Ben!" Mary barked at her brother, placing her hand on top of Ben's. "You had surgery, you idiot!"

"I did?"

"I just told you that! Wow, the drugs must be really good. Honestly, I don't believe this. Hang on a second. And don't take that IV out!" Mary scolded her brother like he was a child.

After Mary called the nurse, she returned to Ben's room. They discussed what they would do after learning about Dylan. It meant the threat they were under had become much more serious. The police suggested the O'Connells go to Ontario to stay with relatives, but Sara was adamant she wasn't going to put her family in harm's way. She also said Dylan could possibly be a suspect in the killing of at least one person, maybe three, in Ontario, which grabbed the attention of the police. She sternly rejected their proposal with disdain. With the memory of Jacob in mind, Sara wasn't going to run. She would stand her ground and protect her children here in Franklin.

Mary had a bit of a turned stomach knowing at some point she would have to tell Ben about Dylan being under suspicion for Shelley Randall's murder. And he could also be implicated in the murders of Diane and Andrea, which would light Ben up. Mary would be the one to tell him because she seemed to be able to keep Ben from raging out of control, more so than anyone else.

The Quinns' and O'Connells' new reality was that they were all in danger from one source, but multiple hands were involved. In Dylan's criminal record, Evan saw his connection to Joe Miller from the days they lived together at the same halfway house in Toronto. Evan knew quite well that the police wouldn't accept their accusations about these men as fact. And coincidences wouldn't pass muster as real evidence. It would just be speculation to the police. But both families now knew the truth of who had been behind these attacks. It started with Sara at the Marriott in Vancouver and continued on through to Mary and Carol and then to Ben's shooting just the day before. They came to accept the reality that without proper evidence, the police would help them only if something happened.

42

The Weight

Evan chose to allow construction to begin on the warehouse expansion while Ben remained in the hospital. He thought the same as Sara, in not letting Dylan have control over their lives. He also considered it a good distraction from the constant worrying. Evan hoped if Ben could relax enough and let his body recuperate, it might just calm him down or distract him from his desire for retribution. Following the doctor's orders, Sara enforced the rule that Ben stay home and heal.

Ten minutes into the dig for the footings at the warehouse, the machine was shut down. Evan was called out from the warehouse to come inspect what the excavator had inadvertently exposed. Evan was aghast and speechless, standing over the hole in the ground where some of the pallets had been stacked. He looked like he had seen a ghost. In a way, he had.

Staring down into the excavation, Evan numbly pulled his phone out. "I'm calling the police. You should probably call your boss and tell him the project is going to be delayed for a while."

Evan couldn't have sounded or behaved any more vacant than he did in that moment. He knew very well who the corpse was from its clothing. He also knew who the killer was. Evan let himself fall backwards and sat on the excavator's bucket. The machine's operator assumed by logic, and from Evan's body language, that whoever they had found in that hole was someone close to him. The atmosphere was untenable for the simple-minded operator. He crawled out and down from his machine and went to his truck to call his boss, leaving Evan by himself.

This was the proverbial straw that broke the camel's back. Evan uncharacteristically bent over, burst into tears, and began bawling into his hands, seeing his younger brother in this undignified burial site. Evan realized why Dylan had thrown such a hissy fit at not getting a heads-up about the construction.

How am I going to tell Rose? She's going to fall apart over this. I have to find this evil piece of shit and bury him myself, be dammed the consequences!

Understandably, Evan's emotions were getting the better of him, and he was unsure of what to do in this moment. His thoughts became scattered, thinking about everyone and how he could best protect them. He also envisioned how poorly his parents would take the news. The misfortunes surrounding all of them put Evan at a tipping point. The group would have to quickly come to terms with the totality of what had brought them together. They needed to put a plan in place that they could control, without consideration of the police. Although they knew the police would now be a part of their lives, and not without tension.

The animosity between Evan and the local precinct wasn't going to bode well for the Quinns, so a call was put through to the supervisor covering this region of the province. Evan knew the drill. They will look first to the family for suspects, but he had no patience for it, not now. He would point them in the right direction, but he wasn't going to divulge anything beyond what the police already knew. The Vancouver police had their own ongoing investigation into Michelle Matthews's murder, and Dylan was currently one of their main suspects. Before long it would be understood that nothing surrounding that man moved in a straight line, they were looking at a serial killer.

Carol informed Sara about the shocking discovery of Ryan's body. She politely asked her to try to keep Mary and Ben out of the loop for a day or two while Evan dealt with the initial shock. Intellectually and emotionally, Evan had already buried his brother after the countless times he had stolen from the family and left town. And there were the overdoses and many trips to rehab that had failed. With all that was going on, Evan somehow managed to deal with Ryan's death more easily than he had with Vic's.

43

Friend or Foe

PART 1

The drive into Franklin from the north provides an elevated perspective of the beautiful surroundings of this old western-style town of fifteen thousand, give or take. The rising and falling mountain ranges to the west, the various farms and cattle ranches in the foothills to the south, all provide a breathtaking view. The river that bled out through the mountain's base approaching the outskirts of Franklin cut through the landscape comparable to a sidewinder rattlesnake leaving its mark on the desert sands. Nearing the town's core, the river widens and runs straight to the south, splitting the commercial area from the quiet residential neighbourhoods on the opposing east side. A small, wooded area with footpaths crisscrossing through it stood as a buffer from the bustling sounds of business for its primarily peaceful residents. Train tracks crossed the southern end of town, and they moved a great deal of commerce, and many a sightseer, east and west through the mountains.

An old warehouse and shipping facility had been converted to the new farmer's market one street east of the main drag. It also accommodated commercial businesses, including Quinn's Cider & Wine. The street facing the entrance had diagonal parking. A newer, black Dodge pickup truck was parked in front of the store. A tall man in his mid-to-late twenties got out and paused for several seconds before moving toward the building. He raised his head and began inspecting the falling sky to the southwest with a look of uncertainty and apprehension. The horizon looked like it was on fire, and the sky was filled with clouds, all nearly symmetrical in size. The clouds looked strange though, an odd colour of baby blue shifting to light purple, and only their outer edges maintained a common colour of stormy grey.

Eugene Brownstone shook his head, disturbed by what he thought of as a comic book sky. He watched as the sun quickly fell, and the horizon's colours began to give way to a rapidly encroaching darkness. Eugene wasn't quite sure how to judge the speed at which the atmosphere was changing, leaving him feeling wistful. He wondered if it was an omen for what lie beyond the threshold he was about to cross. When he noticed the sign for Quinn's store he suddenly had a craving for the taste of real apple cider. But as a stranger to town, he didn't think anything was out of the ordinary.

The miniature cowbell over the door clanged, letting those who may be in the back of the store know they had a customer. It was Mary O'Connell who came out from behind the coolers to greet Eugene. Her dark auburn hair was highlighted by the thin, crossover white top she was wearing, completing an attractive look with skin-tight dark blue jeans.

"How may I—" Her words to the customer stopped abruptly. The second Mary made eye contact, looking up from drying her hands, she was frozen.

"Sorry, did I disturb you?" asked a calm and confident Eugene.

He was a ruggedly handsome man with thick, black hair, hazel-brown eyes, and smooth, light brown skin. He had a smile that completely caught Mary off guard. It wasn't Eugene's good looks alone that startled and stammered Mary's speech and movements.

"Ah, no. No, I just ... for a minute, I thought you were someone I knew. Or know. How can I help you?" Mary was unable to hide her nervousness. Her words came out in a near stutter, and her motions were awkward.

Inside, Eugene giggled at her nerdish behaviour, fumbling to pick up a spray bottle and paper towels to clean an already clean countertop. "I was just going to ask you which one's the best cider, just regular cider." Eugene was still sporting an irresistible smile that wasn't letting up.

"Uh … I think it's the one in the blue box on the end, just there." Mary, not quite sure if she was right, pointed to the first cooler at the front of the store. She cleared her throat again, failing to portray any sense of cool.

Mary had never met this man, but he was no stranger to her. Lately, he had been a regular visitor to her dreams, day or night. This interaction truly struck her as nothing less than amazing. However, she didn't want to admit that just yet. He pulled a six-pack of cider out of the cooler and caught Mary checking him out in the reflection of the glass. He quickly twisted back to the counter, hoping to catch her in the act. Mary was awkwardly trying to divert her eyes.

"That's fourteen seventy-two please," Mary said after scanning the case, still unsure how to react.

"Is it made of gold? There's not even any alcohol in it." The tone of Eugene's voice was in jest, good natured as he passed her a twenty dollar bill.

"I don't really know. I'm just filling in for a friend. We're taking turns for a sick family member," Mary said, easing a bit and reaching her hand out to return his change.

"That's okay. Just kidding," Eugene responded, unable to relinquish his smile.

PART 2

Mary was most certainly charmed by Eugene. His presence, his smile, gentle voice, and overall appeal had Mary intrigued and attracted. A normally reserved person in the romance department, Mary shyly took a brave step forward.

"I never say … I would never usually say this, but you seem very familiar to me. Have we ever met? I know, I know, that sounds corny or cliché, but I just wondered if I've seen you before." Mary fought to get every awkward word out feeling she would regret it if she didn't. She timidly reached out her hand. "My name is Mary O'Connell."

Eugene was truly surprised by what Mary said, and he realized how difficult it must have been. "Eugene Brownstone. I think I'd remember meeting you. But I am very pleased to meet you now, Mary O'Connell."

Eugene gently squeezed her hand with a slow shake. They smiled at one another, and the handshake lasted a little longer than a typical greeting between strangers. Mary put her trust in her own intuition as to why he had been in her dreams. She trusted whatever had brought him to the store was for a good reason. There was definitely an instant connection shared between them, and Mary was quite smitten with the man standing in front of her.

Mary was a beautiful young woman, now in her second year at university. Eugene, a solid and strong steel worker, was about seven years older. The age difference would be insignificant for the pair, but it would raise Sara's motherly instincts in a hurry. At least at first.

"So, Eugene, why are you here in Franklin?" Mary asked, much calmer now.

With a three-week shutdown on his jobsite in Calgary, Eugene told her that he was looking for an uncle he never met, a Vic Armstrong. He was trying to find his father's brother as they had been separated when they were kids.

Eugene was fascinated that Mary had a connection to Vic. She empathized with Eugene after telling him that Vic had died before Eugene had the chance to tell him about the family he had never known. It had been something that bothered Eugene's father, Teddy. He tried to piece together the family he came from after being ripped apart and separated as children by the Catholic Church. Undiagnosed too long with diabetes, Teddy had fallen ill. After an accident at work, he had one of his legs amputated at the knee after an infection went untreated too long. It was a hard time for Eugene's father, himself a proud steel worker for years. Teddy was fearless and was a sought-after high-steel welder and fitter and had worked on some of the highest projects all over Canada and some in the US.

Eugene's parents had been looking for Vic for years. Eugene searched persistently and had finally discovered what province he lived in. Eugene was an old soul with an uncommon perception of people and his surroundings. His belief was to always trust that his instincts would lead him the right way, and they led him to Mary.

Eugene walked to his truck with butterflies in his stomach. *Wow! She's something else, that one. And totally hot!* he thought to himself before backing out of his parking space. He had to admit to himself that there was something familiar about her.

Mary was inside with the same sentiment. And while Mary had the courage to ask Eugene who he was and engage in conversation, Eugene summoned the same courage and left his number after making a date for coffee. A connection was made.

44

Before the Storm

PART 1

The detectives from Vancouver did a thorough job investigating Ryan's murder, but only one conclusion could be found. Dylan Matthews was the prime suspect. He was the last person seen with Ryan before he disappeared. At least he was according to Maury Babich. The police had also learned Ryan was getting some of his drugs through Dylan. And they concluded the prime suspect in Michelle Matthews's murder was her very own son.

However, there was no physical evidence and the only witness, an elderly woman, provided a description that was questionable, at best. The investigation had almost been stopped cold. Even though there had been a fight earlier in the day Ben was shot at Quinn's Orchards, there was no physical evidence to be found linking Dylan to the shooting. The former Quinn employee was under suspicion for the most serious of offenses, and the police were under immense pressure to find him. The only hope of proving Dylan was their man required finding a weapon or getting a confession. That was very much a longshot. Meanwhile, they continued their search.

In Clarington, back in 2006, Paul Kelley had been left with only his gut instinct to consider Dylan for Shelley Randall's death. Months after her murder, when discussing Shelley's death with Paul, Sara had seen only an old driver's licence photograph of Dylan from when he was seventeen. Now that she knew who Nathan really was she was convinced that he was connected to Ryan's disappearance. No different than her suspicions about what happened to Shelley and the two girls in Clarington. The fact that the coroner couldn't find a cause of death for Ryan, didn't change anyone's suspicions.

Not long before Dylan left Toronto for Clarington, several men were under suspicion for the murder of Barry Kitchen in southeast Toronto. Joe Miller climbed to the top of the list of suspects for Kitchen's murder after he ran from parole. His connection to Dylan put them both on the radar. With the police stopped in their tracks, notices were sent out to pick up Joe, Dylan, and all of their known associates for questioning. At this point, the only associates available were Lenny Bonacorso and Rick Jackson. Lenny and Rick knew the system quite well and simply kept their mouths shut and stayed away from each other. It took the police quite some time to bring all of these facts together.

Evan had no idea who Bonacorso was, even though he had seen him picking up Dylan in his red Ford Ranger a few times. Although Evan was trained to detect drug use as a cop, he never picked up on Dylan's recreational use of various drugs. These details were slow to emerge for Evan, slowly coming out of the fog related to his ex-foreman. Rick's life had been a mess for years before he was busted for drunk driving and narcotics possession. Nonetheless, he blamed Evan and hated him for it. The police were unable to make an arrest with nothing other than suspicion and bad feelings. While Lenny and Rick were questioned, the rest were doing a good job of staying out of sight.

Without a warrant, one of the officer's used his banking connection to check out Dylan's finances. His inheritance was surprisingly significant, but that trail ended when Dylan liquidated everything he had. There were no properties or rentals to be found, and very few witnesses to identify him. He didn't have so much as a library card.

He didn't even have a vehicle in his name. For all intents and purposes, he had fallen off the grid.

§

Jonathon Vargas was the epitome of evil. Dylan followed his father's example in every aspect, polishing his methods of hunting and stalking his prey. Dylan delved into his father's journals and scrapbooks as his talents progressed. In those books, he discovered references his father made to him by name. Dylan began to believe that he was the chosen one meant to evolve in his father's avocation. He believed this would make the devil proud. It was a frightening and dangerous world inside the mind of Dylan Matthews.

When Jonathon moved from B.C. to Ontario, he had two extremely subservient, sycophant men in Vancouver tracking Michelle Matthews's every move. After Jonathon raped this poor, unfortunate young woman, he discovered Michelle was pregnant, making him ecstatic that she was carrying his seed and a possible protégé.

Michelle was a virgin and a devout Catholic, so she wouldn't abort the child. Jonathon thought he had struck gold. In his deranged mind, he believed Michelle was nothing more than his concubine. If she delivered a son, he would have someone to follow in his footsteps. However, Jonathon was so obsessed with the O'Connells, he waited too long for the chance to develop his apprentice. With his father's literary guidance, Dylan mastered a skill in darkness that helped him to avoid detection. He could appear as average, unappealing, and unnoticeable, able to disappear in a crowd. He had left Evan feeling foolish, but he needn't despair. Dylan's was an art in the darkness of manipulation that could cause guardian and seer alike to miss it. And for a time, it worked until something or someone shook him from its hypnotic grip.

Through Glen Simon, Evan learned what he could about Dylan. When he heard the revelation of what Sara and Paul Kelley had suspected regarding the murders in Clarington, he knew exactly what he was dealing with. Once he was free of Dylan's presence, and the spell he held over him, he could see Dylan in a light that had been dimmed for almost a year and a half. As each day passed, everyone became more sensitive and keenly aware of their surroundings. Evan felt responsible for everyone. After Ben's shooting and Ryan's memorial, Glen and Evan stayed in close contact.

PART 2

In the week following Ryan's memorial, life slowed with a sense of calm around the Quinns and O'Connells. After Ben's shooting, Mary chose to stay on at Quinns' store in town. She worked on weekends, and any other free days she had, to help Evan and Carol through a difficult time. Mary and Ben occasionally found themselves working together, which everyone liked for safety reasons. During this period, Mary and Eugene spent a lot of time getting to know each other. Their age difference was irrelevant to them.

At a dinner with everyone present, Mary introduced Eugene. The evening became a moment for celebration as Eugene revealed himself as Vic's nephew and the very same boy Evan saved on the highway. It was especially emotional for Evan, all things considered. However, everyone sensed goodness in Eugene and believed he would be a strong person to have by Mary's side, which brought additional needed relief to the group. After all the experiences of late, Eugene was a breath of fresh air.

Attempting to resume a sense of normalcy, Sara returned to her nighttime painting classes and invited Carol to join her. Safer in pairs, they thought. Sara confided in Carol and told her about the events that dramatically changed her life before and after Jacob's death. When she and Jacob were being stalked and had to be hyper-vigilant, always watching out for their safety, they both refused to stop living their life because of it. Even though it had been hard enough, giving into fear was not something to be considered.

Almost a month after Ben's shooting, Evan invited everyone to join him at Glen's cottage for a weekend. It was off-season, so it would be quiet and peaceful. The weather was decent and it was a well-deserved time of fun and relaxation. Ben, Eugene, and Mary went out on the lake with Sea-Doos while Glen, Evan, and Trevor went fishing.

They had a fish fry dinner, enjoying some rainbow trout the men caught. Afterward, they spent the evening around a roaring campfire, telling jokes and sharing stories. This proved to be a fascinating trip through nostalgia for Sara and her children. The connections between everyone drove Mary crazy with excitement and wonder, and it filled Ben with fascination. The conversations were emotional for Sara at times, reliving moments of her life with Jacob, but it proved to be cathartic for her. While it may have appeared awkward for Sara to speak of Jacob in such terms in front of Trevor, he remained engaged and supportive of her throughout the conversation. Mary and Ben listened intently, at times shedding tears with their mother. The others listened in amazement at the near impossible set of coincidental circumstances coming together with so much at stake, a small world indeed. These were stories Sara either avoided or barely skimmed over with anyone, but now much of it was being brought out into the open.

Evan stood up with a pronouncement of the importance of what was being revealed on this night, convinced it was a matter of life and death for everyone in their group. For Evan, being reunited with Eugene, the little boy he saved all those years ago, was a sign of a parallel congruence appropriately arriving in this moment in time. He insisted everyone around that fire was meant to be there and needed to watch out for one another. Falling into a lull of complacency could prove fatal for any one of them.

No one gave a look of simply tolerating Evan, nor did they think his perception of the situation was off. They all looked on and listened as though they were receiving instructions on how to make land from a sinking ship. Individually, they all realized the gravity of what had happened. What could be coming next was more a probability than a possibility. Evan found himself unable to settle his emotions. The pain from losing his brother was still raw. With the recent spate of attacks on his family and friends, Evan's baser instincts made him want revenge, but common sense prevailed. And with that logic came a need for prudence that everyone around that fire needed to be a part of.

PART 3

"Things have been awfully quiet lately. Too quiet," Evan said, resuming the conversation. "I'm glad you're around, Eugene. For several reasons, not just as a bodyguard to Mary. Not that Mary needs one. It's just nice you're around." Evan lowered his head momentarily. "I just want to make sure everyone is aware and prepared, that's all," Evan said, turning his attention to Ben. "If you end up face to face with this guy, Ben, walk or run away. I know that goes against everything you are, but this is beyond a back-alley scrap. But if it happens that you're forced to protect yourself or the girls, I just know how you would react. You can beat him senseless, but don't kill him!"

Eugene looked on with an odd reaction as Evan spoke, wondering why or how Ben would kill a person, not being filled in on that detail yet.

"You can even stomp him to the point of being a vegetable and break his bones. You can even leave him so he has to have his meals through a straw for the rest of his life. But you can't kill him!" Evan exclaimed, louder than expected.

Sara finally spoke up. "Okay, Evan. I think that's enough. Ben understands what he can and can't do," Sara said, coming to Ben's defence and putting an end to the shock and awe.

"Sorry, Sara, I get a little excited about this stuff. Just make sure that under no circumstances … well, you got it. Right?" Evan asked, looking Ben in the eye.

"Right. I got it," Ben said respectfully. "But the same applies to you, right?" That statement caught Evan off guard.

"Yes, Ben. It applies to me, too," Evan responded, slowly backing up and sitting in his chair.

Evan took the opportunity to tell Ben about his first experience hunting. He told them that when he was young, he shot a deer but had only wounded it. By hunter's rules, a person ethically had to track it and end its suffering. When Evan found the deer lying on its side, taking its last breaths, he brought the deer back to life. He intentionally missed every shot he took after that.

Ben shared his first encounter with his gift as a child. He spoke about visiting a friend who lived on one of the neighbouring farms outside of Clarington. The farmer sold farm fresh eggs and free-range chickens. No one knew where this dog had come from, but this shabby-looking black lab was constantly coming onto the property and killing the farmer's chickens. On the day Ben was there, the farmer shot the dog and dragged it to a drainage ditch and left it there. For a ten-year-old kid, this was traumatic for Ben, but the action he took next was almost pre-programmed. Ben healed the dog. Oddly, it never returned to the farm for another chicken dinner. Evan and Ben's bond only increased after sharing their stories.

The following Saturday, Carol and Sara were headed out for a much needed day of pampering to be followed by an overnight stay at a spa. The spa was located at one of the developments Sara was designing in The Narrows. Trevor was still working for the developer of the site and had arranged for the day and night of luxury. He knew the women could use some time to try and get their minds off everything.

With Ben as his handy assistant, Evan used the time to get caught up on a long list of duties he found himself behind on, so Carol had no need to worry about him. Trevor was clear to Sara there was no need to keep checking in with him and her kids as he was spending the night with them at her house. It would give him time to develop a more personal relationship with Mary and Ben. He assured Sara all was fine, and they would talk the following morning.

As Carol and Sara neared The Narrows, the conversation lulled. Carol turned to look at Sara. "Are you getting a bad feeling at all?"

"Lately, too often, but not enough to stop us from going. Let's just get inside and let the pampering begin. They can massage the bad vibes away. I'm not giving this up," Sara said with a giggle, and Carol was quick to agree.

45

Rude Awakening

PART 1

Sunday

The time was about to roll past five o'clock on Sunday morning when Evan was startled awake by Carol's ringtone on his phone indicating she sent a text message. The room was dark and quiet. The lit phone screen on the dresser provided the only illumination to guide him to it. Half asleep, he fumbled the phone several times before it finally fell into his hands. He poked the screen a few times with his thick, calloused digits, finally opening the message from Carol.

{*Sorry Evan, but the girls won't be making it home. Ever.*}

Evan flew across the room to reach the switch for the bedroom light. He looked at the message again before typing.

{*What's going on Carol?*} Evan inquired, scared for Carol and shaking.

{*How's Ryan?*}

This was the only reply, and it was the last message to come through the phone. Evan's call went straight to voicemail, so he sent another text.

{*Let me speak to Carol. Put Carol on.*}

Evan didn't bother saying anything else, knowing full well it was Dylan. He threw his clothes on, sliding the phone into his back pocket. He stomped through the house at high speed, falling over into the wall while slipping his shoes on and then slamming the door behind him. Gravel crunched under his feet as he raced to his truck. Evan's first thought was to call Glen and have him contact the police to start a search, but at the last second, he cleared the phone, started the truck, and screamed out of the lane and onto the road to the O'Connells'. His body was shaking, weak with fear and pumped full with adrenaline. He almost drove the truck off the road while trying to call Trevor. He put the speaker on, and it dialed through, ringing several times.

"Evan?" Trevor was confused, awakened by Evan's call so early.

"He's got them, Trevor. The son of a bitch has Carol and Sara. I'm stopping by." Evan thought if the police cornered Dylan in a hostage situation, he wouldn't hesitate to kill everyone.

"How? Sara sent me a goodnight text last night. When was this possible?" Trevor asked, confused and quickly becoming scared. Dylan was smart enough to go through the girl's text messages and conclude they would at least say goodnight to their men.

"Yeah, I got one too, but it could've been him. He had to get them yesterday because the girls weren't getting up at five this morning. It's him. He told me in so many words," Evan growled out. He knew Dylan wanted him there for whatever game he was playing. What Evan was about to do was something he believed may not be in Trevor's character. It was decided that Trevor should stay with Mary and Ben for now. Once Evan had a location, Trevor would get a call to come. Then they would go after them together.

Evan's thoughts went back to Glen. After Ryan's memorial, Glen told him that if he needed any help locating this "Dylan guy," he would be all in. Evan knew his friend would do whatever it took to bring Dylan down. For now, however, having everyone flying off in different directions would prove futile.

It took Evan, Trevor, and Mary to convince Ben of this. Evan asked Ben to walk him out to the truck after their quick meeting was over. "Be ready when I call you, Ben. Okay?" Evan said, holding Ben by his shoulders and looking him in the eye.

"I'll be ready. But why don't you want me with you now? What if—"

Evan cut Ben off. "We have no idea what this asshole has planned. And one of his flunkies might try to come here for you and Mary, so they might need your help. Until we know something, the three of you keep watch. I mean it, Ben. Keep your head on a swivel and watch out for each other. Don't forget what we talked about. Don't try and take any of these guys on. Trevor has one of my rifles in the house. Don't use it. It's for him. Are we understood, Ben?" Evan couldn't have been firmer in his instruction to Ben.

"Yes, sir," Ben said sincerely.

"You know what can happen. And I can't have any one of you hurt. Not again! Not again." Evan choked out the words then gave Ben a gentle shake.

Evan left to take Glen up on his offer. And even though Glen wasn't hesitating to go, he felt it important enough to ask Evan to keep an eye out for his grandson, Greg, in their travels. "He was at a party at a campsite and probably just stayed an extra night, but if you see him, tell him to get his ass home before his father has a heart attack," Glen said to Evan over the phone. It was agreed, eyes wide open for each and all.

PART 2

Their plan was for Glen to locate Rick Jackson and keep tabs on him. During Ryan's murder investigation, which was still active, Evan also learned of Dylan's association with Lenny Bonacorso who recently came under investigation for dealing. Just beyond Lenny's house is a deep ravine that cuts across before the street resumes on the other side. It was a well-maintained street with the ravine acting as its dead end. It was a somewhat isolated place. The house was a small bungalow built in the sixties, with a detached garage. It had white horizontal aluminum siding with green trims, but it was in rough shape, with a poorly maintained yard.

It was approaching seven a.m. and Evan had parked on the opposite side of the street minutes before Lenny returned home with two large coffees in hand. Evan couldn't know if Lenny actually had information that would help him, but his instincts drove him there.

Dylan had quickly turned Lenny into an underling with significant amounts of cash. Lenny had just returned from his dealer in Calgary, picking up his supplies the day before and spending the night. It finally dawned on Evan that this was the same red Ford pickup he'd seen Dylan either driving or being picked up with. The light became brighter now. Evan recalled Babich in Vancouver mentioning Ryan being picked up in the same truck. Evan was painfully aware that the current situation only affirmed how well Dylan kept him in the dark. He realized that Dylan would have to have gone to Vancouver to seek Ryan out in order to do what he did, with the only outcome hurting Evan. It just happened sooner than Dylan planned on. All of this angered Evan that much more.

The knot in Evan's stomach twisted with what he was experiencing in this moment. He planned on going straight away to try and catch Lenny off guard before he got comfortable in his routine. The second coffee Lenny was carrying bothered Evan, and he wondered if there was someone else inside. But he needed answers now.

Evan crawled his truck across the street and parked it half a car's length from Lenny's driveway. He had just stepped out of his truck when a massive explosion blew three-quarters of the gable-end wall off Lenny's house. The wall landed on top of the pickup parked in the driveway with a loud crash. Pieces of the house and shards of glass from the front windows flew clear across the street at such velocity they embedded in some of the maple trees in the empty lot. The explosion generated enough concussive power to knock Evan back like he was a rag doll. It took the air out of him and his legs were a little rubbery, but he slowly gathered himself. Evan ignored the onlookers in the distance and walked through what had been the front entrance. He needed to find any information that could point him toward Dylan, no matter what he had to do or who he had to go through to get it. As spectacular as the explosion was, Evan wouldn't let it slow him down.

The front door of the house was on the lawn as Evan stepped over the debris to get inside. The gas stove was lying on top of the blown-out wall sitting on the collapsed roof of the truck. The intentionally disconnected gas line had been filling the place with natural gas. Standing inside the kitchen, Evan looked down to see a small flame still coming out of the gas line. When he did so, he caught sight of Lenny lying on the grass in the backyard. When Lenny came home, he walked in the back door as he always had. He realized his mistake in the half-second it took for the spark of the three-way light switch to ignite the gas in the house. The pressure from the explosion blew him straight back from the back door and over the barbeque before landing in a pile on the ground. Pieces of wood and glass bored into him throughout his torso and face. The force of the explosion killed him instantly. The glass that had penetrated his face and head left him disfigured, an insult to injury. Evan flipped his body over and pulled his phone from one of his pockets. Emotionless, he wiped it off and walked back to his truck to see if it could help him locate the girls. It had Rick's phone number in it, which would prove useful.

46

Shock and Awe

Saturday

Ben's school friend, Greg Simon, had bought and made roadworthy an old '79 GMC Blazer, which he intended to restore to its original glory. For now, he enjoyed driving it through the mountains, testing its four-wheel drive capabilities, and generally having fun. It was the Saturday morning before Evan's rude awakening when Greg was heading home from an overnight camping trip that was nothing more than party around a bonfire. His day was planned out for him, thanks to his father's list of duties to be accomplished around the house. He didn't whine too much as one of the few showers they had this summer finally arrived, dampening the campout/party. Heading east on Highway 2, Greg was approaching the dirt road to the logger's camp when he saw a Jeep Cherokee turn in. He was confident he caught site of Carol Quinn and was sure the woman next to her was Ben's mother. He thought Carol looked nervous, and he didn't recognize the two men in the front seat, nor had he seen that vehicle around before. It bothered him enough that in less than half-mile away, he turned around and headed back toward the dirt road to take a closer look.

Greg had learned much over the years from his grandfather, a retired cop with over thirty years of service. Greg planned on joining the army after high school, and he was considering the possibility of becoming a cop after military service. Greg knew his fear was making him move far too slow to catch sight of the car moving down the dirt road, but he had no idea what was waiting ahead. The road was almost completely overgrown. He looked at the tree branches and bushes, barely cut back, as he crawled his truck forward. Finally, he saw the rooftops of the two old barrack-style cabins the loggers once used. His nerves were frayed now, and he could feel something was wrong. He was starting to feel the pins and needles of uncertainty, so he sat still, momentarily questioning himself. There was an overgrown trail, only partially cut out, to the right, but it clearly hadn't been used in years. Greg thought it good enough to keep his truck there and walk up closer to the buildings to see what was going on. The closer he moved toward the cabins, the shakier he became, fighting his instinct to simply run for help. He decided he had to know first. If he made a call to someone about this, it could very well backfire, getting him in trouble for sticking his nose in where it didn't belong. Especially if it was a rendezvous that two couples were having. But he wanted to know.

Greg crawled up the berm adjacent to the river that flowed between the dirt road and the cabins and looked over. That very second, he was aghast as he watched a man's head come off in one fell swoop from the violent swing of Dylan's broadaxe. Joe Miller didn't see it coming. Watching Joe's body fall with blood spraying from his headless neck was too much for Greg to absorb. Frozen with his hand covering his mouth, he watched as Dylan calmly stood over Joe with a blank look on his face and pushed Joe's body over with his foot. Dylan appeared to be annoyed that he had been sprayed and covered with Joe's blood. He picked up the rifle Joe had been holding in one hand and looked at the blade of his axe in the other. He shrugged his shoulders and headed back into the cabin.

Keeping his hand to his mouth, Greg struggled to muzzle his gasp. Just then Dylan raised his head to look in his direction as he ducked below the rise of the berm, completely terrified. His hand was still over his mouth and his eyes widened in shock and fear wondering if he'd been spotted. His legs felt like rubber from weakness, but his sprint quickly turned into a full-out run back to his truck.

Once he was in his truck, the panic increased dramatically as he fumbled his keys around in sweaty hands. He mistakenly put the four-wheel drive in low gear after he started the Blazer. With all that torque, the truck leapt forward as he hammered his foot down on the gas pedal, pulling the truck to the edge of the riverbank. Greg tried to regain control but pulled too hard on the steering wheel and felt the back of the truck slide laterally and begin to shift down the bank. Because of the rain, both wheels on the passenger side of the truck easily slid off the wild grass and slipped farther down the steep riverbank. Physics took over and the truck rolled completely over the edge. Understandably, he forgot his seatbelt under this kind of pressure.

With the truck lying on its side at the bottom of the shallow river, Greg shook his head to regain his focus and composure. He reached up and grabbed the passenger side door and started pulling himself up. Just as he had his hips out of the opening, he sat on the side of the truck, taking a calming breath. As he was about to climb down the side of the truck, he looked up and saw the blood-soaked maniac with a rifle in hand. The last thing Greg ever saw was the evil smile on Dylan Matthews's face.

47

Expensive Lure

PART 1

Dylan made his way back and walked inside the log cabin, slammed the door and turned to Carol and Sara with that same nauseating smile. The girls were facing each other, handcuffed to a ring bolted on the wall between two army-style cots. He continued to stare them down, his face frozen with that frightening smile.

"Well ladies, Joe won't be here for the remainder of the festivities. His head wasn't in it. Bad joke, I know, but I couldn't help myself."

Dylan had that axe sharpened to the point he could shave with it. The women were horrified and sickened to see such an enormous amount of blood on Dylan's face and the beard of his broadaxe held in his equally blood-covered hands. His forearms up to his elbows looked like they were dipped in blood, along with the streaks and splatters on his shirt and pants. Joe had served his purpose, and Dylan viewed him as an annoying witness who had to go. Dylan was in his endgame now. But for the moment, he thought it would be fitting to picture killing Joe as a comparison to felling a tree. A sort of tribute to being in a logger's camp, and a salute to the many lumberjacks who came here before him. But Joe being as disagreeable as ever, fell backwards almost landing on Dylan's thighs, spraying him in copious amounts of his blood. Dylan was unable to drop Joe in the direction he wanted, unlike the professional lumberjacks who could fall a tree in whatever they pointed it. Joe's final insult to his partner in crime was little victory for the now deceased Mr. Miller.

Sunday

Chains hung from one of the horizontal ceiling timbers that ran from side to side parallel to the rafters above, as a ceiling joist. There were six old metal army cots with rolled up grey-and-blue-striped musty-smelling mattresses inside the rectangular-shaped room. The place resembled an army barracks. The old wood plank floor was smooth in the high traffic areas from years of dirt on the floor acting as sandpaper. Between a set of beds at the far end of the building, Carol and Sara were cuffed against the wall, sitting on cots facing each other. This was one of the few reprieves the girls received in the last twenty-four torturous hours of being strung up by their hands, off and on throughout the night. Dylan and Joe had fondled and abused the women to the point of terror-filled screams. Each scream was responded to with a long, thin cut along the small of their backs. The screaming stopped, and Dylan couldn't decide whether it angered or impressed him that the women remained defiant in the face of torture and the threat of death, which was surely coming. When and how remained to be determined.

Carol silently prayed for Evan to come and save her while Sara wished for Ben and Mary not to feel her distress and hoped they wouldn't come. She thought of her children's safety as the priority over her surviving this maniac. The only saving grace was that Dylan wouldn't allow Joe to rape and murder Carol until he was done with his fun. But being a whining and annoying prick hastened Joe's death. Deep inside, Sara felt that she and Carol would prevail somehow; it was just a matter of time. She believed this in her heart. If she could survive Jonathon Vargas, she could survive his punk kid.

Earlier when she woke in the back of the Cherokee, coming out of a heavy dose of chloroform, Sara's first thought was about Mary. She recalled Mary's comment about something being wrong with

Dylan the day they saw him working at Quinn's. *You couldn't have been any more accurate than that sweetie. I can't believe I let this sneak up on me, on us. Damn it to hell!* Sara thought to herself, furious over the reality of the moment, furious when she was handcuffed from behind, hooked into the base of the Cherokee's seatbelt.

"Just sit up like good girls taking a ride on a lovely Saturday morning. That is unless you want everyone to die," Dylan said to Carol and Sara, showing them his insanely long hunting knife. She was unable to release her rage at being caught, and she was groggy from the chloroform — it was a horrible feeling. Once Carol saw the knife, she froze in fear.

Even after the night of torture, Sara quickly shared a silver lining with Carol. "Well, at least Joe won't be doing what he said he was going to do," whispered Sara. Looking at Carol, she shrugged her shoulders and made a slight smile. "Hey. We're going to get out of this. Just hang in there," Sara said.

There was a crack of light through an old burlap sack being used to cover one of the windows in the cabin. Sara rested her head against her arm for a moment and thought she could see a figure outside through that sliver of light. She wiped her forehead across her arm a couple times to stop the sweat from dripping into her eyes, hoping to stay focused. Her stomach was rumbling from hunger, and her low blood sugar was blurring her vision. She kept looking, squinting to make out who it was. A warm feeling rushed through her body, something intimately familiar, telling her who it was. Dylan caught her efforts to look out through the crack. He sauntered over to her, dragging his hunting knife across the sandstone.

"What are you looking at?! Do you see your saviour out there? Is Jacob going to magically appear and put a bullet through my head like he did to my father?" Dylan tilted his head and leaned so close to Sara she was repulsed and nauseated by his disgusting breath. "Well, Sara? What do you have to say?" he asked, attempting to move a strand of her red hair from her face. Sara jerked back and looked at him, showing her revulsion.

"Don't touch me, you bastard! And Jacob didn't shoot your father in the head," Sara said, twisting her body to keep herself as far away from him as she could.

She struggled in a futile effort to release herself. Dylan looked at her and smiled, shaking his head. As he made a slight movement away from her, he hauled off and backhanded her, splitting her lip. But Sara didn't make a sound, not a cry or whimper. In a challenging posture, she looked him in the eye and became belligerent again, turning back and glaring at him. Her pupils grew black with rage.

"I got to hand it to you, you're as hard as the old man said in his journals. Oh, and I'm not a bastard, I have a father. But I can see why the old man had a thing for you, though." Dylan kept his twisted smile pointed at Sara, and she held her look of disgust.

PART 2

"Fuck!" Sara screamed with an exhale of exhaustion, shaking her head. "Jacob didn't shoot him in the head, he put four bullets through his chest. You fucking little imp of a prick!"

"Sara!" Carol pleaded with her to stop antagonizing, but it didn't work.

"And he wasn't your father, he was a sperm donor and a murdering rapist. He was a sick, evil piece of shit! And I can see the apple didn't fall far from the tree." Sara couldn't seem to control her anger at this point, and the words continued to come out of her mouth. She took a gamble that by keeping Dylan off kilter for as long as possible, it would keep him distracted from his final goal. She concluded that by not raping either of them yet, he would try to take them individually, from performance insecurities. And that's when she would battle him to the death, no matter the result. She couldn't tolerate any more of this man.

Dylan walked back over raising his hand to hit her again, but this time it was Carol to yell out, swinging her legs in an effort to block him from reaching Sara.

"Leave her alone! What's the matter with you?" she asked, like a mother scolding her child. It seemed to throw him off momentarily. "Why are you doing this?" Carol was more susceptible to giving away her naivety and the emotions that came with it, more so than Sara. But she was still boldly protective of her best friend. Dylan looked at her, then to Sara.

"Pff. You people will never learn," he said, turning around and walking away.

Sara's anger was still rising. She wasn't going to stop. "You killed my friend, Shelley Randall, too, didn't you?"

Dylan turned back to Sara, but said nothing, keeping a disturbing smile on his face.

"It's a little late for denials now, don't you think?" Sara scoffed.

"Oh, I'm sure you've known the answer to that for a long time now, Sara. You and your friend, that fat asshole Kelley. I'm sorry I didn't smoke that prick, but killing a cop brings too much attention," Dylan said, shuffling through a cardboard box that held some of his possessions. He pulled out another hunting knife, not much smaller than the first, and took it out of its sheath briefly admiring it while looking back at Carol.

"Remember that feeling, Carol?" he asked, enjoying seeing her frozen in terror. He slid the blade slowly through his fingers. "Oh, joy!" he said, licking his lips and enjoying the moment.

"You killed Diane and Andrea too. Didn't you? You weren't in Vancouver the whole time. But you got to finish your vacation and stop in long enough to kill your mother. We know what you've been doing." Sara was pushing the envelope, to Carol's dismay.

"Well, look at that. Give the little detective a gold star. And before we're done here, you're both going to have an experience similar to that. But we have time before that comes. Besides, we have to wait for the family to come. I mean, sooner or later, they'll figure out something. I did leave Evan a couple of clues. I'll invite them if I have to," Dylan said as a matter of fact, still rummaging through the box. Carol feared the worse as Dylan came back over to them, having attached the sheath for the knife to his belt.

He took the girls one at a time, still handcuffed, and stood them on two old rickety, wooden chairs with woven twine for the seats. Using a rope, he tied their hands above their heads, looping the rope through the chains above, and tying it off to a double-sided cleat fastened to the wall.

"There! Now, girls, it's up to you whether you rip your shoulders from their sockets or not. So, I suggest you don't fuck around. I'll be doing that with both of you later … the fucking around part." The girls considered Dylan's laugh as repugnant as it was ominous.

In preparation for the coming events, Dylan had taken the time to acquire explosives from an odd source. An acquaintance of Brian Gundry's, Dominic Becker, had worked off and on in the mountains with avalanche control and blowing rocks too large to be moved for road construction or landslides. Being in Gundry's circle, it wasn't a surprise Dominic had his own addiction problems. Of course, being stuck up in the mountains on jobs that lasted for long periods of time had its consequences. And that was the opportunity Dylan seized upon. Dylan educated himself well, between what he picked up from Dominic and the ridiculous amount of information accessible online, in order to set the charges under the cabin. He placed them nearest the four corners so he wouldn't have an issue getting his signal through to blow it remotely. It was his worst-case scenario contingency plan. If everything went sideways and he had to run, he would blow the cabin, and if he got lucky, take someone else out at the same time. However, as Dylan was experiencing today, plans have a will of their own to change in unexpected directions.

PART 3

Believing the girls secured and dissuaded from attempting an escape, Dylan left them to go outside. Before taking a seat, he took out his phone and a remote with an antenna to make sure they were in working order. He used the remote to activate the receiver for the bombs placed around the cabin. For a trigger, all he had to do was make a phone call to the cellphone wired to the interconnected explosives and the objective was complete. Confident enough, he sat on a chair propped against the wall of the other smaller cabin that was used as storage and to salt meats, with one part smokehouse at the rear. He leaned his head back against the wall and attempted to rest, confident the girls would be injured and scream out if they tried to wriggle free. He was tired from all the activities in preparation and execution for abducting Carol and Sara.

For everything to work out, he had to lure out Evan and the O'Connells. Dylan set up camp at the abandoned logger's cabin before he killed Vic and took his job at Quinn's. He hadn't seen a sign of anyone remotely close to the camp, so he was convinced he had been safe up to now and for however long it took for Evan to arrive. He knew the police wouldn't fill out a missing person report for twenty-four to forty-eight hours after a disappearance was first reported. But Dylan believed he knew Evan well enough to expect him without the police. He believed that would be his advantage.

Dylan's consideration of Evan as docile was a major underestimation of the man. However, he had seen a different side of Evan the day he was fired. He also underestimated Carol, viewing her as a scared, timid woman who would be easy to control. Back inside the cabin, Carol looked at Sara with her eyes raised, expressing a look of optimism. "He's not very good at this."

"What do you mean?" Sara asked, recoiling from any explanation. Carol tilted her head with a brief smile.

"Can you hear him? Can you see any shadows around the door or anything?" Carol asked nervously.

"No, Carol. Why? What are you trying to do?" Before Carol said another word, she partially dislocated her thumb at the wrist and slid her sweaty hand out of the cuff.

"Listen for him," Carol said while she held the other cuff and repeated the same maneuver, taking advantage of the same deformity of her basil joint.

"Jesus, Carol. He could be right outside the door. Get out of here. Now!" Sara ordered her friend in a strained whisper.

Carol spun around to scan the room, then gently crept across the floor. In mid-stride she froze thinking she heard something outside the door. She twisted her torso to look back to Sara with her eyes almost popping out. Her neck muscles strained, veins bulging and jaw muscles flexed from biting down. Terrified Dylan might come through the door sooner than expected, she didn't know what to do. The rifle was at Dylan's side, and he placed the axe outside the cabin door, just in case. Carol realized there was nothing she could hit him with if he were to come back at that moment. She was shaky, weak, her growling, empty stomach hurt, and she felt nauseated from fear.

Sara again called for her to leave. "Carol, please go. It's just an old wooden frame with a screen," Sara nodded in the direction of the rear window. "Pull the burlap off, pop the screen, and get out of here now before he comes back. Jesus, Carol. Go! Go and get help, it's our best chance."

Sara could see the shape Carol was in, clearly too overwhelmed in the moment to act. Worried Carol would freeze in fear, Sara nodded to the window one last time. Carol reluctantly floated across the floor.

"I can't see anything to use to unlock your cuffs."

"God damn it, Carol! If you don't leave, we're both dead. Go now!" Sara said, exhausting her breath and strength, emotionally stirred from yelling at Carol in a restrained voice. Carol finally realized she might be out of time, and possibly out of luck, if she lingered another second. Tears began to stream down her face as she made her way past Sara to the window, desperately wanting to help her friend. She tore the materials off the window frame and slid her body out, ever so delicately and silently.

Sara almost fell off the chair, weak with fear, anxiety, and relief that Carol got away. She quickly gained control and a renewed strength held her up, straight and steady. Ten minutes had passed before Dylan came back into the cabin. The second he saw the window open, and Carol gone, he turned around with rifle in hand

and jumped out the door. He cleared the three rotting steps and hit the ground running. Sara prayed Carol had gone far enough to be out of sight and not just hiding nearby. She screamed at the top of her lungs for her to run. Moments after she screamed, a shot from the rifle rang out. Shortly after the echo of the shot faded, Dylan calmly walked back inside the cabin. He leaned his precious axe and rifle against the wall and remained silent, continuing to dig through his box. He pulled out a stapler and affixed the burlap back over the window, saying nothing.

48

Interrogation

PART 1

After Evan left the Bonacorso house, he received a call from Glen. He had parked down the street from Rick Jackson's residence and saw that he was home. In short time, Evan parked ahead of Glen's truck.

"Any sight of Greg on your way through town by chance?" Glen asked Evan, with an undeniable look of concern for everything that was happening.

"I'm sorry, Glen. No, nothing. Hey, Glen. Look, stay here for now. If you hear any screams … well, a lot of screams, then come in."

"You're kidding, right?" Glen asked, indignant Evan wouldn't have him by his side.

"If anything goes wrong, it will only be me they haul in. And if that's the case, you can keep going and find the girls. If we're both in jail—"

Glen cut Evan off, acknowledging and agreeing with the logic. Evan quietly approached a row of overgrown red maples and holly bushes that lined the side of the dirt lane that was Rick Jackson's driveway. His property was at the south end of town, down the road from the original wood-clad train station. It had been abandoned for a new station in the nicer west end back in the '70s. The rest of the block had two houses, one empty and one occupied, at the far end of the block. Evan thought it appropriate to call the place the wrong side of the tracks.

Evan wasn't concerned with making any noise other than his approach to the house that would give Rick a chance to run. At first Evan thought of calling him from Lenny's phone, which would provide a good distraction while he entered his house. The small wooden porch was dilapidated and falling apart just like the rest of the white cedar–sided bungalow. The cottage roof was showing its age with the interlocking asphalt shingles curling up around the edges, pieces missing, and a lot of moss all over it. Evan decided to forego any distractions, so he ran up and onto the porch, kicking the door in and catching Rick by surprise. His face was a mix of shock and anger with his drugs and paraphernalia in front of him all over his coffee table. The second Rick realized it was Evan, he stammered a few words and froze, remaining motionless for several seconds before he could get something out.

"Hey! I have no idea—"

Evan was on Rick before he could finish his sentence. He picked him up with one hand clasped like a vise around his throat. With his other hand, he grabbed Rick's arm and threw him across the room. He landed in a pile on the filthy carpeted floor. Evan stomped over to Rick and hit him in the face with such energy that blood spattered up Evan's arm. Rick was knocked out and he dropped to the floor. Evan flipped him over like a fish on the beach and handcuffed his hands behind his back, tightly. As Rick came to, he began complaining of his sore wrists.

"Shut the fuck up, sit down, and stay put! I saw the police report in Ryan's investigation. So I know damn well you, Bonacorso, Miller, and the Gundrys all hang together. Don't waste my fucking time trying to deny it!" Evan said, after throwing Rick into his filthy living room chair.

Evan remained silent, slowing his breathing down. He squinted his eyes, leering at Rick. "My wife was attacked and is only alive because of a friend being there. Did you have anything to do with that?" Evan asked, becoming heated again, not waiting for an answer. "Look, I'm gonna run this by you one time. And if you look at me sideways, making out like you don't know what the fuck I'm talking about, I'm just gonna put a bullet through your head. Then I'll just figure this out on my own because I really don't like looking at you. Got it?"

A nod came back in acknowledgement instead of words through his bloody mouth.

Evan pulled his Glock semi-automatic handgun from the back of his jeans, slid back the top rail, and loaded the first bullet into the chamber. He noticed Rick looking beyond him to the closet by the front door where a sawed-off shotgun leaned upright on the inside corner of the wall.

"Holy fuck, I missed that! Good thing I'm not a cop anymore, eh? Okay … this works," Evan said, picking up the shotgun and checking to see if it was loaded. "Now, you fucking worthless piece of shit, be very fucking careful how you answer these questions because they're only coming once. Where is he? Where did he take my wife and friend? And how many are with him?" Evan asked, sliding his Glock into the waistband, grabbing the shotgun, and cocking it. "This is a sweet little unit. I bet this will take your face clean off your head, leaving a real nice Jackson Pollock on the wall behind you. See the connection there? Jackson … you're a Jackson. Shall we test that theory? Where the fuck is my wife?"

Startled by Evan's screaming voice and demeanour, Rick jumped up in the chair.

"You know what? I don't like messes," Evan said, setting the gun on the floor next to him and pulling his pistol out from his waistband. "This is much cleaner."

Evan took a step toward Rick, showing him the insignia on the side of the gun before smashing it across his face. Rick's head snapped to the side, blood dripping from his eye and down his cheek. Evan watched his feeble attempt at defiance quickly slide down off his face after the second backhand with the butt of his gun slammed into his teeth.

"Jesus Christ, man! You knocked my fucking teeth out."

"Wrong answer," Evan said, putting the nozzle up against his forehead and pulling the hammer back.

"He's at the old logger's camp off Highway 2, outside of town, a couple miles past Pell's Landing. Joe Miller's with him and maybe Lenny Bonacorso. I don't know about Gundry, I haven't seen him."

"Oh, Bonacorso isn't with him. He's dead. Like not even an hour ago. I'm guessing Dylan is cleaning up loose ends before skipping town. You should have better friends, Rick," Evan said, smashing the gun against the side of Rick's head, knocking him out again.

Evan flopped Rick over onto the floor and took the cuffs off. He threw Rick's phone on the floor and destroyed it with several stomps from the heel of his boot before walking out the door.

PART 2

Stepping outside of Jackson's house, Evan nodded to Glen, holding up his finger indicating to him to wait. Evan emptied the shotgun of its shells and smashed its handle several times against one of the maple trees in the lane rendering it useless before throwing it into the long grass next to the house.

Evan walked to Glen's truck and told him what happened inside and what he had learned. After informing Glen where they were going, Evan got into his truck and paused for a moment. He watched the raindrops hitting his windshield as he composed himself, trying to digest the moment. There was no joy for Evan in what he had to do. Just after he started his truck, he heard the familiar click of a handgun being cocked just behind his left ear. In a millisecond after, a blast from a gun deafened Evan. Blood sprayed all over the side of the truck, his face and arm, and covered the phone he was holding. Evan thrust forward in his seat. He pulled himself toward the centre console and turned to look out the driver's side window.

He saw Glen standing there with his gun in his hand. On the ground next to Evan's truck, Rick Jackson lay face down. Just in front of Rick was his own five round, forty-five calibre revolver lying next to his face, which had a gaping, bloody hole in it. Evan was disoriented, a high-pitched ring was stinging his ears. Glen stepped closer to the driver's side of Evan's truck, holding his gun at his side, a small vapour trail escaping from the end of the barrel.

"Get out of here, Evan."

"What?" Evan was in shock. His ears were still ringing, making it difficult to hear.

"Hang on." Glen reached in the back door of Evan's truck and grabbed an old t-shirt and wiped the blood from Evan's driver's side door. "The stupid son of a bitch snuck up on you, walking right past my truck. What a complete idiot. Could he not see me there? And if I said, 'Hey, what are you doing?' he would have turned and shot me. I'm sorry, Evan, I had to."

Glen looked down to Rick's body and nodded in the direction Evan's truck was pointed, repeating himself. "Get out of here, Evan. Now! Go get them. I'm more help to you here. I'll clean this up," Glen said, putting his gun in the rear of his waistband. He pointed down the road, giving Evan a look of assurance in a moment beyond reason. No one in the area stirred. Possibly nobody was home, or they were too far away to hear. Evan started his truck and headed west through town toward Highway 2.

Glen looked around again to see if anyone was outside. He grabbed Rick by his ankles and dragged his body past an old oak tree, into the tall grass and weeds of the undeveloped property opposite his house. Once Rick's body was far enough in, Glen dropped his legs.

"Good enough for a piece of trash like you," Glen said, dragging his palms along the butt of his jeans in disgust, wiping away what remained of Rick Jackson. This was self-defence as far as Glen saw it. Except he was defending Evan. It was the same thing to him. And at this point Glen couldn't care less what the police might say or do to him. He knew the system.

Driving out of town Evan pulled out a handful of napkins from the centre console and with a bottle of water, he wiped as much of the blood off his cheek and arm as he could. He was vibrating, struggling with what just happened. He then made his call to the O'Connells, reaching a panicky sounding Ben. Evan directed him to tell Trevor to come with his rifle.

"I'll see you on the highway by the old logger's road," Ben said.

"No, Ben. I don't want you up there," Evan weakly pleaded, still shaken that he almost died minutes ago.

"There's no way I'm not going out to look for my mom, Evan. I won't do what we talked about. I'm heading up there now with Trevor and Mary."

Evan knew objecting was futile. He just hoped Trevor was the kind of man who would do everything in his power to ensure Ben and Mary remained safe.

49

Gambit

About thirty yards east from the entrance of the logger's road, Evan ran across Dylan's jeep. The conspicuous placement of this still-mint-condition Jeep — pointed in the direction of the cabin — was a note for Evan to come and play. Not entirely odd for Dylan, a builder's grade, clear plastic sheet lined the trunk area, sending another message. It wasn't surprising to discover the doors unlocked, a grey and black notebook conspicuously located on the floor behind the driver's side seat in an otherwise spotless interior. This was the final indication the car was Dylan's, and what was inside those pages was specifically for Evan. When he opened the notebook, he was shocked and shaken to see paper photos of Carol and Sara pasted to the pages with times and locations captioned above or below each photo. The discovery sent chills through Evan. A few more pages in, Evan found older crime scene photos of different women who were murdered in the most vile and horrific ways. Dylan added them for affect.

Evan picked up the notebook and tore a few pages out, lightly balling them up in his hand. He curled up the book into the shape of a cone and stuffed its narrow end into the top receptacle of the gas tank like a funnel. He placed some of the scrunched-up pages into the cone, lit them on fire and swiftly walked away. Ten seconds hadn't passed before the Cherokee's gas tank exploded, lifting the car five feet into the air. The noise of the explosion echoed throughout the forest as the fireball rose nearly twenty feet above. This was Evan's message to Dylan, letting him know how far he was willing to go to end this. He wanted to let him know that he was now in this game and ready to play for keeps.

The cabin was at a higher elevation than where Dylan left the jeep. Hearing the explosion, Dylan grabbed his binoculars and ran out of the cabin hoping to spot Evan. He had to admit to himself he didn't expect Evan to blow up his car. He could see the black smoke from what he assumed was his burning jeep. Instead of being angry, he scanned the area with a smile on his face. Although earlier than expected, Dylan received Evan's message loud and clear. He began to calculate his next play.

But he was outside too long. When he returned to the cabin, he was stunned to find Sara gone, just like Carol. With both women gone, he panicked in his anger. He ran to look north behind the cabin, and then to the east. He had to give up for the moment. He realized he had little time to load up his pack, grab his weapons, and head out to find her. And hopefully Carol. He ran out of time. Simply killing them wasn't good enough. They had to suffer, and he wanted an audience. If he couldn't find Sara or Carol, he would move into the battle with Evan, and hopefully Ben. Just before entering the woods, Dylan activated the explosives receiver and his phone was close at hand. His worst-case scenario was coming uncomfortably close to being put into play. If nothing else, it would serve as a good distraction should he be in an untenable position.

Dylan didn't know it wasn't just Evan coming for him. Rick Jackson wasn't going to be able to provide the transportation back up Dylan thought would be there if he needed it. He could certainly use it now. By the time Dylan left the cabin, he was frustrated that there was no response from Rick. This was a day Dylan desperately wanted to get right, so he needed to clean up loose ends, and that would include Rick after his usefulness was over.

During a late-night visit with Lenny Bonacorso a while back, Dylan discovered an unmarked car watching his house. Knowing Lenny's house was high risk to be raided for drugs, Dylan knew Lenny would sell him out in a second to save his own skin.

The one thing Dylan didn't expect was Evan blowing up his car, thinking he would see the logger's road and start searching. For Dylan, it was Brian Gundry who was the wild card. Knowing he might have to rely on him for help now, Dylan wasn't sure if Gundry would be a worthy assistant or an adversary. Dylan considered himself in the master class of murderers, but he had doubts when it came to taking out Brian. He knew his aim would have to be true. But for now, he had to concentrate on the task at hand and quickly ready himself for the hunt or battle that was unfolding in real time. What was a terrorizing event for the Quinns and O'Connells was a joyful day of hunting as far as Dylan was concerned. He was his father's son.

50

Escape

Earlier in the morning, Dylan covered the cabin window that Carol escaped through, but he didn't bother fixing the screen on the exterior. This told Sara he didn't plan on staying long enough to be concerned about her escaping, which in turn was disconcerting to say the least. After everything else Sara had been put through, she prayed for escape or for Dylan's death. After getting slapped around by Dylan earlier that morning when he wanted to know how Carol escaped her cuffs, she reached her end.

Sara's white top was barely hanging on at the back after he cut and ripped it open to expose her skin, cutting her bra away and dragging his hunting knife up and down her spine. He occasionally applied enough pressure to break the skin. He showed her the knife with her blood on it. Inside, Sara was going berserk, desperately wanting to scream out every expletive she could summon. It took great courage to remain quiet and not give him the satisfaction.

Before Carol escaped, she tried her best not to provoke him any further than she already had. The small cuts were painful. When they filled with her salty sweat, they burned and itched all the more. *God help me through this. Don't let this maniac anywhere near my children,* she thought just before passing out. It wasn't a surprise after so many hours of pain and exhaustion from the totality of physical and psychological torture. The constant wondering of when he would sexually assault her and ultimately kill her kept her on edge. So far his sexual assaults on her had been through touching, but they were still repulsive and demoralizing. Sara kept the strength to put it out of her mind, knowing what she must do. Small mercies came when she passed out. But unlike the black void that comes from being put under with anesthetic, horrible dreams still came, giving Sara little rest.

Precious seconds before going out, she had glanced one last time out the window where she had first seen Jacob through a small opening. Even at a distance, she was confident it was Jacob and his familiar look of serenity and gentle confidence. He didn't speak, he simply looked at her as if he knew she needed to shut down, if only for a short time.

Copying his father, Dylan was furiously writing in his journal, trying to document the details while he could. He didn't appear adept at what he was doing in his attempts to emulate his father. He was so easily distracted. Regardless, he kept writing, trying to sensationalize what were moments of humiliation and agony for the girls. At the same time, he flipped through his phone, looking at the many pictures he had taken of Sara and Carol and becoming aroused. Carol getting away started to wear on him.

She couldn't make it out of those woods. But if she managed to find her way to the highway or conservation area. No way! Couldn't happen. She was heading north, and no food or water for all this time. She's fucked! She's not going anywhere. Despite the back and forth in his mind, erring on the side of caution jumped front and centre. *Gotta get these entries in before I forget,* he thought, his head tilted over like a student writing a test.

Dylan wasn't your typical drug user, but over the last month he started using meth more frequently for the extra energy. But before long the delusions returned. He was remembering his father's teachings. He believed his father was praising him through auditory hallucinations. First on his list of instructions was to never trust everything to electronics. Writing his experiences down on paper allowed him to relive the moments. This was crucial. His instructions were meticulous in their detail. *What kits to bring with: Rape – minimal – lock pick, knife, nylon, and condom (maybe, – depending on mood). Don't forget to shave everywhere, bring a toque. Map out your area well, with several options in and out. Killing – Know how you want to do it long beforehand...* And on it went. Sickening details for different scenarios, who to pick, when, where, and how. His father even gave a point system for blonde, brunette, and redhead. The latter gave the most points because true redheads are harder to find. That was obvious from Vargas's obsession with Sara.

Engrossed in chronicling his handy work, Dylan paid no attention to Sara beginning to stir. She was relieved for what little mercy Dylan gave her by lowering her rope from the chains overhead to lay her down on the floor, so she wouldn't die on him before it was time.

PART 2

As Sara slowly regained consciousness and control of her faculties, she was overwhelmed with her senses lighting up to full strength. If she closed her eyes, she could see Mary and Ben standing together on the back deck at home. A brief rest, a few deep breaths, and again she closed her eyes to see the kids standing with a forest as their backdrop. The more she tried to push them away, the more they refused, standing tall and approaching her. The image became stronger as each minute passed. As Mary and Ben came closer into view, suddenly Trevor was there, with Evan and Eugene close behind. Standing at a fair distance back from everybody, Jacob came into sight, his appearance no different than it had ever been. What she was seeing gave her comfort that she would get through this. But something told her she wouldn't be seeing Jacob in this manner for much longer after this day. It was a sad feeling, but it made sense to her and gave her the energy to attempt an escape. She had been lowered to the floor, right next to one of the old cots. With Dylan sidetracked with his journal, Sara managed to pull off a bent piece of rusted wire hanging from the bottom of the cot.

God love you, Evan Quinn! I hope this works, Sara said to herself, thanking Evan for teaching the group how to get out of a pair of handcuffs if they had the right material. In this case, a rusty piece of heavy gauge wire off an old cot would suffice. Sara clutched that broken wire in her hand for all she was worth. She was wondering how she could possibly fight Dylan if she were free and he came in the room. She had next to no strength left. She was dehydrated and hungry, but she had a renewed sense of purpose after seeing her children so clearly in her thoughts. It was only adrenaline, and it wouldn't last for long if she had to struggle through Dylan to make it out that door alive.

Sara's thoughts were jumbled as she calculated the distance to determine if she could make it to the axe or the rifle before Dylan turned around from the picnic table to stop her. If she ended up in a struggle, would she have the strength to get away from his grasp? If she ended up with the axe in her hands, could she swing it? The axe leaned up against the wall on one side of the cabin door. The rifle was on the other side, closer to Dylan's back.

Sara's throat was dry, and her stomach was sore and spasming. Her body was vibrating from weakness, and her palms were sweaty. This was the moment. She believed that when he was finished writing in his book, he would turn his attention to her. The cot was partially blocking Dylan's view of her, so she began to move at a snail's pace to pull her hands partially under her chest. Click. One cuff was open. She began to shake even more, wondering if he heard the cuff release. The only distracting sounds in the room came from Dylan's police scanner, his feet scraping across the sandy floor, and an occasional page being flipped. Every movement he made either gave her cover to get free from the cuffs or terrified her, thinking he was coming for her. *He heard me. Oh, God, stay there. Stay there.* Sara was frantic, her senses heightened, fearing the worst.

She moved the piece of metal wire between her slippery fingertips, but it fell a couple of inches to the floor. Again she panicked, worried that her movement to pick it back up might catch his attention. Ever so gingerly, she picked the wire up between her fingernails to pull up onto the skin of her fingers when she heard what turned out to be Dylan's jeep explode.

The explosion penetrated the air and seemed to echo around the cabin. Click, the other cuff was released, covered by the noise. Dylan grabbed his rifle and launched himself out the door. Sara moved like a trained black-ops agent as she got up and raced to the window, knowing she might very well be caught in the act. The inside of her left arm was scraped raw and bleeding after she dragged it across the bottom of the windowsill as she slid out.

Sara was a runner for many years of her life, and she had battled the pain of healing broken bones after multiple surgeries on both her legs when she was younger. It may have been a short distance to the edge of the woods, but she ran full out alongside Carol's tracks. She noticed Carol's tracks had disappeared in the grass before the thicket of bushes on the edge of the forest. Sara's stomach dropped again, after seeing Carol's tracks, it automatically raised her fear of coming across the dead body of her best friend. It was a frightening image to penetrate her thoughts, believing the possibility that Dylan shot her.

Where is she? How far did she get before he shot her? Was she wounded and got away? Oh God, I hope so! I hope she made it out of here. Sara prayed for that to be the case, but she was no tracker.

Moving as quickly as she was didn't allow for any inspection of the trees, branches, or plants on the forest floor for signs of blood. She had to set that aside and stay in the moment, which was about survival and nothing else. Any other thoughts were fleeting as she tried to negotiate the thickly dense forest, not sure what direction to go in, but knowing she had to keep going.

51

Recovery

PART 1

Ben and Trevor had to get through the woods that stood between them and the dirt road on the east side of the cabin. The area was a mishmash of some tall cedars, firs, and pine trees, along with low-growth plants, wild ferns, and endless seedlings covering the forest's floor. The rain came to an end and the sun slowly started to show to the south, mist rising through sun beams.

In among the mist, thousands of flies, gnats, and mosquitoes buzzed about, alive and well. Ben — who hates bugs of any kind — would have to fight his way through them and do so quietly. Strangely, he barely noticed them. Various birds could be heard singing to each other, squirrels fought over prime real estate in which to bury their nuts for hibernation. He heard the occasional sounds of woodland creatures making their way across the forest floor, hunting and mating, or both. It was increasingly difficult for Ben and Trevor to make their way over, under, and around some of the dead trees that lay on top one another or leaned against new growth. The collective density of that forest between the taller trees was mostly from young pine and spruce trees. At times, it was nearly impossible to see any detail beyond ten to twenty feet in front of them.

They were making their way as swiftly as possible when Ben had to stop for a second to catch his breath and wipe the sweat from his brow. Just as he took his next step, the whoosh of a branch went swinging over his head. Ben ducked just in time. When a terrified Carol realized it was Ben, she leapt into his arms. She saw Trevor and began frantically trying to tell the two everything that happened at once.

"How did you find us?" she asked between gasps for air, covering her mouth to muffle her cries and fighting back tears.

"Evan found out you were up here. He's here." Ben pointed west toward the cabin. "Where's Mom?" Ben was anxious for an answer and wanted to keep moving.

Carol became emotional again. It was difficult for her to keep her composure, almost hyperventilating from the trauma. After all, she had been wandering around in the woods for the last few hours, as weak and exhausted as Sara.

Carol's eyes were darting back and forth between Ben and Trevor. "She was in the cabin. I don't know if she's still…" She broke down again, flopping down on the dead log behind her, her head falling into her hands.

"If you're too weak to walk you should probably wait here. The cabin is only a little farther to the west, and Evan's coming from the north down on the other side. We're going to meet at the cabin." Carol took notice that Trevor was holding a rifle but Ben wasn't. Knowing about Ben, it was a comfort to her.

"I'm not waiting here. I'm coming with you. I'll stay behind and out of the way," Carol said, but she looked too weak to keep up. Trevor insisted she wait for them, telling her they would come right back for her.

As the pair resumed their trek toward the cabin, the sound of an explosion went off so loud everyone instinctively crouched to the ground. They could hear the sound push through the air like a passing plane in the sky. Pieces of timber and dirt rained down on the leaves of the trees not far from where they stood.

"Mom!"

"Sara!"

Ben and Trevor yelled in the same moment. Carol was dumbfounded with a look of despair and confusion on her face. Ben wailed for all he was worth. "Mom!" Over and over, he screamed it out as he jumped over logs, branches, and plants.

Trevor wasn't far behind him. Both moved at a high speed for these conditions. Ben's young, strong legs were lifting like he was running hurdles at a track meet. His thoughts were racing. The horrible fear that his mother had just been killed gave him an unbelievable burst of adrenaline, like speed directly into his veins. Worry for Evan also ate at his nerves. Thoughts of killing Dylan if he ran into him between here and the cabin also ran through his mind. His anger and rage were on high, envisioning himself crushing the man's throat until he died, not caring of the consequences. A dangerous emotional toll.

Trevor was filled with panic and confusion, trying to absorb all that was happening. His first concern was reaching Sara while making sure Ben stayed safe. Ben made it to the dirt road seconds before Trevor as Evan came jogging down the same road from the north to meet them, covered in dirt and splinters.

Ben fell to emotion, grabbing Evan. "Where's Mom. Is Mom...?"

"No, son. They're both out there somewhere. They weren't in the cabin that just blew up. I know, one of the logs almost took my head off not long after I looked in there ... and I was all the way over there on the road!" Evan exclaimed, nodding his head north toward the trail and holding Ben by his shoulders, trying to settle him down. Dylan had heard the voices of Trevor, Ben, and Carol, so he took a chance and blew the cabin. His hope of taking somebody out didn't work, but it came too close for comfort. Maybe Evan was lucky or maybe his work that the day wasn't quite done yet.

"There are two separate sets of small tracks, most likely the girls, heading northeast into the woods from the cabin ... and one male set not far apart. They're okay, but he's either with them or in pursuit, so let's go," Evan said, speaking without a breath, confidently and sternly while he brushed the dirt from his hair and off his shoulders. Ben was overwrought with emotion, wiping his eyes dry, not moving.

Then Trevor stood in front of Evan, placing his hand on his forearm. "Carol's fine. We just found her. She's just over here. Come on." With just a hint of the direction Trevor and Ben were heading from, Evan took off like a rabbit, jumping any object in his way toward Carol. Trevor placed his hand atop Ben's shoulder. "Let's get your mom."

Ben looked at Trevor, breaking a little smile. "Yeah," he dryly choked out.

PART 2

Once Evan and Carol caught sight of each other, neither of them could control their tears. Carol tripped trying to run to Evan, but he closed the distance quickly, and they embraced like long-lost lovers. The reunion didn't last too long, and the joy that was on Evan's face quickly dissipated. His reaction became subdued because they still had Sara to locate and a psychopath on the loose.

Evan walked, supporting Carol, with Ben and Trevor right behind. Evan stopped momentarily when he recognized what was an old overgrown trail that cut southeast, coming out between the waterfall and the Franklin Valley Gorge. Evan stopped for a moment and walked east a few yards before coming right back. Evan could see the damage to a few plants, indicating someone cut through there. "That's where the little fucker went, I bet. He's out here, I know it," Evan said quietly to himself, not wanting to startle the others. He could now sense Dylan like a scent to a bloodhound.

It didn't take long before they had Carol back to Trevor's truck where there was another emotional reunion between Carol and Mary. Mary had to stay in the truck in case the girls came out of the woods, then she would honk the horn. Ben and Trevor jumped into Evan's truck, and the three drove to the far entrance of the conservation area before going north as far as they could. Once there, Evan asked Trevor and Ben to cut into the woods on the west trail before turning north and eventually arc back east to the gorge. Moving a little slower, Evan headed straight north so they would eventually be on a parallel track.

"Ben, text me every couple of minutes to let me know you guys are okay or if you see anything. Now ... what's the deal?" Evan asked Ben with one eyebrow raised. Standing behind Ben, Trevor winked at Evan, thankful it was him trying to keep Ben from making a poor decision.

"Yeah, I know. If I see Dylan, or anyone else, call you instantly! Watch, report, but don't approach," Ben said begrudgingly.

"Ben, I know what you're capable of, in both worlds, without question. So, it has to be this way. You get that, right? You're too important to take any chances. You're meant for better things, Ben." Evan said in a loving manner, and it wasn't his first time he said that. Ben nodded, and he and Trevor headed into the woods once again.

§

Trevor took the lead. As the one with the rifle, he wanted to keep Ben behind him so he could protect him the best he could. They walked at a steady pace, doing their best not to create a great deal of noise in doing so. Shortly after they turned north, Ben became distracted by something he thought he saw to the west of their position. Before he knew it, he was out of sight from Trevor. When Ben took his next steps, he walked around a huge cedar tree and discovered Dylan standing about fifteen feet from him pointing his rifle at Trevor.

Ben yelled out, "Trevor, get down!"

Dylan slowly lowered his rifle. He turned toward Ben and began to raise his gun back up to his shoulder. Ben leapt through the air, landed at Dylan's feet, and knocked him back. Ben reached out his left arm and grabbed Dylan by the strap of his pack and swung for all he was worth. He made two solid punches to Dylan's jaw and cheek, leaving him stunned. Dylan still had the rifle gripped in his hands but his grip weakened and the barrel fell, pointed to the ground. Ben didn't hesitate. He opened his right hand and slammed it against Dylan's chest. Dylan finally expressed fear when he saw Ben's eyes begin to glow brighter than they had on the day he had first seen them at Quinn's Orchards.

Ben heard his name being screamed out by Trevor at the top of his lungs, distracting him. "Ben! No! Ben! Don't do it, Ben. Your mother. We have to find your mother!" exclaimed a panicked Trevor, trying to shake Ben by invoking his mother. Trevor had a grip on the rifle, ready to pull it up in a moment's notice. Ben wasn't completely aware that Trevor knew about his hidden ability, but he quickly released his hand from Dylan's chest, not having the time to cause him any harm.

The short distance between the two left Dylan only one choice, so he rapidly swung the butt of his rifle into Ben's cheek, knocking him back on his rear. Dylan wiped the blood from his mouth with the back of his hand as it was rolling down to his chin. He started to pull the rifle up to his shoulder to shoot Ben. Dylan managed to raise the gun only a few inches before there were two loud whacks where Trevor struck the big cedar right next to Dylan's head causing him to crouch down. The loud cracks from the rifle, and the following echo in the woods, was enough to make Dylan turn. In a kneejerk reaction, he fired a few quick shots in Trevor's direction.

After his third shot, Dylan realized he best turn the gun back on Ben, but it was too late. Ben was gone. When Dylan had turned to shoot at Trevor, Ben bolted up and raced as fast as he could in the direction of the gorge, putting several trees between him and Dylan.

I should have killed him, God damn it! I hope your aim is true, Trevor, Ben thought as he continued on. He realized Dylan had again got the upper hand. Ben couldn't compete against a bullet, so he did the only thing he could do and ran. It was only a couple of minutes later when Ben heard a noise from a branch cracking near him. He was relieved to see Trevor walk past a tall Douglas fir.

"Ben. Stay there, I'm coming," Trevor said, in a raspy whisper, hopping over hostas, ferns, and dead branches as quietly as he could.

"Tell me you shot him," Ben said, still trying to lower his breathing.

"No, I didn't. After he shot back at me, we both left. I saw you run away. Damn it, Ben, that scared the shit out of me. Jesus, it looks like you have a broken jaw for Christ's sake."

"I can't feel a thing. Let's keep going. We'll keep an eye out for that fuckhead, but we gotta get to Mom before he does," Ben said, getting his breath and composure back, sporting a swollen cheek and jawbone. Unknown to Trevor or Ben, Dylan continued north, believing that's where he would find the girls. That is until he heard the faint sound of the water from the gorge to the east.

52

Merge

PART 1

Sara continued to hobble herself away from the logger's camp, pulled in a direction that she could only hope was away from the gunfire she just heard. She had also heard the explosion less than thirty minutes ago. However, she was far enough away that the location of the blast was indistinguishable from the echo in the forest, so she kept moving. Shortly after entering the woods, Sara's foot slipped into a burrowed hole, seriously twisting her ankle, badly enough it felt like she broke something. Putting the pain aside, she was moving by instinct now with no indication of where she was. At this point she was out of breath and, thanks to the plants and bushes, the bottom half of her pants were soaked. Her top was filthy and torn, stained with her own blood. She was trembling from weakness, and the possibility of being shot was an intolerable and constant anxiety. While painfully pushing forward, she kept replaying the last twenty-four hours through her mind like a film reel caught in a loop.

Sara kept repeating to herself, "If I get out of this, I'm going to hunt that bastard down and kill him. He's not going to get another chance to hurt any of us! It's not going to happen again, honey, I promise you that!" she said, as if she were speaking to Jacob directly.

Then with all decorum gone, she blurted out, "That sick fucker! Damn him straight back to the slimy hole he came from." She kept looking behind her, trying to control her breathing and to brave the next steps ahead of her. "My God, Carol, I hope you made it out okay," Sara said through puffed breaths, limping forward to keep her escape in motion.

Up ahead, she could hear the faint sounds of running water, like a strong river. She became aware that the gorge was nearby. In the distance she could see a gap in the trees and realized she was close to one of the many trails around the gorge. Stopping and leaning against a tree, she started to cry tears of joy, knowing she would be breaking out of the woods alive. Even with the fear of being shot, she still worried about Carol. It was a difficult trudge to the opening in the shape she was in, having to limp barefoot across a forest floor of roots, branches, and twigs. When she made it to the opening, seeing the cleared area around the gorge's swing bridge, she was near delirious.

She could see it was about one hundred feet from the forest's edge, through the tall wild grass to an area of patchy, clover-filled grass, around the gorge. The moss covered most of the rocks alongside the gorge nearest to the bridge. They were dangerously slippery as indicated by the surrounding signage. Sara felt secure where she stood, but then she felt a sudden uneasy feeling of being exposed when she walked out into the open, moving toward the gorge. At the opposing entrance to the bridge, a large boulder stood in front of a four-foot by eight-foot sign indicating the bridge was built and maintained by the provincial conservation authority. When Sara looked out, she could see entrances to trails leading north and west. To her left below, there were valleys on both sides of the Bone River and not far beyond there were a couple of large ranches and a few smaller farms.

Sara's head was pounding. Her ankle hurt, and her body ached from being strung up in the cabin. Concentrating on her surroundings was becoming increasingly difficult, but she found the strength to keep going. With only a sleeveless shirt on, her arms were significantly cut up from fighting her way through the bushes and trees of the forest. A portion of the scrapes and cuts on her body came from Dylan's hunting knife. She hoped the thick forest behind her would now provide cover between her and her abductor if he were close behind in pursuit. It took what little remaining strength she had inside her, but she made it to the cliff's edge. Completely exhausted and almost unrecognizable, she flopped onto the grass.

An even stronger and overpowering link to her children began to return. She sensed their presence nearby, and she knew they were searching for her. It gave her the strength to get to her feet again and limp toward the swing bridge a fair distance away. The sun was coming out again in the south sky now, but a sudden cold wave enveloped Sara, stopping her movement.

Evan walked out of the forest through one of the lesser travelled footpaths from the southwest. Sara, from the opposite end of the gorge's opening, looked straight on to Evan. They both broke out with the biggest of smiles. Sara's shoulders sank, her body ready to collapse in the comfort of Evan being there. He yelled out to Sara to stay put, and he would come to her, but the noise of the rushing water at the bottom of the gorge made it difficult to hear at that distance.

Sara squeezed her eyes closed for a moment in relief. She was closer to being safe and away from this ordeal. In that moment she could see Jacob as clear as if he were standing in front of her. "Sara, be careful," Jacob said with a concerned look on his face, looking just beyond her. Sara turned to her right to look at the woods where she had come out but saw no one. She looked back to Evan and saw him waving at her to get down as he pulled his father's old slide bolt 30 aught 6 rifle up to his shoulder and took aim to the right of her. For the third time in Sara's life, a brief moment in time became suspended and everything turned to slow motion. The first time was when she was escaping Vargas's hold on her the morning of Jacob's death, and the second was during her vision in the upstairs hall at the farmhouse in Clarington. And now it was happening again.

With horrible chills running up and down her back, she wanted to duck down and turn to see what was happening. Before she made any move, she saw Trevor walk out of the woods from the west trail, between her and Evan, with his rifle already aimed in the same direction as Evan's. Her face turned white, panic stricken, when Ben stepped into view just to Trevor's side. Sara twisted back around in the other direction to see Dylan had snuck up behind her, pointing his rifle at her. She looked back at Trevor and Ben one more time. She knew Dylan could fire at will, using her as cover, and neither Evan nor Trevor would risk shooting back once he got too close to her.

"Trevor!" Sara yelled out. Trevor took one step in front of Ben and at the same moment, Sara's body went limp, falling to the ground.

Three separate shots broke the air. Two were less than a second apart from each other and the third following shortly after, sounding like they came in a circle around Sara. She spun herself around on the ground in time to see one bullet enter Dylan's chest near his right shoulder, resulting in the rifle falling out of his hands as blood shot out from the wound. She heard Dylan's shot go off, almost deafening her, but it went wild. The third shot rang out, hitting Dylan in the chest near his heart and snapped him back around to his left. Sara watched the look of shock and surprise on Dylan's face as his body appeared to go limp, with blood filling his shirt. His knees hit the cliffside rock, and his body fell to the side. The impact bounced him off the rock and over the edge into the river below at the bottom of the gorge. Out of sight.

PART 2

Shortly after Dylan fell, Sara could hear those very familiar and comforting words once again. "It's going to be okay, sweetheart. You and the kids are going to be okay." Sara looked back to the woods and there stood Jacob with a long-held smile, slowly fading back into the forest. She was torn over her feelings when hearing what Jacob said next. "I have to go now, Sara. You're going to be okay. You have someone to help watch over the kids and each other. I have to go now, Sara. I love you always." Tears began to pour down Sara's cheeks, but she smiled and watched Jacob fade away, absorbed by the colours of the forest.

Ben had screamed out for his mother after the shots rang out, then ran to her aid with Trevor right behind him. Evan looked on in amazement. Like everyone else, he had heard three shots crack out, but one of those shots didn't belong to him. He watched Dylan's intended shot go wild after taking a bullet in the chest from Trevor's first and only shot. Evan could clearly hear the third shot come from behind him to his right. When he stretched himself around to see, there stood Eugene, cool and calm, slinging his rifle back onto his shoulder like it was an average day out hunting. Evan looked at the boy he had saved, now a man, who had just protected the people he loved and cared for. Eugene had become a part of that list before today, but it was certainly cemented now. Evan simply nodded to Eugene in thanks and received a nod in kind. Not much was made of it. Eugene was a soft-spoken man who knew when words were needed.

Through Mary, Eugene had recently learned about Jacob, Ben, and Evan's abilities. He knew if he could help stop Ben and Evan from making a fatal mistake, they could survive the day and continue to thrive with their families. Eugene had several reasons for doing what he did today. One was revenge on the man who cowardly murdered his uncle, a blood brother to his father. The other reason was to return a favour to the man who placed his hands on his head and made sure he survived what would have remained a fatal accident when he was a child. Eugene understood a guardian saves a life for a multitude of reasons. He believed that at the top of that list, they saved lives to ensure that an individual is not errantly deprived of the chance to fulfil in their life what they were meant to. Eugene discovered that Mary's world was parallel to his in many ways. Age difference or not, the pair were falling deeply for each other.

Within minutes of the shots ringing out, Trevor was quick to Sara's side, leaving the rifle for Evan to take and carrying her back to his truck. Holding his rifle like a soldier and the other slung over his shoulder, Evan walked in front of Trevor and Sara with Ben and Eugene following up the rear. Trevor had a serious look of concern on his face, unsure how to feel about just killing a man. But Eugene believed it was his experienced shot that was the fatal one for Dylan. Eugene told Trevor he needn't carry that weight for stopping the man who had tortured his partner. They might have been able to stop after the first shot when Dylan dropped the rifle, but Eugene saw it necessary to remove this darkness from everyone's lives for good. It was his decision.

When Sara was back with Mary and Carol, they had an emotional reunion. When Sara had learned Carol was alive, the news brought tears of joy. Ben was shaking. His emotions were at the surface about to burst, but he held it in the best he could in the moment and let it out when they made it back home.

Evan delicately helped Carol to move into his truck. Trevor and Ben did the same with Sara. Eugene and Mary followed behind, all on their way home. There would be much to discuss about the events that culminated in Dylan's death, but for now, it was time to get some distance away from all of this. Both women demanded care at home. They didn't want to go to the hospital, where too many questions were sure to be asked.

A few days passed before the first group discussion occurred. It was a short conversation. They would leave the discovery of Dylan's body up to the police. The authorities would receive no help with any investigations that could possibly take place. Clothes were burned, guns were cleaned, and mouths remained closed on the subject. All evidence from that horrible day had been erased, less the physical and psychological scars that Sara and Carol would carry.

Disconcerting to all, Greg Simon remained missing from the day of Sara and Carol's deliverance. The next day, Ben was spurred into action, having joined the Simon family and friends to go on a search for his school friend. It would be a week before the discovery of Joe Miller's body, which was of no surprise nor concern to anyone, especially Evan and Carol. However, the police finding a murdered Greg Simon farther south of the cabins was more shocking than mysterious. Sara and Carol could only speculate on what happened to Greg, but there was little guessing as to who carried out such a heinous act.

With the time passed, everyone thought it more frightening than odd that there was still no news of a body being found anywhere along the river. Nothing else would be spoken about Dylan Matthews until such a discovery was made. Most were hopeful he would be eaten alive by wild animals, a fitting end.

Epilogue

The second farm south of the gorge is where the Bone River splits with the larger body of water making its way southwest and through the town of Franklin. The smaller secondary branch flowed southeast for a kilometre before shooting straight south with its many snake-like bends along the way. The water was utilized by the ranches and farms whose properties the river ran through. There is a small farm along the river that has been owned by the Jenkins family for years, mostly growing crops. But the elder Jenkins were forced into retirement because of health reasons and the couple was moved into a senior's home in Franklin. Times changed, and the only remaining family member interested in keeping the farm was the youngest daughter, Allie. Not interested in farming, she leased out the surrounding acreage to share growers. The old-fashioned, storey-and-a-half, classic farmhouse with gable ends and two gable dormers was cleaned up. Fieldstone was applied to the bottom four feet with horizontal white half-lap siding above. The gable ends were finished off with cedar shingles.

So, after an inside-and-out remodel to the house to make it a little more modern, Allie lived alone in that little farmhouse she had grown up in. The old, two-and-a-half-storey, pine-clad barn was the only other building remaining on the property, which was converted to an art studio, with vehicles kept below. The contractor thought her crazy for not incorporating the natural wood of the barn when building her studio. But she was adamant that it was to be a building within the building. Framed, insulated, and white painted drywall everywhere. It was her blank slate, as she liked to say. After the end of a long week, Allie was making her way up the stairs into her art studio carrying a box of supplies. She stepped inside the room that had one large easel with a painting in progress, next to the west-facing window. There were pictures of different landscapes on the walls and art supplies on the shelves and tables in her utility-styled art studio. She pushed the door shut and used her key to lock the double-sided deadbolt, which she installed recently.

She walked to the far end of her large studio and into a small kitchen area built in the corner, where she set the box of supplies down on the countertop. She spun herself around, pushing her backside up to the edge of the counter and held onto it. She was wearing tight blue jeans and a red polka-dot button up that was tied in a knot above her bellybutton. Her blonde hair was in ponytails. She had a bit of a pant from walking up the stairs, and she grinded her hips into the countertop, back and forth. She carried a come hither look on her face as she slowly stepped, toe and heel, toward the opposite side of the room to an unconscious man lying in a bed hooked up to an IV. Off to the side of the room, a raised table was covered with pans full of bloody gauze, used surgical gloves, scalpels, and different sized clamps. Allie stood next to this unconscious man, tied down to the bed, and looked down at him with an adoring smile.

"I'll have you all fixed up before you know it. And things will be just wonderful with you staying here. You just wait and see," Allie said, walking around the bed toward the rocking chair sitting by the north-facing window. Before she would take a seat with her sketch book, Allie grabbed her binoculars, as she often did, and looked up the valley to the swing bridge over the gorge where her gift had come from.

Not a great amount of detail, but enough that she could make out a man standing in the middle of the bridge. She could see well enough that his skin was darker, like he worked outdoors, and he stood tall above the bridge's rail. She thought it looked like he had a rifle resting on his hip, with the barrel pointed to his side away from him. He held it with the scope facing him. And if Allie didn't know any better, she could swear that tall, dark stranger was looking right back at her.

Lightning Source UK Ltd.
Milton Keynes UK
UKHW010757081021
391877UK00002B/304